Oliver stared at me. "What the devil are you doing here?"

I gave a shivery laugh. "Is that how you greet me after eighteen long months?"

"Anne!" he said hoarsely, and held out his arms.

I threw myself upon him and felt his arms tighten about me. He soon released me, however, and remarked, with a touch of sadness, "You've cut your hair. It reminds me painfully that you're growing up."

"You'll like me better grown up. Just wait and see."

His voice was gruff, with a touch of anger that I thought was directed more at himself than at me. "I like you well enough already."

Berkley books by Elizabeth Mansfield

Elizabeth Mansfield

Love Lessons

BERKLEY BOOKS, NEW YORK

LOVE LESSONS

A Berkley Book / published by arrangement with
the author

PRINTING HISTORY
Berkley edition / May 1983

ISBN: 0-425-05938-3

Chapter One

IF YOU, GENTLE READER, expect me to blush with shame when I admit at the outset that by the age of ten I was already fully acquainted with the vicissitudes of *amour,* you should put my story aside before you begin. I felt no shame then, nor do I now. Nor am I put in the least out of countenance when I add that, even at so precocious an age, I'd already found *amour* to be detestable.

By the age of eighteen—with the added experience which almost a decade of living inevitably must supply I had not seen fit to change my mind.

I did not choose to make *amour* the subject of my childish concerns, of course. The subject was thrust upon me, much as the French noun was. (My mother chose never to use the English word when she spoke of love, despite the fact that she was as English as ale.) Only *amour* interested my mother. She was my first teacher of the subject. My last was Oliver.

I first laid eyes on Oliver Fleming, Earl of Pentargon, at my mother's funeral. I was not yet thirteen. I had discovered my mother's body three days earlier, when I'd come to her bedroom to urge her to take some tea. She'd had a particularly dreadful quarrel with her *cher ami*, Sir Averil Luton, and had closeted herself in her bedroom, not permitting me or anyone else to enter.

(I already knew the true meaning of *cher ami*. I'd learned years before that it was a *ton*nish circumlocution for a paramour—itself a frenchified circumlocution for an illicit lover. I couldn't undertstand then, nor do I now, why my mother insisted on the French phrase. The blunt fact was that she was Luton's mistress, and everyone knew it. They weren't "dear friends" at all. When they weren't actually making love, their time together was filled with hurling screaming vituperations at each other. *Cher ami*, indeed!)

My mother had not been happy in her life, but she'd been incapable of changing it. "Anne, my beloved Anne," she would say to me in moments of motherly affection, holding my face between her hands and peering tearfully into my eyes, "you are the one creature in the world for whom I truly care. The rest of my life is meaningless... only *amour, amour.* Silly, wasteful, wearying *amour.*"

"Then why do you bother with your *cher amis,* Mama?" I would ask. "Why can't we leave them all? Can't we go and live in the country and be all to ourselves? Just the two of us... somewhere near the sea?"

"Yes, my precious, my baby, my love, we will, we *will!* One day soon I shall leave all this behind me. This house, London, Averil (or Ian or Alistair), everthying! We shall go away, just the two of us. To the sea... one day soon..."

But the day had not yet come, and I was about to discover that it was now too late.

It was a strangely secluded life we lived in that house. We were in the heart of the busiest metropolis in the world, yet we left our premises infrequently and had no callers other than Mama's lovers. The world was in turmoil that year of 1811, with Napoleon battling the English on the Spanish peninsula, with Parliament making the Prince the Regent of the government in place of his mentally incompetent father, and with large numbers of people joining the religious frenzy of the Evangelicals, but these matters did not touch our household. For my mother, the outside world was of small interest compared to her *amours.*

The day of which I spoke had begun with the angry exit of Sir Averil from the house. For several hours afterward, Mama had wailed, sobbed and thrown things against the walls, carrying on in the impassioned manner which had become her style. Finally, at dusk, the noise from her room ceased. I went upstairs, and after tapping on her door for several minutes and receiving no response, I turned the knob and tiptoed in. "Mama?" I whispered into the dimness of the room.

There was no answer.

Perhaps I'd better explain at this point that my mother was a woman whose strong passions dominated her intellect. It took little provocation to set her on a path of self-indulgent emotional excess, and the scene which she'd just played had not disturbed me more than her others. I'd become accustomed from early childhood to hearing her vent her rages, suffer her agonies and indulge in her amusements in all of their uncontrolled extravagance. Therefore I was not particularly discomposed by the histrionics she'd exhibited earlier nor by her present silence. "Mama?" I asked again.

My grandmother had often explained to me (during the semi-annual visits which I was required to pay to her household) that my mother's lack of restraint in exhibiting her emotions was vulgar in the extreme. "*Restraint,* my child, is the mark of quality," she would repeat like a litany. "Your mother's commonality shows in her excesses. But what can one expect? Her upbringing was nothing better than shabby-genteel. Vulgar she was born and vulgar she will die."

I shook the memory of Grandmamma's words away and peered at the figure on the bed. "Mama? You're not asleep, are you? Wouldn't you like to come down to tea? I've ordered Eva to keep the muffins hot for you."

I could hear nothing, not even breathing, although I could make out her form sprawled on the bedclothes. I fumbled for the tinderbox on her mantel and lit a candle.

She lay upon the tousled coverlet, legs and arm akimbo, her rose-colored dressing gown inadequately covering her nakedness. Her head was turned away from me. A stemmed wine goblet was clutched in the hand that hung in terrifying lifelessness over the side of the bed, and an almost empty bottle of spirits lay on the floor below it. There was an ivory-framed hand mirror lying on the pillow beside her cheek, and from my place near the doorway I could see reflected in it the pained grimace which had frozen on her face.

"*Mama?*" I asked again in sudden urgency, my heart seeming to stop. Somehow I knew she wouldn't answer.

Later I wondered whether the expression on her face had come from the sight of her aging, dissipated appearance in her mirror or the spasm of pain with which her weakened heart had assaulted her in its last twitch to grasp at life. But at that moment of my dreadful discovery, my mind and my emotions were too benumbed for reflection.

Yet I was capable of action. Like someone who'd seen death many times (although in truth I'd never before looked upon a lifeless body), I busied myself with what I instinctively knew were necessary undertakings. I shut her staring eyes, adjusted her lewdly sprawled limbs (which required a horrifying struggle to loosen the fingers which gripped the wineglass with fearsome strength), covered her gingerly with the bedclothes, picked up and hid the bottle, cleaned up the room as well as I could without dustmop or broom, went out into the hallway and closed the door. Then, in a voice which I think sounded calm enough, I called for Eva, informed her of the event, sent the slatternly maid to fetch Sir Averil, walked down the hall to my room, shut the door and was sick.

"Mama," I mumbled brokenly over and over again as I cleaned up all signs of my sickness and stationed myself at the window to watch for Sir Averil's carriage. I'd never before felt so bereft. My mother might have been a foolish and passionate woman, but she'd showered me with a generous share of the devoted affection which she'd offered to those whose lives touched hers. There had never been anyone else who'd loved me so. Now I was alone in a completely uncaring world.

I soon discovered just how uncaring that world was. Sir Averil sent Eva back with a note to me in which he expressed his "most sincere regrets on my tragic loss," and added: *You will understand, my dear Miss Saunders, that as much as I should like to offer you my assistance in your period of grief, it would be quite inappropriate for me to be present at this time, since I am not a member of your family. I suggest you send at once for your grandmother, the Lady Marietta Saunders, who will know just what needs to be done. With sincere good wishes for your future, I remain, Averil Luton, Bart.*

I immediately sent Eva on this second errand (although I didn't believe that my grandmother would be any more willing to come to my assistance than Sir Averil had been). Then I sat down near the fire and read my mother's lover's note again. The strange detachment of its tone puzzled me. Why had he called me "Miss Saunders" and written the message as if he were a mere acquaintance? But I soon grasped the reason. He'd worded the letter in cautious self-interest, so that, if it fell under the eye of any person of significance, the reader would be unable to find in it any incriminating evidence suggesting an attachment to my mother or any reason to suppose that the writer had the slightest responsibility for her or for her offspring. Even his *wife* could have read this missive without becoming aware that she'd been in the least betrayed.

My hand trembled as a wave of revulsion swept over me toward him. It was a feeling so strong that it included all my mother's *cher amis* and every man who walked the earth. I crumpled the sheet into a little ball and threw it into the fire.

To my surprise, my grandmother came at once. She lived within a mile of our house but hadn't stepped within its door or looked upon her daughter-in-law's face for almost a decade. At the time of my father's death, she'd sworn never to have anything to do with "the wanton who'd married my son." But now Death had voided the pledge. She'd come to me, and I wanted to run to the door in a rush of relief and gratitude.

But I did not. My grandmother, Lady Marietta Saunders, was a woman of strong character. My feelings for her were, at the time, a strange mixture of awe, affection, admiration and dislike. Her words had always been cutting and cold, yet I sensed under her unemotional demeanor a real attachment for me. I didn't know what to expect from her that night, and, my heart beating in alarming rapidity, I hung back in the doorway of the drawing room and watched her entrance with both eagerness and fear.

She appeared to be perfectly composed as she entered the shabby little townhouse we occupied in York Place. Tall and thin as a stick, she came through the door leaning one arm on that of her butler, Hewes, and supporting herself heavily with her other hand on a round-headed, unadorned wooden cane. The simple, serviceable cane made a ludicrous contrast to the Saunders' diamonds she wore at her throat and the magnificent sable pelisse she'd thrown over her black lace dress. The black costume, I knew, had not been donned to indicate mourning— she wore black all the time.

She was followed into the room by her companion, Mrs. Panniers, a pallid, obsequious woman who was never far from my grandmother's side. Mrs. Panniers blinked at me with a false solicitude and murmured, "Oh, Anne, you *poor* dear," in a tone which made me clench my teeth in irritation. But Grandmamma merely looked at me and said nothing.

I stared back at my grandmother, my chin raised in stiff-necked pride. If she thought I would fall on her neck in a paroxysm of tears, she had much mistaken me. Although she knew how much I now needed her, something in me desired to show her that I, too, had a touch of strength in my character.

The corners of her mouth seemed to twitch. I studied her face with interest. When I'd been very young, I'd felt twinges of fear when I'd looked at her. Little children are often alarmed by the physical signs of extreme age and infirmity. Lady Marietta had had, for as long as I could remember, transparent, almost blue skin which stretched over her bones with a taut fragility (except around the mouth and eyes, where it lay in folds and wrinkles so numerous and puckered that it scarcely seemed to be skin at all), long fingers on which the joints stood out in skeletal prominence, weak legs which couldn't support her frail weight, and an odor of staleness and decay. By this time, the evening of my mother's passing, I'd outgrown these childish revulsions (for I was old enough to see in her straight carriage an admirable dignity and in her direct, light-eyed stare a kind of beauty), but I, nevertheless, could not like her. For she despised the mother I'd loved.

"Dead, eh?" Lady Marietta asked sourly after she realized she could not stare me down. "Her heart, I suppose. I'm not surprised. Knew all along that dissipation and degeneracy would take their toll."

I clamped my jaws tightly shut and didn't answer. If my mother had been dissipated and degenerate, my grandmother had been at least partially to blame. Why hadn't she tried to pull my poor Mama from the mire of dissolution in which she'd thrown herself? But I knew it wouldn't do my mother any good if I now made that accusation.

Lady Marietta's watery blue eyes remained on my face for a moment, easily reading my unexpressed animosity. Then she turned to her butler and ordered him to go upstairs and see to the body. She signaled to Mrs. Panniers to assist her into the chair beside the pier table at the right of the stairway, and when she'd lowered herself upon it, waved the woman away. "Go up and see if Hewes has any need of help," she muttered. "And as for you, child, come here and let me look at you."

I approached her with a disdainful swagger. I would rather have died than let her see how close I was to terrified, unrestrained hysteria.

"Sullen as usual, I see," she said, her eyes ranging over me from top to bottom. "Good God, child, don't you ever comb your hair? It's as wild and unkempt as a gypsy's, if ever there were a gypsy with such crinkly red locks. And that frock! Creased and stained and shabby as a beggar's. Didn't your mother take interest in anyone's clothing but her own? She spent a King's ransom on her own back, God knows."

"I have *dozens* of dresses," I said defiantly.

"But none, I'll wager, suitable for a funeral. Your mother's taste in colors was appropriate for no one but a trollop. Don't throw me those dagger looks, Anne Saunders. I didn't hide my disapproval when the woman was alive, and I shan't now. I knew from the moment my son brought her home to me that he'd made a dreadful mistake. But Reggie'd already married her, so what could I do? I wasn't surprised when I learned she'd cuckolded him within the year. Poor boy, it was her faithlessness that killed him more than the apoplexy." She put a hand up and smoothed my hair. "Reggie never could have been certain that you were his issue, but he acknowledged you just the same. And that, granddaughter, is good enough for me."

She proceeded to reminisce for a quarter-hour, recalling my mother's amorous transgressions in detail. None of it was news to me...I had lived through it all. Child that I was, I had understood very early that my mother lived on the fringes of society because of her shocking reputation. "While your father lived, he protected her with his name and his character. Loyal to her 'til he died, Reginald Saunders was," Grandmamma reminded me. "But once he was gone, she was doomed. Mowberly wouldn't give her his name, though she'd given him her best years, and after he grew tired of her, it was all downslide. I tried to warn her, but she never did know how to put head above heart, so I washed my hands of her. And now it's all over. She's gone to an early end. Perhaps it's just as well. There's nothing in life for a wanton once her looks are gone."

I regretted that I'd sent for her. I wanted to shout out, *Stop it! You are speaking of my mother! And she's dead!* But aloud I said nothing. I knew that I'd had no choice but to send for her; I had to have help from *somewhere*. What did I know about dealing with death? How was I to make funeral arrangements by myself? I didn't even know what was to become of me. Unpleasant as it was to have to listen to my grandmother's cold assessment of my mother's life, I realized with despair that I had to endure it. I needed her.

Grandmamma didn't permit me to spend the night in the York Place house. I was soon ordered to collect my "necessaries" with dispatch, and she ordered Mrs. Panniers to bundle me into her carriage. Then Hewes assisted her into the carriage—staying behind himself to deal with the details—and we set out for her mansion in Mount Street.

The room she gave me, with its huge four-posted bed and dark-red hangings with their gold Greek-key border (for Grandmamma liked the impressive dignity of Grecian designs in furniture and ornamentation), was a painful contrast to my tiny room in Mama's house. It reminded me sharply of my uprooted, alien condition. I felt lost in its enormity. I yearned for the simplicity and hominess of my yellow bedstead, but I knew that I would never again spend a night in my old room. At the same time I was fully aware that this room in Grandmamma's house would not likely become my home either.

Mrs. Panniers, clucking her tongue and making conventional murmurings of sympathy, assisted me to undress and put me to bed. I don't know if I slept that night, for my memory of those few days in grandmother's house is now but a fog of vague impressions. I recollect endless mealtimes at a long, forbidding table in a dark dining room where I was confronted with an epergne so large and ornate that I could see nothing beyond it. I also recall standing impatiently in the middle of my grandmother's sitting room while her seamstress fitted me into one of Grandmamma's black dresses which she'd cut down for me.

But I do remember the day of the funeral. I dressed myself that morning (Mrs. Panniers being occupied with assisting Grandmamma and making her own toilette), and I remember studying my reflection in the mirror as if the girl looking back at me were a stranger. *Who is that pitiful creature?* I wondered. The face that stared back at me was thin and white, with a pointed chin and huge brown eyes that were red-rimmed in spite of the fact that I'd not been able to shed a tear. The face looked ghostly under the ugly, oversized black bonnet Grandmamma had ordered me to wear. Beneath the hat, two disorderly, uneven braids of frizzy red hair hung down pathetically, for I'd had neither the desire nor the ability to plait them properly. The body under the mourning dress was scrawny and angular; the ill-fitting, loosely hanging neckline and overlong sleeves only emphasized its awkward spindliness. The dress had been cut off and hemmed at midcalf, and two gangly legs clad in black worsted stockings were visible below, the ankles so bony they seemed sharp enough to work their way right through the wool of the stockings. Was this poor creature Mama's daughter? Was the child in the mirror someone I knew at all?

At the graveside, while the unfamiliar clergyman mouthed words which held no meaning for me, I looked round at the tiny circle of mourners gathered about the gaping pit. My grandmother, of course, stood right beside me. She leaned on her cane with both hands and stared fixedly at the mound of freshly dug earth at her feet, seemingly oblivious of the voice of the clergyman, of the wind, the flying clouds, the other mourners . . . of everything but her own thoughts. I couldn't tell from her expression what those thoughts might be. If she stood there regretting her failure to open her heart to my mother during her lifetime, I never learned of it. I could only *hope* that her thoughts were taking that direction.

On Lady Marietta's other side was Mrs. Panniers, wearing a fittingly doleful expression. Right behind her, our maid Eva stood sniffing loudly into a dirty handkerchief as if to convince all the onlookers of the sincerity of her grief. Only I knew how grudging had been her sulky service to my mother.

On the other side of the gravesite stood Hewes, my grandmother's butler, in his impeccably suitable black coat. His hat was in his hand and his head respectfully lowered. At his right was Mr. Cushing, who'd been my father's solicitor and who had given my mother legal and financial advice from time to time. His long, unkempt white hair blew about in the wind, and he wore a black armband on the sleeve of his coat. It seemed to me that his expression was the only one showing sincere regret. My heart swelled in gladness to see him there. In gratitude, I forgave him his maleness, but that forgiveness was only for him. Toward the rest of *man*kind, I felt an overwhelming abhorrence; not one of the *amis,* the lovers on whom my mother had lavished so much of her life and her emotions, had seen fit to make an appearance.

I looked down at the box of dark, polished wood (my grandmother had not stinted on the expense of the casket) which held my mother's remains, but I couldn't cry. Even though the unshed tears seemed to be lodged in a painful lump in my chest, they wouldn't come out. None of the ritual seemed real to me. Dry-eyed and bewildered, I almost managed to convince myself that I was living through an extended nightmare . . . that I would wake in my old room to the sound of my mother's hysterical weeping or excited laughter. Standing there at her grave, with my grandmother at my side, it occurred to me with a shock that such an awakening would not necessarily be a happy one . . . that my life in my mother's house had, in its way, been a nightmare, too! It had only seemed less nightmarish than this because I'd grown accustomed to it.

While mulling over this discovery, I became aware that a stranger had walked into the circle of mourners and was removing his hat. He was perceptibly taller than anyone else in the circle, had thick, dark hair and was not dressed in mourning. He wore a coat of country tweed, sturdy breeches and a pair of riding boots. And he was heavily bearded, an almost unheard-of characteristic in a gentleman; the only men I'd ever seen with beards were religious zealots or eccentrics. However, having had my fill of fashionable gentlemen, I found the stranger's appearance fascinating. The beard, black and curly, gave him an air of piratical mystery and drew attention to the two features of his face which the beard could not disguise—his nose and eyes. The nose was strong, pronounced and straight, while the eyes were light and keen and seemed to look upon the world with a critical detachment.

Even as the diggers prepared to lower the casket into the ground, I couldn't help speculating on the identity of the stranger. Was he one of my mother's old lovers, from a time before the days I was able to remember? What had brought him here? Could it be that there was one man in the world who loved her still?

Across the dark pit, the gleaming casket and the mound of moist earth, his eyes met mine. It was surely my imagination—an impression created from my hungry need for solace—that made me read a message in his look: *Take heart, don't despair . . . you are not alone.*

I felt a burning in my throat and wondered if I was about

to cry at last. But before the burdensome lump within my chest could begin to melt, I noticed my grandmother start. She lifted her head, gaped at the stranger and gave him a nod of satisfaction. "Thank God," I heard her mutter to herself.

Then he can't be an old lover, I said to myself, crushed with disappointment. No lover of my mother's would be welcomed by my grandmother with such gladness.

The casket was lowered into the ground. In a fog of pain I dropped a handful of earth on it. My mind was benumbed and my eyes unseeing. I was aware only that no one in that circle of faces looking down at the grave was truly grieved but me.

My grandmother let me stand there for a while after the others had turned away, but when a few mintues had passed I felt her hand on my shoulder. "Her spirit is not there," she said with quiet sympathy. "It's gone to some other place."

With a firm arm about my shoulder, she made me turn. "Come away, child. Give me your arm. I want you to meet your cousin Oliver."

Chapter Two

MR. CUSHING SAT behind the long table in Grandmamma's library, frowning over the calculations he was making from notes taken from a sheaf of papers spread before him. Grandmamma had sent me to the far corner of the room, instructing me to "sit there quietly and drink your tea, if you please. And don't jump up and down, kick your heels or do anything else to cause a disturbance. Your elders have several serious subjects to discuss, and we won't brook any distractions." She then went away as if my presence in that room was no longer of any consequence.

She and my cousin Oliver (the only other person in the room) ensconced themselves on the deep armchairs near the fire and talked together in low voices while they waited for Mr. Cushing to conclude his examination of the state of my mother's affairs. They were talking about me. I knew it because I managed to overhear a great deal of what they said. "She's an unkempt little gypsy," my grandmother said, adding that I had "no more moral sense than a Hottentot."

I suppose I should have been disturbed by what I heard. And somewhere in the back of my mind, a little voice *did* urge me to take offense—to jump to my feet and demand of them by what right they could make judgments of me. *What do they know of you at all?* the voice in my head asked. *Your cousin has never before laid eyes on you, and your grandmother saw you only twice a year, despite the fact that she lived a mere mile distant.*

This was quite true. Grandmamma had demanded my presence at her domicile twice a year to attend her for afternoon tea. During those strained afternoons, she ordered me to kiss her on her forehead, made disparaging comments on my hair or dress, quizzed me on my studies and requested that I play the piano for her. I'd usually managed to win her approval of my knowledge of English history (for I loved to read), but she'd clucked disdainfully at my inadequate French, and she'd winced in pain when I played (for no one in Mama's household had ever cared enough to see that I practiced with sufficient regularity and dedication, so that my technique was nothing short of deplorable).

Nevertheless, during those interviews, I had always been impeccably polite, restrained and well-behaved. Therefore, what did she know of me to judge me deficient in morals?

But I ignored the voice that urged an outcry. I didn't care what my grandmother or my cousin Oliver thought of me. I seemed to have no feelings at all. The sense of unreality which had enveloped me earlier that morning at the funeral persisted. The world around me seemed askew, unreal and disordered, as in a nightmare. And as in a nightmare, my feelings, too, were strangely muffled and vague. I knew that a terrible blow had befallen me—that somewhere deep inside I was bruised and sore—but the sensations of pain had not yet reached my brain. My relatives might sit there across the room and malign me to their hearts' content...I didn't care. They might even disown me and throw me out into the streets. Nothing seemed to matter very much.

Mr. Cushing looked up from his sheaf of notes and figures. He cleared his throat. "It's not a pretty picture," I heard him say in a subdued voice which nevertheless managed to reach me in the far corner of the room. I heard snippets of his remarks, like "...cannot estimate the exact value...jewels and personal effects...rough estimate...after the sale of the house and the carriages...debts of four or five thousand pounds still remaining..."

"Good God!" Grandmamma ejaculated in disgust.

"Never mind," Oliver said sharply, throwing a quick glance in my direction to see if I'd heard. I pretended to be fully preoccupied with stirring my tea.

"Never mind?" Grandmamma exclaimed loudly. "How can I not mind? If Luton kept her in virtual penury—as these figures seem to indicate—he will scarcely be receptive to any suggestion that he make good her debts."

"Yes, but it makes no difference. I'll take care of her debts," Oliver said. He kept his voice low, but my hearing is very keen.

"That is most generous of you, Oliver, and I appreciate the offer, but I'll take care of my daughter-in-law's debts myself."

He looked at her with eyebrows raised. "Will you? Then why did you bother to send for me? If you don't need my help in these exigencies, why did you send me the urgent summons to come to you with all speed?"

Grandmamma seemed to hesitate. Mr. Cushing drew two chairs up to the table and, placing them opposite his, urged them both to be seated. From this moment until their discussion concluded, they seemed to forget that I was in the room. I took advantage of their absorption to inch my chair closer to the table so that I would not miss a word of their discussion.

Grandmamma tapped her fingers nervously on the carved wooden arm of her chair. "I sent for you, my dear, first, because you are the head of the family, and second, because I require your assistance in a matter far more difficult to solve than mere debts."

"Oh?" Oliver lowered himself into the remaining chair and studied her face with more interest than before. "What matter is that?"

Grandmamma threw a quick glance at Mr. Cushing. The solicitor passed a hand over his white hair as if he suddenly felt unsure of himself. "It concerns the child, your lordship," he ventured when he realized that a response from Grandmamma was not forthcoming. "Lady Marietta feels, quite understandably, that her age and ill health make the rearing of a young girl a task too arduous for her to undertake."

"Age and ill health? What sort of folderol is that?" Oliver asked suspiciously.

"I'm *seventy-four*, Oliver," Grandmamma said with dramatic emphasis. "Seventy-four! (Although I shall deny it loudly if you should ever repeat that to anyone. I don't own up to a day past sixty-two.) But I must be frank with you, my dear, and admit the truth. Seventy-four is my real age, and that's too old to endure having a twelve-year-old scampering about underfoot. There's the problem in a nutshell. You can see, can't you, that I'm faced with a quandary."

"What I see, ma'am, is a spoiled old beldame who's using her age and the state of her health as a pretext to avoid responsibility," Oliver said with a bluntness I found startling. No one else in the world, I knew, would have dared to speak to Lady Marietta Saunders in that way.

But Grandmamma only laughed. "I won't deny it," she said without shame or rancor.

"You *can't* deny it. Not to me. For I know exactly how old you are, and you're seventy-six if you're a day, and as fit and spry as you were at thirty, notwithstanding the cane you pretend to require."

"Very well, perhaps I do exaggerate my infirmities. But you must agree that at my time of life I've become too set in my ways to adjust to having a child about."

"Yes, I can understand that, of course."

"Besides, my sort of life wouldn't be good for the girl . . . and the sort of life she needs would not do for me."

"But I had the impression, Aunt Marietta, that you're fond of the child."

"So I am. *Very* fond of her. Too fond to wish to install her in this mausoleum of a house with a crotchety old hag who sleeps all day and plays cards with her cronies half the night. I've decided that it would be far better for the girl to move in with some other relation."

"Some *other* relation?" Oliver's brow furrowed in puzzlement. "You can't mean Richard in Scotland, for he has too many of his own to raise, and as for the rest of the family, there *is* no one else except—"

She looked at him archly. "Yes, Oliver? Except—?"

"Good God!" He rose from the chair in horrified astonishment. "You're not suggesting, are you, that I—?"

"That's *exactly* what I'm suggesting."

Oliver gaped at her. "You want *me* to take the child in? Me?"

"Yes, my dear. Who else?"

He let out a snorting laugh. "My dear aunt, you're jesting."

"Not at all," was her quick rejoinder.

"Then your wits are surely addled, ma'am. What do I know about bringing up a little girl?"

"No less than I do, Oliver, I assure you. I had only a son, you know, and *he* was raised more by his nurse than by me."

"But if you think *your* home is too quiet and secluded for a young girl, what then is *mine*? Here you are in the heart of the world's largest, gayest metropolis. You've a circle of friends and a staff of more than a dozen, I'd wager, to help you run this establishment. I, on the other hand, live in a decaying castle in Cornwall with only an elderly couple to do for me. I spend my days on my horse, with my books or in my greenhouses. I'm four miles from my nearest neighbor. I'm a confirmed bachelor who has barely spoken a full sentence to a child in my life and who finds all children strange and incomprehensible. Is that the sort of guardian you wish to bring up your only granddaughter?"

"Yes, Oliver, it is. Living in the country will be the very best thing for poor little Anne."

"I don't see why. There's no special advantage to living in the country, unless 'poor little Anne' is sick and needs country air. *Is* she sick?"

"No, she's not. Not that I know of." Grandmamma cocked her head and looked at him speculatively. "If I'd said she was, would you have taken her?"

"No, I can't take her at all, sick *or* well. The whole idea's impossible."

"Then you're refusing me?" Grandmamma asked calmly.

"I *must* refuse." Cousin Oliver ran his fingers through his tousled hair and took his seat, frowning, obviously troubled at his inability to comply. "You must realize the suggestion is preposterous. If taking her into this house will be too much for you, why don't you send her to one of those schools for young girsl? That would probably suit the child best. She'd have other girls her age for companionship, and proper teachers to train her in all the maidenly nonsense that females are expected to learn—"

Grandmamma sighed. "Yes, I suppose that's what I must do, if you're adamant."

"Don't sigh so despondently, Aunt." He patted her shoulder comfortingly, relieved at having solved the problem, at least to his own satisfaction. "You can't pretend that you expected me to agree to so impractical a plan as the one you suggested.

What do I know about dealing with young girls? Those schools, on the other hand, are run by experts. They'll feed and clothe the child properly, supply her with suitable surroundings and give her all sorts of beneficial instruction. I can't imagine why you ever conceived the notion of *my* taking her when a school is such an obvious—and obviously superior—solution."

She glared at him. "Oh, you can't, eh? That's because you have a male mind. Men can never understand the subtleties of domestic problems."

"Subtleties? What subtleties?"

"Never mind. Too bad poor Anne isn't a plant or a tree— if she were, you'd see the problem quickly enough, and you'd be the first to take her home to transplant in your Cornwall soil. As it is, however, there's no point in going further into the matter."

"Out with it, Marietta," he insisted. "I've come all this way to do what I can to help. If I don't understand the problem, how can I assist with the solution?"

"The problem, numbskull, is the child's mother. Poor little Anne has my daughter-in-law's blood in her veins. I don't want the girl to follow in her mother's footsteps."

Oliver frowned at her. "What nonsense is this? Why should you even *think* of such a possibility?"

"The apple doesn't fall far from the tree, as you know better than most. I don't wish my granddaughter to grow up a harlot like her—"

"*Harlot?* See here, Aunt, I can't permit—"

"Don't you see how it will be?" Grandmamma persisted. "If little Anne goes to a school, sooner or later someone will learn of her background and begin to whisper about it. It will spread, as all such vicious gossip does. She'll be insulted at best, ostracized at worst. She'll grow sullen and rebellious, and soon she'll tell herself that if she's already won herself a sullied name she may as well play the game. She'll begin to *earn* the bad reputation that she, at first, did not deserve, and—"

"*Enough!*" My cousin Oliver rose from his chair. I think he'd completely forgotten my presence in the room, because he spoke in a full, furious voice. "Never, Aunt Marietta, have I heard you speak such drivel. In the first place, your daughter-in-law was *not* a harlot. In the second place, even if she were, it would be ridiculous to believe that her offspring would follow the same road. Harlotry is not something one inherits, like the family nose or a tendency to hemophilia. Confound it, Aunt, you know as well as I that *moral looseness is not handed down!*" He took a couple of angry strides around the table before wheeling on her again. "In the third place, ma'am, if girls' schools are such dens of gossip mongering and callousness, I'll be damned if I'll agree to permit the poor child—"

As he swung his arm to point a finger in my direction, my presence seemed to return forcibly to his consciousness. His arm froze in midair, and he flushed. "That child has probably heard every word of this monstrous conversation," he muttered to Grandmamma, abashed.

Grandmamma shrugged. "She may as well grow accustomed to hearing herself spoken of in this way."

"She will *not* grow accustomed to it!" he barked. He glared down at my grandmother for a long moment and then strode across the room to me. He circled my chair, his eyes sweeping over me as if he were showering me with darts. Then he turned away, wandered to the fireplace and stood leaning on the mantel, staring down into the flames. "Girl," he ordered at last, turning to look at me again, "go and collect your things at once. You're coming home with me."

A tremor of feeling shot through me at his words, but I couldn't tell what sort of feeling it was. Fear? Excitement? Relief? Dismay? Perhaps a little of all of them. But I calmly put the teacup down on the little Grecian table beside my chair and went to the door without a word. As I stepped out into the hallway I heard Grandmamma chortle. "I knew I could count on him," she said gleefully to Mr. Cushing.

I didn't quite close the door behind me, and I lingered for a moment at the door to catch my cousin's response.

"Feeling proud of yourself, ma'am?" I heard him ask my grandmother drily. "I shouldn't gloat, if I were you. You handled me very cleverly, I grant you that. Well, you've won your wish. I'll take her. But whether this scheme will be good for your granddaughter's future is something I very much doubt. I only hope, my dear, that we shan't spend years regretting what we've done today in haste."

Chapter Three

"YOU'RE NOT A very talkative child, are you?" my cousin Oliver observed after we'd ridden in silence for two hours.

"No, sir, I'm not," I told him shortly.

"Good, I've little use for chatterboxes."

He resumed his perusal of the newspaper which had been occupying him since we'd left my grandmother's house. I'd spent the time staring out of the coach window, watching the density of the closely packed houses thin, the streets disappear and the landscape begin to take on the green expanse of countryside. I should have been thrilled, for I was traveling away from London at last. Instead, I was trying very hard not to be sick.

The coach was racing rather wildly westward, for Oliver had ordered the coachman to make every effort to reach Basingstoke by midnight, and although I was fascinated by the changing view outside my window, the constant rocking of the vehicle was making me feel decidedly queasy. I'd never traveled any great distance in my life before, although taking a trip away from London had always been my fondest dream. Yet now, this achievement of my dream filled my soul with bitterness. My mother wasn't with me and would never be. Instead

I was imprisoned in this musty-smelling, dizzily rocking carriage under the guardianship of a saturnine, forbidding gentleman who didn't want me and who had shown not the slightest interest in me or my state of mind.

I'd never realized before that travel could be so unpleasant for the stomach. I'd read, of course, that shipboard travel often made one ill, but no one had prepared me for the nauseating motion of a coach. I began to feel more and more uncomfortable. The queasiness filled me with terror, for I knew that my cousin already found me a burden which he would have preferred to do without. If I became sick, his disgust would be absolute.

But the disturbance in my stomach was not my only pain. The agony of the loss of my mother still lay on my breast like a lump of ice. Worse still, my future seemed to me to be even darker than my past, for it was to be intimately bound to that of the fiercely frowning gentleman opposite. The prospect offered no hope of my ever feeling happy again.

The late afternoon brightness faded rapidly as twilight fell abruptly over the green hills. My cousin was forced to put his paper aside from lack of light. "We're passing through Hampshire," he remarked, stretching his legs out before him and yawning. "We'll reach Basingstoke quite late, I'm afraid, but we'll be rewarded by the accommodations at the Three Elms. Have you ever been to Basingstoke?"

"No, sir, I've never been anywhere," I muttered glumly, one hand pressed against my heaving stomach and another on my head to keep my dreadful bonnet from falling over my face because of the rocking.

"At twelve years of age I hadn't been anywhere either, so you needn't sound so put-upon. I've little use for children who are sorry for themselves."

I put up my chin. "I'm not a child. I'm almost thirteen."

"So much the worse. You're too old to rail against your fate."

I wanted to retort, but my stomach heaved. "Yes, sir" was all I could manage.

"You needn't call me 'sir,' girl. Nor 'my lord,' nor 'cousin,' nor any other title. I've little use for titles either."

"What shall I call you, then?"

"Call me by my name, of course. Oliver. And I'll call you—"

"Poor Little Anne," I muttered under my breath.

"What?" He looked at me curiously. "Is that what you want to be called—Poor Little Anne?"

I threw him a look of disgust. "That's what everyone's been calling me ever since . . . since my mother died."

"Not I, surely?"

"Yes, you. Twice."

"I take it you didn't like that very much."

"*Like* it?" Sick as I was, I couldn't resist mocking him. I imitated the way he held his head. "I've little use for pity from my relations," I said, aping his tone.

He instantly caught the mockery and laughed. "Saucy little imp, aren't you? Very well, girl. I shall never call you so again. You have my word."

"Thank you, s—Oliver."

His lips twitched. "You're welcome, poo—Anne."

We rode on in silence for a while, a silence for which I was most grateful. Every word I was forced to say brought me closer to being sick. But soon my cousin spoke again. "I suppose you're looking so glum because you're sorry not to remain in London with your grandmother," he remarked in a rather kindly way.

"No, I'm not. I don't much care for London. Nor for Grand-mamma either, if truth be told."

"Indeed?" He frowned at me. "Are you always so brutally frank?"

"I try to be."

His eyebrows rose in disapproval. "You say that with a distinct tone of self-pride. But arrogance is not becoming in a child of twelve. I wonder, my girl, if you would enjoy hearing others speak of *you* in that same, brutal way. If, for example, your grandmother said she cared little for you, you'd probably burst into tears."

"I would not. I'm quite accustomed to hearing unpleasant truths without bursting into tears."

He studied me shrewdly. "Yes, I suppose you are. I haven't seen you shed a tear all day, although you've had plenty of reason to do so. But tears are not the only way to express self-pity. Statements like the one you just made, even when they are muttered so belligerently, reveal quite clearly that you're feeling sorry for yourself."

I felt myself pout. "But as you said yourself, I've good

reason to feel sorry for myself."

"Yes, you do. But if you show it, you must expect people to be tempted to call you Poor Little Anne."

"Hummmph!" I muttered sullenly. "I suppose *you'd* be brave and not show a touch of self-pity if you'd lost *your* Mama and your home, if no one wanted you and if . . . if . . ."

I could feel his eyes on my face. "Go ahead, girl," he urged. "What else?"

"Nothing." My sulky outburst had made my queasiness even more pronounced. I turned my head to the window and tried to settle myself.

"I don't deny that your circumstances are difficult," he said quietly, "but you're not the only creature who's had to endure pain and loss. I've had to face some unpleasant truths in my time, too, and I managed to—"

"Can you face one now?" I cut in, my hand at my mouth.

"What?"

I turned from the window in desperation. "Can you face an unpleasant truth now?"

He blinked at me in confusion. "Yes, I suppose so. What is it?"

"You'd better stop the carriage."

"Stop the carriage? But why?"

I wanted to die of shame, but I brazened it out. "Because the unpleasant truth is . . . that in one minute . . . I'm afraid I'm . . . going to be very, very sick."

After throwing me a startled glance, he rapped sharply at the partition to the coachman's box and the carriage slowed and stopped. Without waiting for his permission, I pulled off my bonnet, thrust it into his hands and leaped out.

I lingered behind the hedge for a few minutes afterward, trying to catch my breath and steel myself to face him again. I felt a great deal better in body, but my spirit was battered with humiliation. My cousin, I surmised, must have been overwhelmed with disgust and was undoubtedly berating himself for having permitted my grandmother to saddle him with such an ungainly, sickly, arrogant, self-pitying nuisance as myself. But there was nothing to be gained by a long postponement of the inevitable confrontation. I turned round.

Oliver had followed me out of the coach and was standing beside the hedge watching me with an expression of unmistakable sympathy. It was the same look he'd given me that morning at the graveside—the look that had seemed to say that I was not alone. For the second time, I found that look a solace to my soul.

He held out his handkerchief. "Feeling better now?" he asked with a slight smile.

I nodded and walked through the hedge to the carriage. He followed and, with a show of gallantry, handed me up. After he'd seated himself, the coachman climbed up on the step and covered my legs with a thick laprobe. Then we were on our way again, but I was aware that the pace of the vehicle had considerably slackened.

I looked up at my cousin's face, wondering if I should express my gratitude to him for ordering the coachman to slow his speed. But the look of sympathy was gone from his eyes. He seemed, instead, to be watching me with sardonic amusement while he absently twirled my bonnet in his fingers. My feelings of gratitude died, and I felt my hackles rise. What was so amusing about my having been sick? I lifted my chin. "You'll never reach Basingstoke by midnight at this rate," I said defiantly.

"No. We'll put up at Aldershot instead."

"You may please yourself, of course, but you needn't have slowed your pace on my account."

"I'm quite aware of that. But I prefer a slower place to seeing your complexion turn green again."

I should have thanked him, but I have never been the humble sort. "I'll take my hat back now," I said coldly, holding out my hand.

"Must you wear it?" he asked, looking down in disgust at the flat-ended cone of black straw trimmed round the poke with ugly black-silk roses—a style much too old for a child to wear. "I like you better as you are."

"Grandmamma says that proper young ladies must wear hats when out of doors."

"I see. But don't you think it's . . . a bit odious?"

"I think it's the ugliest headpiece I've ever beheld. Mama would never have . . ." My voice failed me at the memory of her, and I dropped my eyes.

"No, she wouldn't have. Your mother's taste in hats was excellent."

I blinked up at him. "How do you know?"

"I knew her fairly well. I remember the day when I first

met her. Your father brought her to Pentargon to meet the family—my mother and father were both alive then—and she wore a yellow straw hat with the widest brim and a cloud of feathers above. I was only a lad of sixteen at the time, but I thought she was magnificent in that hat."

"Yes," I murmured, feeling my throat burn, "she liked . . . feathers . . ."

"This creation," he said, holding my bonnet aloft for inspection, "is an insult to her memory."

He was right. "But you see," I sighed, "Grandmamma said I had to wear something black for mourning, and it was the most suitable thing they could find."

"Nevertheless, it insults your mother's memory." He opened his window and cast the bonnet to the winds.

"Good heavens!" I gasped, watching it fly off like a ruffled crow. "Grandmamma will be *livid!*"

"'Grandmamma' will never know."

I didn't know whether to laugh or cry. "But . . . it was the only bonnet I had. If I go about in public bareheaded, people will think I . . . I . . ."

"People will think what?" he asked, studying my face intently.

"That I'm . . . vulgar."

He frowned. "People will think you're a girl without a hat. That's all."

"But Grandmamma says—"

"Hang what Grandmamma says! Nobody in his right mind would think you vulgar, even if you appeared in public without *shoes*. Nobody! You have my word on that."

"Even without shoes?" I looked at him suspiciously. "Why wouldn't they?"

"Because there's not a vulgar bone in your body, that's why," he growled. "However, if it will make you feel more comfortable, we shall find a milliner in the morning and buy you a hat that would do your mother proud."

"Thank you, Oliver," I murmured, feeling my throat burn again in gratitude and pleasure.

His brow was still knit and his eyes fixed on my face. "You overheard what passed between your grandmother and me this afternoon, didn't you?" he accused.

My eyes fell, and I nodded.

"It was all nonsense. It would be foolish of you to refine on it."

I couldn't answer. Now that my stomach had settled, the lump in my chest seemed all the more painful. Grandmamma had been quite decisive in her opinions about my mother and in her conclusion that I would follow the same path. How could I be sure that Oliver was sincere when he called it all nonsense?

We rode along in silence for a while. I kept my eyes on the window through which nothing at all was visible except an occasional light.

"She was not a harlot, you know," he said suddenly, his tone firm and matter-of-fact.

I turned and looked at him wonderingly. "W-Wasn't she?"

"Not at all. She was a generous, loving woman who never gave herself to a man unless her heart was involved."

My underlip began to tremble. "Did that ... m-make it all right, then?" I asked timidly. "To G-God, I mean?"

Oliver stared at me for a moment and then got up and took a place beside me. "I'm quite certain it did," he said quietly, putting an arm about my shoulder. "With what else would God concern himself except the heart?"

Tears stung my eyes. "I'm afraid I'm ... about to c-cry," I told him.

"Go right ahead."

"B-But you said ... self-pity ..." I tried to wipe away the spilling tears with the back of my hand.

He took out his handkerchief again and dabbed at my cheeks. "It's not self-pity to cry for *her*."

The tears came then in earnest, and suddenly there was nothing I could do to stop them. I turned my face into his chest and wept. I could feel his hand gently stroking my head as my sobs racked me.

It seemed like hours before I'd cried myself out. But when I stopped, I noticed that the lump in my chest had considerably diminished. It would never completely disappear, I realized, but it had shrunk to a manageable size. I could once again breathe without pain.

Chapter Four

I WAS TO learn later that my guardian was an eccentric and that my life at Pentargon was blatantly unorthodox. But to me, after the years with my mother, my time at Pentargon seemed wonderfully carefree. Everything about my new home suited me. My bedroom, on the southwest corner of the third floor, had a view of the sea, a prospect that so delighted me that I barely took notice of the shabby bed-hangings or the unadorned furniture. I could smell the sea everywhere, which made a pleasure of merely breathing the air.

Every season at Pentargon had its own charm. In the spring the blooms on the rhododendrons which edged the road and surrounded the castle were as huge as cabbages, and the sun sparkled in the crisp air; in the summer the weather was so balmy that I was permitted to run about out of doors all day, even in the rain; in the fall and winter the mist from the sea touched the landscape with the aura of fairyland. Even the castle itself was magical to me. It was full of dusty passages, interesting little nooks and secret rooms—the sort of place where a child could wander about exploring or hide away for hours with a book without being found.

Oliver's idea of child-rearing was, to say the least, casual.

He rarely gave orders or made rules. So long as I didn't inflict myself on him—irritate him with questions when he was trying to read or impose myself on him when he was occupied with the business of the land or with his experiments in his greenhouses—he made no complaint about my behavior. He hated arguments, however, and expected all his decisions to be accepted without question. One day, for instance, when he was working over his account books and I came in to beg him to take me riding, he merely lifted me bodily from the floor, tucked me under one arm, deposited me like a bundle of laundry on the floor of the corridor outside his study and closed the door on me. He always seemed to prefer an act of physical decisiveness to verbal confrontation.

But we had little confrontation. I liked being left to myself as much as he liked being able to continue with his accustomed ways without changing to suit our new situation. He led his life and I mine. I was expected to appear at the dinner table on time and in passably presentable garb, but otherwise he required little of me and had little to do with me.

The other members of the household were equally nonchalant about my presence in their midst. Trewin, the Cornishman who was butler, footman, coachman and general factotum, made funny faces at me when he thought my behavior unladylike, but he otherwise treated me like a fond uncle. His wife, who doubled as housekeeper and cook, clucked over me fondly and pressed me always to "eat a wee bit more." Their son Jacka tended the horses, and their married daughter, Eda, came daily from her own little home a short distance down the road (while her mother-in-law tended her two babies) to help in the kitchen, but neither of them would presume to reprimand me for anything I did.

This small household staff was not capable of keeping the sprawling castle in tidy condition—it would have taken a staff of twenty to keep the place dusted, scrubbed and in complete repair. But Oliver, who employed a large number of men on his farms and orchards, cared little about the condition of the house itself. Therefore every room was, to my mind, comfortably disheveled. One could put one's feet up on the furniture, pile books and papers on the floor alongside one's chair, leave one's sweater or slippers on the hearth, or drop one's apple core in a precious, antique vase without ever being chastized or made to pick up.

Oliver, having long ago found his bailiff a useless appendage, now managed his own estates, an occupation which took much of his time. In addition, he had a passion for botany, and he had set up his greenhouses so that he could experiment with the effect of light and temperature on the development of fruit trees. His orchards were the wonder of the region, and he spent much of every day working over his seedlings and noting their changes. He also corresponded with other scientists who were interested in the subject—Robert Brown in Scotland, De Candolle in Switzerland and the Chevalier de Lamarck in France, who had already written a treatise in which he theorized that plants change to adapt to their environment—the very theory which Oliver was working to prove.

Oliver had two other passions—reading and riding—and they soon became mine as well. He had collected a sizeable library, which he housed in a dusty room on the first floor. I had free access to its treasures, among which I managed to find (amidst a great number of tomes of scientific or historical significance far beyond my comprehension) hundreds of volumes of interest to me. There was Malory's *Le Morte d'Arthur*, Chaucer's *Boke of the Duchesse*, the poems of Donne and Marvell, Robert Burton's *Anatomy of Melancholy* (which I read with difficulty in short doses after Oliver had remarked that it would do me good to make the acquaintance of an author of such intellectual depth and rich scholarship), *Paradise Lost*, Dryden, Pope, Pepys *Diary*, and of course, Shakespeare. But what I most eagerly devoured were novels. I found all of Richardson's voluminous stories on the shelves (all of which I read avidly but found rather silly), *Peregrine Pickle*, all the works of Fielding, a copy of *Gulliver's Travels* (which I read and reread dozens of times), and Goldsmith's *The Vicar of Wakefield* (over which I wept many a happy tear).

In addition, Oliver insisted that I peruse the London papers regularly. The war with Napoleon was coming to an end, he said, and the stuff of history was unfolding on those sheets. He followed the progress of events closely and expected me to do the same.

The other passion I shared with my cousin was riding. Oliver was gone from the house almost every morning at the first light, racing across the fields and jumping the hedges on his great roan. He taught me to ride during my very first year at Pentargon, and after I'd grasped the rudiments, I convinced him that I would improve much more quickly if he permitted me to ride astride, like a boy. Thenceforth, a pair of leather breeches that had once belonged to him, a thick sweater and a peaked hunting cap into which I tucked my hair became my riding costume, and there was no stopping me. On my four-teenth birthday, Oliver gave me a sweet bay mare of my very own, which I named Belinda (after Pope's heroine) because of her beautiful mane. I think that day was the happiest I'd ever to that time experienced.

But you should not believe, dear reader, that my life at Pentargon was entirely hedonistic. Grandmamma had seen to it that such should not be the case. I had not been three weeks in Cornwall when she sent an emissary. Discipline arrived at the doorstep in the person of Miss Hildegarde Gribbin. Miss Gribbin, a thin, stiff, angular woman in her mid-thirties, carried with her a letter from my grandmother informing his lordship that the bearer had been carefully selected from among a dozen applicants for the post of governess to Lady Marietta Saunders' granddaughter.

Thus Pentargon's doors were opened to yet another indi-vidual—my governess. Mrs. Trewin, now having another mouth to feed, was forced to suggest to his lordship that perhaps we should hire a housemaid to help with the cleaning so that she and Eda would have more time for the cooking, and curly haired Mabyn was engaged. Oliver's once-quiet household was growing by leaps and bounds.

I could see, during the evening of the day of Miss Gribbin's arrival, that Oliver was not pleased by her presence. No sooner had the three of us sat down to dinner when she began to fidget. She pursed her mouth in disapproval as she took note of the dust which had collected on the edges of the frames of the portraits which covered the walls, and she stared with unmis-takable horror (and for an inordinate length of time) at the cobwebs in the corners of the high ceiling. Then she deliberately picked up each one of the silver utensils at her place and wiped it with her handkerchief. I could hear Oliver growl under his breath.

Oliver was not the sort of man to permit himself to be discomfitted in his own home. As soon as dinner was over, he took Miss Gribbin aside. "I hope you won't take offense, ma'am, if I request that you take your dinner with Mr. and Mrs. Trewin in future. You see, my ward and I have formed the habit of exchanging privacies over the dinner table, that hour being the only one during our busy day when we can be certain to be free of interruption."

Miss Gribbin, standing imposingly tall at five feet six, nevertheless had to look up to meet his eyes. It was the first close look she'd taken of him, and even from my position at the far end of the table I could see her melt. "But of *course*, my lord," she gushed, "I understand *perfectly*, Indeed, I'm touched to the heart that you've taken so great an interest in the child. Lady Marietta was afraid . . . that is, she confided in me that . . . er . . ."

"That I was a most reluctant guardian?"

Miss Gribbin reddened. "Yes, her ladyship *did* hint—"

"Well, she need no longer trouble herself on that score." He threw me a wink. "You may write and tell my aunt, Miss Gribbin, that I've taken to my guardian duties as easily as a frothblower takes to ale." Then, ignoring her effusions of approval, he turned on his heel and strode out of the room.

I found Miss Gribbin to be a great nuisance at first. She made me rise at six and insisted that I start my studies by eight and continue until noon. She would have filled my afternoons as well, but I ran to Oliver for support. He told her flatly that four hours of study were quite enough for me, that he required my assistance in the greenhouses for an hour in the afternoon, and that I was to have the rest of the time for myself. Miss Gribbin was horrified at such an arrangement. "But, my lord, I have a *schedule*," she insisted. "It's been approved by her *ladyship*. We must have time for music, sketching, French history—"

"Are you arguing with me, Miss Gribbin?" Oliver asked forbiddingly.

She had not yet learned Oliver's method for dealing with verbal confrontation. She tried to hold her ground. "I only wish to point out, my lord, how important—"

He took a step toward her. "But you agree, do you not, that a child has need of open air . . ."

"Yes, but—" She was forced to take two steps in retreat.

"And a period of time for quiet contemplation . . ." He advanced three more steps.

She retreated again. "Of course, but an entire afternoon—?"

"And an hour or so for riding?" By this time he'd backed her to the door.

"But Lady Marietta specifically ordered—" She was now standing in the corridor.

"My dear Miss Gribbin," he said shortly, "I don't intend to remind you again that it is I, not Lady Marietta, who pays your salary, and that it is I, not Lady Marietta, who is the child's guardian." And as was his wont in such situations, he closed the door on her.

Thus Miss Gribbin learned whose word was law at Pentargon. The poor governess tried to salvage something of her carefully planned schedule by begging me to spend at least one hour of the afternoon at the pianoforte. I felt so sorry for her in her defeat that I succumbed, but I never developed any real proficiency with the instrument, and whenever Oliver was anywhere within earshot when I sat down to practice, he bluntly ordered me to cease.

As time went on, Miss Gribbin lost some of her starchy air of disapproval and began to surrender to the lackadaisical atmosphere of the household. I grew to like her better as her garb became less formidable, her hair less severely combed and her alarm at any curtailment of her "schedule" less intense. The more she ignored the signs of slovenly housekeeping and the general untidiness, the more agreeable I found her. She has never (even yet) grown completely accustomed to my willfulness and impulsiveness, to living in the midst of chaotic untidiness or to the eccentricities of our lives at Pentargon, but she grew fond of me nevertheless, and she has been my companion ever since.

Perhaps she would never have remained in the unruly, slapdash household of Oliver Fleming if she hadn't instantly fallen in love with him that first evening. Miss Gribbin was, at heart, a true romantic; she took one look at his dark locks, his sardonic expression and his offhand manner and, from that first day, was completely infatuated. As far as I knew, she never revealed her feelings to a soul. Nor did she harbor any expectation that her love would be returned. But I came to know her so well that I could guess he'd become the hero of all her romantic dreams. It is ironic, however, that as well as she came to know me, she never guessed that, in those days, he was also the hero of mine.

Mrs. Trewin and her daughter Eda, too, were enamored of their employer. Mrs. Trewin made no secret of the fact that she was completely devoted to him. In her eyes his lordship could do no wrong. Eda could never bring herself to say a word to him or to pass him in the corridors without turning beet red. Yet the object of all this adulation, Oliver himself, moved among us in complete ignorance of the dreams he inspired and the feelings he provoked. Toward Miss Gribbin he exhibited an impervious if polite indifference, toward Mrs. Trewin and her daughter an affectionate but impersonal familiarity, and toward me an avuncular indulgence. Not one of us had a shred of encouragement on which to base a hope, but that did not prevent us from dreaming.

But Miss Gribbin and I were soon to learn (as Mrs. Trewin and her daughter must certainly have known all along) that his lordship's romantic interests were turned in other directions. One evening a few months after Miss Gribbin joined the household, I was requested by Trewin to take my dinner with his family and Miss Gribbin in the kitchen. "His lordship's entertainin' guests t'night, see," he told me.

"Guests? How lovely! Who are they, Trewin, and why can't I dine with them? I'd like to meet his guests."

"Tain't fittin' fer 'ee," the butler said, hurrying off.

I chased after him down the hall. "Not fitting? Why not?" He stopped and gave me a shrug. "Baan't fer me t'say."

"I don't understand. Who are they, anyway?"

"Baan't fer me t'say," he muttered again, proceeding on his way.

I glared after him. "Well, if you won't tell me, I'll ask Oliver."

"Go on, if ye've no mind of a josing," he called back over his shoulder.

I went to the study, not being at all afraid of a scolding. Oliver had never scolded me. I opened the door and stopped in my tracks. A woman who'd been standing suggestively close to Oliver in the window embrasure moved away from him abruptly. She was a well-shaped woman with dark, glistening hair and unfathomable eyes, dressed rather showily for the country in a low-cut gown of Pompadour silk. It was a woman with *amour* on her mind; I could tell that at once. The look on her face was one which I'd often seen on my mother's when I'd come upon her in such a situation. I felt my heart sink at the recollection. "Oh!" I said awkwardly. "I didn't know—"

"This is my ward, Anne Saunders," Oliver said calmly to his guest. "Anne, this is Mrs. Longmuir. She and her sister and some friends, Sir James and Lady Tregoning, will be staying with us for a few days."

"How do you do?" I asked with loathing.

"What a little urchin!" Mrs. Longmuir exclaimed, crossing the room to me and lifting my chin with her hand to study my face. "How do you do, my dear? Really, Oliver, you must let my hairdresser do something with this wild hair. I don't think it's been cut since she was a babe."

"No, I don't want it touched," he said as I pulled out of her hold. "I rather like it the way it is. Did you wish to see me about something, Anne?"

"No, nothing. That is . . . it can wait," I muttered and backed out of the room. I had suddenly realized that I didn't want to be present at their dinner that night. The talk would probably be what I'd thought of since childhood as *amour* talk, the sort of flirtatious badinage that my mother had always enjoyed and that had always made me sick.

I had dinner that night in the kitchen, with Miss Gribbin, Mrs. Trewin and Jacka at the table and the new maid, Mabyn, serving us. Trewin had eaten earlier so that he could take care of the last-minute preparations in the dining room upstairs. Eda, who had already gone home to feed her husband and babies and was now back to help with the company dinner, stood at the stove keeping an eye on the roast and the bubbling soup while her mother took a momentary respite before the guests had to be served. "Does Mrs. Longmuir come here often?" I asked Mrs. Trewin.

"Too often, if 'ee asks me," Eda muttered from the stove.

"Tain't fer 'ee t'say," Mrs. Trewin said sharply. "'Is lordship can ask 'oo 'e wishes t' dine in 'is own 'ome."

"Hummmph!" was her daughter's comment. "I call it noggleheaded fer 'im t' keep on with 'er. With 'er married an' all."

"Do you mean . . . they're *lovers?*" I asked, appalled, even though I'd suspected the answer from the first.

Mrs. Gribbin gasped. "Really, Anne, it's decidedly improper for you to ask such a question. And Mrs. Trewin, I must make strong objection to your permitting your daughter to discuss—"

"Oh, aye, Miss Gribbin, I'm with 'ee there. Eda, ye jinny-ninny, cease yer prattle afore the chiel."

"I'm *not* a child! And I'm quite familiar with *amours*, so you needn't worry about me," I told Mrs. Trewin grandly.

Jacka chortled. "An' how did 'ee become so clever?" he asked, leering.

But his mother got up and slapped him smartly across the shoulders. "Mind 'ow ye speak t' the lass, ye totle! She's on'y a wee maid, but she's yer better by a long chalk, and don't 'ee ferget it!"

Miss Gribbin seemed to lose her appetite. Putting down her spoon, she stared at her bowl of soup with unseeing eyes and murmured something about his lordship being too much of a gentleman to indulge in such sordid affairs.

"Ha!" Eda laughed, sitting down on the hearth. "I ain't never heared of any gentleman what were too gentlemanly to indulge in 'em."

"Eda's in the right there," Jacka agreed, free of tongue again now that his mother had resumed her place down the table from him.

"Right or no, 'tis the last word I wish to 'ear on the matter from either one of 'ee!" Mrs. Trewin ordered. And her offspring obediently fell silent.

But Eda's last remark remained for a long time on my mind. If Oliver was indeed "indulging in sordid affairs," why didn't *he* have a tarnished reputation as my mother had had? Yet everyone, from my grandmother to the tinker who came to the kitchen door of Pentargon to sharpen the knives, treated him with the utmost respect. It didn't seem right.

Mrs. Longmuir and her party visited Pentargon several times in the months that follwed, as did other parties of ladies and gentlemen among whom there were several females who seemed to me to inspire Oliver's interest. And there were many weeks when he went away from home to visit friends. I hated all these interferences in our usual way of life. When they occurred, I was filled with angry resentment. I was barely civil to him for days afterwards. But I never expressed my feelings to him until one day, just after I became fifteen, when Mrs. Longmuir and her friends were again visiting the house. I had been riding, and when I entered the front door, still dressed in my shabby breeches and sweater, I found Mrs. Longmuir and Oliver standing together at the foot of the stairs. I felt the old, familiar disgust rise up in me.

Mrs. Longmuir looked me over with an almost imperceptible but, to me, clearly supercilious smile. "Ah, Anne, my dear girl," she said with silky cordiality, "I see you are still playing the urchin."

Fully aware of the unorthodox and untidy look of my "riding costume," I pulled off my riding cap and flushed. "Good afternoon, Mrs. Longmuir," I said coldly.

She chose to ignore my obvious dislike. "Still haven't done anything with your hair, I see," she remarked, coming across the hall to me and looking me over critically. "I was just about to go upstairs to dress for dinner. Why don't you do so, too? It's about time we had the pleasure of your company at the dinner table, don't you agree, Oliver?" She turned and walked back to him. "You don't want her to remain an impudent tomboy forever, you know," she murmured in his ear as she drifted by him and on up the stairs.

"Would you like to join the guests at dinner tonight?" Oliver asked me. "Perhaps it *is* a good idea for you to learn to deal with adults at the dinner table."

"No, thank you. I prefer the kitchen," I said, pushing past him to get to the stairs.

"I don't think I like that tone," he said, catching my arm and preventing me from leaving. "Mrs. Longmuir may be right. Perhaps you *are* an impudent tomboy."

I wrenched my arm free. "At least that's better than being a gentleman's *fancy piece!*" I hissed.

"What?" His face hardened. "I can't have heard you properly," he said, not quite believing his ears. "Or else you don't know what you're saying."

"I know quite well what I'm saying. I learned about such things at my mother's knee, remember?"

"If that crude reference was made about Mrs. Longmuir," he said, his eyes darkening, "you'd better remember that she's a guest in this house."

"But not of mine."

"Of *mine!*" he barked. "And you will treat her with respect, and you will come down to dinner in proper dress and with proper humility!"

"I *won't!*" I shouted, making for the stairs. "I won't sit down to the table with that woman, or with you, either!"

I was terrified, despite the rebelliousness of my words and the fierceness with which I shouted them. I knew he hated to engage in this sort of confrontation, and I fully expected him to pull my riding crop from my hand and beat me with it.

But the fury of his eyes was worse than the lash of any whip. "You will do as I say!" he said in a tone so implacably cold that I shivered, and with a gesture that said the discussion was at an end, he turned to walk away.

I was half crazed with agony. I was convinced that, unless I did as he ordered, the wonderful life that had been mine in the past two years would be destroyed. Yet every instinct in me fought against obeying him. I could not resist the impulse toward complete destruction. "There's nothing you can do to make me!" I cried after him childishly. "I'll *die* first! Mama at least *loved* her lovers . . . you said so yourself. But you and Mrs. Longmuir . . . she's j-just a harlot . . . and *so are you!*"

He swung round, enraged, and like many a parent before him who felt futile and helpless in dealing with a hysterical child, he slapped my face.

I cried out in pain and chagrin, staring at him in horror as the mark of his hand burned on my cheek beneath a flood of silent tears. He stared back at me, his face white with shock at my conduct . . . and at his own.

We stood unmoving for a long moment. I prayed that he would relent, embrace me, brush away my tears and tell me he was sorry. But he did none of those things. Instead, he picked me up under one arm as he'd done before, carried me up the stairs to my room and dumped me unfeelingly on my bed. "You're not to go down to supper at all, Miss," he said before taking his leave. "Not to the dining room or the kitchen either. You'll spend the night up here alone, with no food at all." And he slammed the door behind him, locked it from the outside and went away.

The next day, the sun came up in its accustomed way. I got up and dressed as usual, endured four hours of lessons with Miss Gribbin and then went to the greenhouse as was my wont. Oliver wordlessly handed me the record book, as usual, and we walked down the row of *Cydonia oblonga* seedlings, Oliver taking the measurements and calling them aloud as I entered them into the records. When we'd finished, he asked if I would like to ride. Of course, I said I would, and we raced across the fields in silence. When we'd tired our horses, we ambled back toward the house, exchanging desultory, commonplace remarks with a strained but healing amiability.

Oliver never apologized for his behavior of the day before,

and neither did I. And never, in all the ensuing years, did we refer to the incident again.

But Mrs. Longmuir and her friends were gone from the house that day. And I never saw her or any of the other women at Pentargon again.

Chapter Five

By 1815, MY sixteenth year, I'd become a strange creature indeed. I'd grown as tall as Miss Gribbin, brown as a berry from my preference for outdoor activities, wild of hair and spirit, and boyishly free in tongue and movement. Miss Gribbin, who two years earlier would have been appalled at my appearance and behavior, had grown so accustomed to the way of life at Pentargon that she barely noticed that there was anything peculiar about me. And Oliver, who was delighted at my ability to jump a horse, to assist him in his botanical experiments, to carry on an informed yet easy conversation with him at dinner, to help him with his scientific correspondence and his bookkeeping and otherwise to stay out of his way, was quite proud of his success in raising his ward.

I was happy with myself and my life. It did not occur to me that I was an eccentric. I only knew that I was not growing up like my mother, and that realization pleased me. I had no interest in pretty clothes, in the latest hairstyles, in jewelry and frippery adornments, or in *amour*. My grandmother's prediction that I would grow up to follow in my mother's footsteps (a prediction that had hung over me for years like a curse) now seemed utterly ridiculous. There was nothing about me to suggest a future as a courtesan. I was more like a potential *country squire* than a fancy piece!

I was vaguely aware of being lonely on occasion, but the feeling was not very deep or troubling. Most of the time I didn't want for companionship. There was Miss Gribbin, with whom I'd developed a close, comfortable kinship; there was Jacka, with whom I worked in the stables and who shared my love of horses; there was Mrs. Trewin, who always offered motherly sympathy when I bruised a knee or hot biscuits when I came in ravenous from a sojourn out-of-doors; and of course there was Oliver, with whom I rode, whom I assisted daily in the greenhouses, and whom I still regarded with a childish adoration. But none of these was a companion of my own age.

During the late spring of my sixteenth year, the Gilbarts came from London to stay for the summer at Nancarrow, the property just east of ours. Nancarrow had been run for years by a land agent, the owner, Lord Gilbart, preferring to live in London. This was the first time since I'd come to Cornwall that the manor house at Nancarrow had been occupied. Lord Gilbart still remained in London, but Lady Gilbart, her two daughters and her son were now in residence. One of the daughters was my age, the son a year older and the other daughter an old maid of twenty-three.

We learned all this from Eda who, by virtue of her domicile in the village, became the person on whom we relied for all the neighborhood news and gossip. "All three o' the ladies are right fashionable," Eda informed us as soon as the Gilbarts arrived. "They brought more'n a dozen trunks o' clothes. An' the lad's a friendly sort. They tell in the village that when the carriage was passin' through, the lad stopped the coach, got out, went into the Crown t' taste the ale an' greeted all the folk wi' smiles. But the ladies sat in the carriage mopish an' beetle-browed."

Oliver had never had much to do with the neighboring gentry and showed no interest in making the acquaintance of the newly arrived Gilbarts. We at Pentargon, therefore, had no expectation that their advent in our vicinity would have any effect on our lives. But this was not to be the case. A few days after Eda had announced their arrival, I came upon the Gilbart boy during my ride.

"Ho, there!" he shouted at me from across the field, waving

an angry arm and spurring his mount into a gallop so that I should not escape him. "You're *trespassing*."

"I ride here all the time," I responded unperturbed.

"So much the worse," he said as he pulled up alongside. "This is Nancarrow land, the property of the Gilbarts. What right have you—?"

"We've always taken passage through here, young man," I told him arrogantly while I studied him covertly from under the peak of my cap, "just as the residents of Nancarrow have always used our south field to cut through to the Exmoor Road."

The young man seemed to me to be outstandingly handsome and his riding costume was unquestionably the most elegant I'd ever beheld. "I don't care if it's been going on since William the Conquerer," he said, frowning at me sternly. "It will have to stop."

I shrugged. "You'll only be cutting off your nose to spite your face if you start enforcing trespass laws. You'd better think twice before—"

"I don't have to think at all," he cut in. "I don't like having strange fellows cavorting through my fields whenever they please, without so much as a by-your-leave."

"Will you like having to ask leave every time you need to ride northwest? That's just what will happen if you choose to make trouble, you know." I couldn't help admiring the fine figure he cut astride his sleek mount, but his attitude toward the mutual sharing of passageways between Pentargon and Nancarrow which had been established for hundreds of years seemed to me to be extremely foolish. "Besides," I explained, trying to encourage him to behave sensibly, "no strange fellows pass through here. Only Oliver and me."

"Oliver?" He looked at me curiously. "Is that Fleming of Pentargon? I've heard of him from my parents, so I suppose it's all right if *he* crosses through. But who are *you*, fellow? You can't be his son, for I've been told that Fleming is a bachelor."

"Son?" For a moment I was completely bewildered. Then, realizing that I must appear quite boyish with my legs astride my horse and my hair tucked up into Oliver's old hunting cap, I blushed in embarrassment. "I'm his ward," I said, pulling off my cap and holding out my hand. "I'm Anne Saunders."

He blinked at me in astonishment. "I'll be dashed! You're a *girl!*"

"I don't see why you should sound so surprised. One would think you'd never seen one before."

"I've never seen one like you. You're wearing *breeches*." His eyes lit with amusement, and his entire demeanor changed from aggressively challenging to decidedly friendly. He took my hand and shook it energetically. "How do you do? I'm Colin Gilbart. Do you always ride round the place in breeches? Don't people find it shocking?"

"Yes, I *do* always ride in breeches," I said irritably, "and I don't care if people find it shocking or not, Mr. Gilbart. Or is it your lordship?"

"Why don't you just call me Colin? But please, Miss Saunders, can you forgive my rudeness? If I had known you were a girl, I would never have—"

"Why not? What difference does my being a girl make? Trespassing is trespassing, no matter if I'm a girl or boy."

"It makes all the difference in the world," he grinned, "and if you don't know *that*, Miss Saunders, you must be younger than you look."

Something inside me shivered, and I tensed warily. "Good God! Are you *flirting* with me, Lord Gilbart?"

"I'm certainly trying to."

"Well, I wish you will not. I don't care for that sort of thing."

"Don't you? Why not? Most girls seem to like it very much."

"I don't care what most girls like. I suppose I'm different from most girls."

"I'll say you are. I've never met another who wore breeches."

"Well, you needn't make such a to-do over it. I'm not wearing them into your mother's drawing room, after all. I hope you are not a prig, sir."

"I promise you I'm not. And call me Colin, please, won't you?"

"I will, if you stop looking at me as if I were a *lusus naturae*."

"*Lusus naturae?* If I remember my Latin, that means a freak of nature, doesn't it? I do beg your pardon if I gaped at you as if you were. I don't think you at all a freak of nature. But why *do* you wear those shocking breeches?"

"Because I don't enjoy riding like a lady. Sedate little trots, sitting sidesaddle on a slug, are not for me. I like my horse to fly."

"Yes, I see. I watched you jump that hedge. I've never seen a girl take a jump like that."

"There aren't many *boys* who can do as well, I warrant," I boasted. "Can you?"

His eyes gleamed with excitement. "I'll race you down that slope and over to the top of the hill beyond, and we'll see. Are you game?"

I nodded, tucked my hair back into my cap, and off we went. As we raced, I discovered that it would be easy for me to win. I considered briefly pulling back on the reins, for I remembered hearing Mama once say that gentlemen did not enjoy being bested at games by ladies, and I very much wanted Colin Gilbart to like me. But the very idea of using one of Mama's ruses to win a gentleman's affection made me disgusted with myself, and I spurred Belinda on for all she was worth. By the time Colin caught up with me, I had dismounted and was sitting on the grass waiting for him.

I must say, for Colin, that he was not put off by his loss. Breathless and laughing, he congratulated me on my "superb seat" and would not let me go back home until I'd promised to meet him for another ride the next day. By the end of the week we'd become fast friends.

I liked Colin more than I wanted to admit to myself. I wanted nothing to do with *amour,* of course, so I dismissed from my mind even the *possibility* that I might be infatuated with him. But I was uncomfortably aware that the dimples that appeared in his cheeks when he smiled, his light eyes and his dandified, city coats enchanted me. Sometimes I found myself slipping into a lightly flirtatious badinage with him, and I became quite annoyed at myself. Flirting, giggling and teasing were not the sorts of activities of which I approved.

Most of the time we spent together involved riding. Those hours were vastly enjoyable. Sometimes, however, we walked along the craggy cliffs that edged the sea. Twice during those walks, Colin tried to take my hand or slip his arm about my waist. This reminded me of my mother and *amour,* so I slipped out of his grasp and walked on ahead. Fortunately, he was not insistent in these matters, and he'd proceed along the path without showing resentment at having been rebuffed. He seemed instinctively to understand that I preferred our friendship to remain uncomplicated, and he didn't press to change it.

During our walks, he spoke about himself and his family.

He appeared to be very fond of his two sisters and expressed a great admiration for the elder, Eliza. The younger, whom they called Dory, he described as a silly chit, but I could tell he liked her. His had been a conventional, comfortable, apparently happy upbringing—very different from what I'd experienced—and I felt many a stab of envy listening to him describe his home life. In its very ordinariness, it seemed far superior to mine.

After a while I began to wonder why he never brought his sisters along on our rides. Was he ashamed of me? Would his sisters be appalled at a strange creature in breeches? Just as I was beginning to feel offended, he informed me that his mother was going to hold a small party—with dancing—and had sent a card to Oliver, inviting him and his ward to attend. My heart jumped in my breast at the news, for I'd never been invited to a party in all my life!

I went home that day with my head swimming. I couldn't go, of course; I didn't even know how to behave at a party. I had nothing in my wardrobe remotely resembling a party dress. And besides, I didn't care for such things as parties.

Oliver told me at dinner that evening that he'd received the card from Lady Gilbart but had no intention of attending. Dinner parties, he said, were the greatest bore and dancing was worse. "But," he added as if it were a matter of little moment, "you may go if you wish."

If I *wished!* I had to admit to myself that there was nothing in the world I desired more.

I wept myself to sleep that night. Was I my mother's sort after all? How could I not be, if I could allow myself to become so upset over a party?

The next morning I had myself well in hand. I had determined in the night that I should ask Oliver that evening to send my regrets to Lady Gilbart along with his. But Miss Gribbin, who had heard about the invitation (for no message brought into the house was secret from the Trewins, and Miss Gribbin and Mrs. Trewin were as thick as thieves), would not hear of my refusal. "It's time, my love, that you learned how to conduct yourself in polite society," she insisted. "You cannot spend your entire life on horseback, you know. If you don't begin to associate with the proper sort of personages now, you'll only find yourself awkward in society later. I'm quite adamant, Anne. If you oppose me in this, I shall take the matter up with his lordship this very afternoon."

I let her go ahead with her threat, for if I were *ordered* to attend the party, my guilt at acquiescing would be considerably diminished. Oliver listened to Miss Gribbin's argument and agreed that I should go. I went to bed that night a great deal happier than I'd been the night before.

There was, of course, the problem of a gown for me to wear. On this matter Oliver had nothing to say. He told Miss Gribbin that she might spend whatever was necessary but that he didn't wish to be involved in any discussion, since he was completely ignorant on the subject. Miss Gribbin, however, determined to go without sleep, if need be, in order to make me ready for this auspicious occasion. She and Mrs. Trewin pored over a pile of yellowed copies of *The Belle Assemblée* until they found a design they agreed was suitable for a young woman not yet "out." Then Eda and I were dispatched to Tavistock, thirty miles away, where there was a proper linen-draper and where we could choose a fabric worthy of the design. After more than an hour of whispered consultation (with the draper tapping his fingers impatiently on the counter while we deliberated) we chose a cornflower-blue lustring and hurried home with our purchase.

Only three days remained in which to make ready. There followed an orgy of cutting, stitching, and fitting, with every female in the household taking part. Miss Gribbin organized everyone, dashing down to the kitchen (where Eda sat at the hearth sewing lace on the edge of the collar and Mrs. Trewin gathered the tops of the sleeves), up to the sitting room (where I stood in the center of a floor littered with pattern pieces and bits of fabric waiting for the bodice to be pinned), and down again (to pick up the paper of pins she'd left behind). She was indefatigable, and she patiently ignored the sarcastic remarks I made about the whole proceeding.

In the midst of all this excitement, I pretended to an indifference I was far from feeling. I, who had prided myself on my lack of interest in feminine fripperies, was in a tremble over everything. My remarks about the foolishness of lace trimmings, the needlessness of three fittings for the bodice, the senselessness of worrying about whether the sleeves should end at the elbow or the middle of the upper arm were all a pretense, and Miss Gribbin knew me well enough to understand that they were just covering up my nervousness. She had set her heart on making me the belle of the affair, and she let nothing stand in her way. She barely ate her meals and took only a couple of hours of sleep each night so that the gown would be ready on time.

I, on the other hand, continued to the end to pretend to feel complete disdain. Yet inside I worried about every decision. Was the high neck too girlish? Was the fit of the bodice too tight? Would a lace ruffle at the neck be more appropriate for a dinner gown than the little collar Mrs. Trewin was so industriously fashioning? Was the sweep of the skirt too full? Aloud I declared these problems to be too trivial to trouble over, but at night their solutions kept me awake for hours.

The dress was almost ready when the day of the party dawned. Only the lace flounce at the bottom had to be stitched. It was then that Miss Gribbin ordered the final fitting. She was putting pins through the buttonholes at the back when she realized, with a gasp of horror, that we hadn't purchased any buttons. On the verge of hysteria, she ran to her bedroom, ransacked through her wardrobe until she discovered that the buttons on her very best gown were of a blue not too different from the color of the party dress. She cut them off at once and set Eda to stitching them on my gown.

But that was not to be the only crisis. After buttoning me into the dress, pulling all the basting stitches from the hem and sitting back on her heels to gaze up at me with satisfaction, she remarked that, with my white gloves, I would do very nicely. "White gloves?" I asked. "What white gloves?"

The poor governess paled. "Heavens! I forgot to tell you to purchase a pair when you went to Tavistock! But don't you have an old pair tucked away somewhere?"

"No, of course not. Why would I have white gloves? I've never *been* to a party before."

She stared up at me as if she'd heard that the world was about to crumble. "You can *not,*" she exclaimed, her eyes filling with tears, "show your face in society *ungloved!*"

Neither Mrs. Trewin nor Eda could help. Poor Miss Gribbin was beside herself. She set the whole staff searching through the drawers of the furniture in all the unoccupied bedrooms, hoping desperately that someone at some time past had left a pair behind. Meanwhile, she took out a pair of her own and tried to mend them, but they were so shabby she had to give up.

It was Oliver who came to our rescue. Noting the unusual activity around him, he inquired of the maid Mabyn what was going on. Half an hour later he appeared in the sitting room and dropped a pair of elegant, long white leather gloves into Miss Gribbin's lap. "Will these do? I unearthed them from a trunk containing some of my mother's belongings. They're a bit yellowed, I'm afraid."

"Oh, my lord," she sighed, rising to her feet in relief, "they are *beautiful*. The yellowing doesn't matter. If I can't freshen them with neat's-foot oil, I'll . . . I'll . . ." She grinned up at him blissfully, her eyes alight with inspiration. "I'll touch them up with the white paint from my watercolors!"

Thus it was that I was dressed and ready that evening at seven, my gown complete to the last stitch of the hem, my gloves so carefully touched up with white pigment that to my eyes they looked new, and my hair pommaded and brushed to a gleaming smoothness.

My hair had caused the penultimate crisis that afternoon. I had braided it and tied the braids round my head, but Miss Gribbin decreed that the style was too mature for a young miss of sixteen. However, leaving it loose would have been worse, for my hair was naturally so kinked and frizzled that it stood away from my head in dismayingly wild abandon. Therefore, Mrs. Trewin hastily pieced together some leftover scraps of the dress fabric to make a wide, beautiful bow, which Miss Gribbin (after dressing my locks with pomade and brushing them with embattled determination, as if by sheer force of her will she would make them lie in place) used to tie back my hair at the nape of the neck. Thus tamed, gloved and gowned, I stood before the mirror in my bedroom, astounded at my transformed appearance.

But one more crisis had to be resolved before I could depart. I needed some sort of outer covering, for I didn't own an evening cloak. "But it's much too warm for a cloak," I assured the frenzied Miss Gribbin.

"That may be," she responded, biting her lip, "but you must have *something*."

That crisis was resolved by Eda, who ran home and returned with a package which she shyly offered me. It contained a handwoven shawl of white wool which she'd worn on her wedding day. It had an elaborately knotted fringe round its edge, and I found it so lovely that I gasped when I saw it. I accepted her generous offer with heartfelt gratitude and threw it round my shoulders feeling like a queen.

Mabyn came upstairs to announce that Trewin had brought the carriage to the door. Mrs. Trewin and Eda hugged me excitedly. After a last look at myself in the mirror, I embraced the tearful Miss Gribbin and hurried downstairs.

Oliver was waiting for me at the foot of the stairway, a little nosegay of rust-red roses in his hand. At first he didn't say anything, but from the look in his eye I could tell that my appearance pleased him. He held out the flowers. *"Rose rubiginasa,"* he said. "A sub-species of my own."

"They're beautiful," I murmured, lowering my face into them so that he wouldn't see how I glowed with pleasure. Then, unable to stop myself, I reached up, pulled his head down and kissed his cheek.

"I'll send the carriage back for you at ten," he said gruffly.

"Ten!" I objected loudly. "The dancing will barely have *begun!*

He frowned. "Eleven, then."

"Twelve," I bargained quickly.

"Eleven-thirty," he compromised with a sudden grin. "You're not Cinderella, you know."

I laughed, blew him a kiss and ran out the door. I may not have been Cinderella, but this was as close as I would ever come.

Chapter Six

THERE WERE SO many carriages in the drive at Nancarrow that Trewin, in his role as coachman, had to wait in line to draw up at the door. Jacka, dressed in footman's livery for the occasion, helped me down from the carriage as soon as we managed to reach the door, winked at me encouragingly and hopped up on the box beside his father. With a tip of his hat, Trewin called out, "Back for 'ee at 'alf past eleven sharrrp, Miss Anne," and drove off.

I stood alone at the bottom of the stone steps leading to the front door of the Gilbart manor house, clutching my roses in nervous hands, my emotions swinging uneasily between eager anticipation and fearful dread. In her effort to deck me out in proper rig, my governess had not had time to advise me how to go on at a party. What mysterious rituals of behavior, manner or speech would be practiced in the rooms above? Was there some special way of greeting my hostess, of holding a teacup, of taking a dance-partner's arm that I had never been taught?

I hesitated, feeling an urge to lift my skirts and flee on foot across the fields. But the Gilbart's butler, standing at the open doorway, was looking down on me with eyebrows oh-so-slightly raised, and I squared my shoulders, tucked my roses into my sash, looked him disdainfully in the eye and marched up the steps.

I could tell at once that I was not to be a Cinderella at this ball. There were signs from the very first that I and my various "fairy godmothers" had gone wrong on every count. And it took no more than a quarter-hour before I found myself wishing I had never come.

First there was the scene in the hallway. I gave the haughty butler my name, and he passed me on to a footman, magnificently powdered and liveried in white and gold, who took my shawl (which I had handled with the care one would give to a most precious work of art) and threw it over his arm with such carelessness that the fringe swept the floor. "Look *out!*" I cried indignantly. "It's a friend's *wedding* shawl!"

The butler, the next arrivals and two other footmen turned to stare at me, their expressions clearly indicating that I'd already made a *gaucherie*. The offending footman, as impassive as a statue, begged my pardon with indifference and indicated that I was to follow him down the hall. He led me to the drawing room. Within the doorway, the Gilbarts were lined up to greet the guests. The room, enormous as it was, already was crowded. (Lady Gilbart's conception of a "small" party, it seemed to me, was most peculiar; there were at least thirty people in the drawing room already and more than a dozen were lining up behind me.) I gave the footman a warning to take good care of my shawl, and I stepped inside.

Colin was the first to greet me. "I say," he whispered, grinning, as he led me to his mother, "I hardly *knew* you in a dress."

He was flushed and excited, very conscious of being the "host" in the absence of his father. He introduced me to his mother, Lady Gilbart, and disappeared. I stared up into the face of an intimidating woman wearing a gown of purple silk with a dazzling brooch of precious stones on her bosom and a feathered, bejeweled turban on her head. Her eyes swept over me, her penciled eyebrows arching in subtle but unmistakable disesteem. "How do you do, Miss Saunders?" she queried with cool politeness. "I was sorry to learn that your guardian, Lord Fleming, would not be with us this evening." She threw a look at a young woman standing beside her. "We—my family and I—were looking forward to meeting him."

"How do you do, ma'am?" I replied with my sweetest smile,

hoping by an unexceptional demeanor to make amends for Oliver's absence. "Lord Fleming is not given to social pursuits, I'm afraid."

"Yes, so I'm told," She frowned sourly. "I find that completely reprehensible of him."

"But Mama," the young woman at her side cautioned in a low voice, "that cannot be Miss Saunders' fault."

Her mother would not be silenced. "Nevertheless, I can't help feeling offended by his lordship," she said, glowering at me. "Tell me, Miss Saunders, doesn't your guardian hold with the maxim that one should love one's neighbor?"

"I believe that here in Cornwall, ma'am," I quipped, "the maxim reads: *Love thy neighbor but pull not down thy hedge*."

No one laughed, and I could feel my smile grow stiff. Her ladyship scowled more fiercely at me. "I don't believe you've met my daughter," she said icily and without another word or glance in my direction, turned to the guests who'd come in behind me.

Her daughter took my hand. "It's a pleasure to meet Colin's Anne," she said with what seemed to be sincere warmth. "He speaks of you so often and says you're a bruising rider. I'm Eliza, you know."

I had guessed she was Colin's eldest sister. Slim, pale-faced and gentle, she had silky blonde hair tied back from a well-chiseled face and long, graceful hands. I liked her at once. But before I could answer her, her mother demanded her attention to greet the next guest, and I found myself in front of the younger sister, Dory.

"You're Miss Saunders, aren't you?" she asked, looking at me with frank surprise. "I thought it must be you, even though you're not what I expected. I'm Dorothea, but everyone calls me Dory."

She was my age and about my height, but there our resemblance ended. She was quite lovely in spite of being somewhat plump, with the sort of complexion that inspires observers to use the expression "peaches and cream." Her light eyes and hair were very like her brother's, and she wore a dress of white jaconet which was cut modestly low over the bosom and trimmed with ornate embroidery done in silver thread. There was a silver fillet in her hair, a silver ribbon round her neck with a cameo at the center, and a silver bracelet on her wrist. I suddenly realized that I looked the complete dowd.

"Why am I not what you expected?" I asked, feeling un-accountably belligerent.

She cocked her head and surveyed me with critical appraisal. "Colin told us, of course, that you were not in the common way, but I didn't expect you to be quite so ... so ..." But she seemed to think better of it and paused.

"Yes? Go on," I urged.

She shook her head. "Oh, never mind. We can talk about it later, if you like. Now, however, you must take a glass of ratafia from one of the waiters and look over all the young men Mama has invited. She's seen to it that all the gentry for miles around—and their offspring over the age of sixteen—would be here tonight. We shall have a splendid time of it, don't you agree?"

I didn't agree at all, but I didn't say so. As she turned to greet the next visitor in line, I walked into the press of people milling about the room and tried to determine what I was to do next. There were several young men and women in the room who were, like me, not yet of age, and I studied the younger girls with interest. All of them seemed to be wearing white gowns, and all of the gowns were cut low at the neck and shoulders. My dress, I realized with a sinking heart, was not at all the thing for an evening fête. Miss Gribbin, in her concern to dress me in a style appropriate for a young miss not yet out, had bent too far backward. I was attired in a style more suitable for an afternoon visit to the vicarage than for an evening dance.

My hair, too, was wrong. Not one of the other girls had tied her hair back with a bow. Even the youngest of them had contrived an elaborate coiffure, with tight curls gathered at each side of the head and falling jauntily about the ears. Mine, I now realized, was too innocently girlish and casual. The Cinderella feeling that had tingled my spirits only a short while earlier now deserted me, leaving behind only a miserable em-barrassment and a wish to hide behind a potted palm.

I caught the eye of a young woman standing near the window with a girl slightly younger than herself. They were both dressed in the white that was evidently *de rigueur*, and they looked properly stylish. The one who'd been looking at me nudged her companion, who turned to stare at me also. Then they leaned toward each other and giggled.

I was thoroughly enraged. *How dare they laugh at me just because of the clothes I wear?* I asked myself indignantly. I put up my chin and turned my back on them, determined to prove to them, to my hostess and to the world in general that there was more to me than the style of dress on my back. Mama may have believed (as she'd often said) that she'd rather be dead than out of fashion, but I'd spent the last four years trying to outgrow such foolish concepts. I would show them all that character was worth more than fine clothes.

With head erect, I made my way through the crowd to the nearest waiter and took a glass of ratafia from his tray. The cordial was thin, warmish and smelled strongly of almonds. One sip told me that it was exactly as I'd once heard Oliver describe it—a drink of weak tea in which a maximum of aroma converts itself to a minimum of taste. "One can't call it a cordial." he'd said. "It's so *un*cordial that it should be called *rude*."

I looked about me for somewhere to rid myself of the drink, for the waiter had disappeared into the crowd and I did not see another one within easy reach. At that moment, someone pressed against me from behind and jogged my elbow. *"Blast!"* I cried aloud as the liquor splashed from the glass right on the bodice of my dress.

I ignored the shocked stared of the people around me and tried to brush away the spill before it set itself into the fabric. But I had no opportunity to check on the result of my hasty brushing, for Colin was hailing me. "I say, Anne," he called, wending his way gracefully through the crowd with a tap on a shoulder here and a smile there, "I've been looking for you." With what seemed to me to be admirable ease, he cut a path right through the crowd, ushering a young lady along with him. I kept my left hand over the stain on my bodice, looking, I was sure, like a dowager trying to catch her breath.

"I want you to meet Miss Inglebright, who's come all the way from Devon with her brother, Henry, who is my closest friend. Miss Laura Inglebright, this is our neighbor, Miss Anne Saunders."

We smiled at each other with strained politeness. Miss Inglebright was by far the prettiest girl in the room, and I could see at once that Colin was smitten. His color was high, and he couldn't seem to take his eyes from her face. We said our howdedos, and Colin, feeling a responsibility for me, tried to find a way to keep both me and Miss Inglebright under his wing. "I've been telling Laura—Miss Inglebright—and her brother all about you, Anne. About what a smashing rider you are and all."

My earlier distress was not lightened by the realization that Colin had found more fascination in Miss Inglebright than in me. "Is that all you can say to people about me?" I asked him nastily. "I've been known to do other things beside ride."

"Yes, of course you have," Laura Inglebright said sweetly. "But do come with us, Miss Saunders, and meet my brother. Colin has whetted Henry's curiosity about you to an extraordinary degree."

I knew she was only being polite, and her complacent sweetness set my teeth on edge. "One would think I were a circus freak," I muttered, turning to find a waiter with whom I could deposit the half-spilled glass of ratafia.

"Not at all," Colin said, taking the drink from my hand and signaling a waiter with admirable aplomb. "I spoke of you in the most glowing terms. Now don't be so out-of-reason cross, my dear. Come along and let's find Henry."

There seemed no choice but to accompany them. Just as we started across the room, two footmen threw open the windows ahead of us, revealing a long, balustraded terrace with stone steps leading to the lawn beyond. Twilight falls late in Cornwall in early summer, and there was still enough daylight to see that a table had been set out on the terrace, running almost its entire length and covered with enormous platters and bowls piled high with all manner of delicacies. The open windows admitted a light breeze and the tantalizing aroma of the food, and a gasp of appreciation rippled through the throng. Everyone moved toward the windows which, reaching as they did from floor to ceiling, gave easy access to the balcony.

Miss Inglebright clapped her gloved hands with pleasure. "Oh, we shall be able to find Henry quite easily now. He's bound to be near one of the punch bowls." Her eyes sparkled with animation as they met Colin's, and I knew it would probably not matter to him whether or not *she* had a "superb seat" on a horse. He probably wouldn't care if she couldn't ride at all, or even if she didn't know a roan from a grey.

I followed them out to the terrace, wondering in a rush of panic whether I dared remove my hand from my bodice. If the deuced ratafia had soaked into the fabric, perhaps this exposure to the evening air would dry it quickly. (There was bound to be a stain, but I hoped it would not be noticeable in the dim twilight.) My best course, I decided, would be to keep my hand where it was and wait for darkness to fall.

I glanced covertly at Colin as we walked along. Although he was not yet eighteen, he seemed to my besotted eyes to be a man-of-the-world. His evening coat and elegant neckerchief were the equal of any man's in the room. His shirtpoints were high and stiff, but he carried his head with such grace and ease that one would think he'd been born in evening dress. I believed at that moment that I'd never seen anything so handsome, and I yearned to be able to win back his admiration, but I felt inadequate to the complexities of this social situation. And I was certainly no match for the pretty Miss Inglebright.

Her brother was indeed at the punch bowl, but he put down the laddle with alacrity when Colin addressed him. He turned to me at once, and before I could properly brace myself for this newest confrontation, Colin had made the introductions and Henry Ingelbright had lifted my limp hand to his lips.

I found myself looking at a rather stocky, dark-haired young man with a prominent nose, thick lips and an articifically cynical look in his eyes. Mr. Inglebright had adopted the style of weary disdain and careless nonchalance which had become so popular with young men since Lord Byron had published his *Corsair* a year earlier. Mr. Inglebright's hair was carelessly tousled, his coat and waistcoat carelessly unbuttoned, and his left hand carelessly pushed into the pocket of his breeches so that his stance might seem carelessly negligent.

If I had not been so familiar with my cousin Oliver (who by nature seemed to have the qualities which young Mr. Inglebright was so assiduously trying to ape), I might have been fooled into believing that he was as world-weary and cynical as he was trying to pretend. But compared to Oliver, this youth's attitude was so patently exaggerated and so inappropriate to his years that I wanted to laugh.

But Mr. Inglebright read nothing of this in my face, taken as he was with his own performance. "So," he said, his eyes sweeping over me superciliously, "you're the famous horsewoman Colin has been speaking of."

I pulled my hand from his grasp. "Colin must be sadly in need of subjects for conversation if the best he can do is prattle on about my horsemanship."

"I didn't only talk about your horsemanship," Colin said in laughing self-defense. "I also said you have a spirited tongue."

"Oh," I said, feeling foolish and completely tongue-tied. "Did you?"

"Yes, and I warned Henry to watch out for its bite."

Henry Inglebright looked me over measuringly. "He said you have a stinger in your tongue, ma'am. Shall I prepare to defend myself?"

His tone and his amused contemptuousness annoyed me. "Do you think you can, sir?" I retorted.

"I think I can. If you won't take my word, you may ask Colin if I'm not your equal in that *dis*respect."

His sister and Colin laughed at his pun, but I merely shrugged. "If that's a sample of your wit, Mr. Inglebright, your defenses will *not* be adequate, I'm afraid."

Before he could come back at me, the music started. It emanated from a room at the far end of the terrace. Colin turned to Laura eagerly. "Shall we go in to dance, Laura? I think we can safely leave Anne and Henry to insult each other in private."

I watched them walk off down the terrace with a sinking heart. Colin had introduced me to his friend merely to be rid of me. But I had no desire to bandy insults with Henry Inglebright. Whatever remained of my happy expectations of the evening died completely away. All I could wish for now was a quick end to the evening and a return to the blessed peace and privacy of my bedroom. But a few more disasters were in store for me before I was to have my wish.

"It would be too much to hope," Mr. Inglebright said, his voice cutting jarringly into my bleak reverie, "that you are as skilled at dancing as you are at riding, but I'm quite willing to stand up with you, if you wish to dance."

If that's the sort of rudeness which comes of adopting the 'Byronic manner,' I thought with teeth-gritting irritation, *then Lord Byron has a great deal to answer for.* But aloud I only acquiesced. And keeping my left hand clutched over the stain on my bodice, I put my right hand on his arm.

We walked along the length of the terrace without conversing, but before we arrived at the row of windows which gave on the ballroom, we passed Dory Gilbart, who was laughingly parrying the attentions of two eager young men, both of whom were trying to feed her bits of lobster patty. Her laughter faded as her eyes met those of my escort—I could see a spark of interest flash between them. But Dory's eyes fell as soon as she realized that I was on his arm, and Henry and I continued on our way.

The ballroom was brilliantly lit, and although most of the guests still remained outside on the terrace, two sets had been made up for a country dance. The few dancers seemed to be enjoying themselves greatly. Mr. Inglebright and I paused on the threshold to watch. It was then that the amazing fact burst upon me that I had no idea of how to dance!

I blinked at the dancers in astonishment. Each of the participants before me seemed remarkably well schooled in the intricacies of the steps and turns which they were executing. They had evidently practiced diligently to learn the complex and elaborate series of movements they were now performing with almost casual effortlessness. It would take me *years*, I was certain, to learn to dance like that!

How incredibly stupid I had been! Had I imagined that I could stand up on the dance floor and cavort to the music as I had done as a child when Mama'd played gay little tunes on the pianoforte? What had I been *thinking* of? The answer was that I hadn't thought at all.

Feeling the hot color creep into my cheeks, I said to Mr. Inglebright that I'd changed my mind. "I think I'd rather have a . . . a bite of supper first," I murmured.

He looked down at me knowingly. "Lost your pluck, Miss Saunders? Turning craven?"

"Not at all." I lifted my chin. "I'm merely hungry. But you needn't miss the dance on my account. I'm sure there are dozens of other young ladies who would turn handsprings of joy to be asked to dance by so witty and worldly a gentleman."

"Yes, that may well be true, but I promised Colin I'd look after you," he said, taking my arm smugly and turning back toward the buffet.

I pulled my hand loose. "There's not the least need, I assure you. I can very well look after myself." And I walked hastily away from him.

He followed. "A promise is a promise, Miss Saunders. I don't wish to do anything to incur Colin's wrath. He's my best friend, after all. I suppose I shouldn't have revealed to you that he asked me—"

"It doesn't matter," I said, angry and impatient. "I don't have any more desire for your company than you have for mine."

"Oh, I don't mind your company," he said with a fatuous air of generosity that made me want to box his ears, "even if you *are* a bit eccentric—"

"*Eccentric?* I am *not* eccentric!"

"I don't know what else you'd call someone with such peculiar attributes."

I glared at him furiously. "Just because my gown and the way I've dressed my hair do not meet the standard set by the *haut monde*—"

"It's not just your clothes," he said cold-bloodedly, turning to the table and beginning to heap two plates with lobster cakes, cheese buns, Italian truffles, candied turnips, little souffles and all sorts of sweetmeats, "it's everything about you."

"*Is* it indeed? For example—?"

He studied the contents of a chafing dish and wrinkled his nose. "These mushrooms look inedible. For example, my dear, you stride like a boy rather than mince like a girl, you lift your chin in a decidedly bellicose manner whenever you speak, and, for some reason which I haven't been able to determine, you always keep your left hand clasped on your bosom. If those qualities aren't eccentric, then I don't know what is."

I wondered how eccentric it would seem if I kicked him in his shins. "I don't *always* keep my left hand clasped on my bosom," I said defensively, removing the hand and dropping it to my side. "It's just that someone made me spill—" I looked down to see how badly the spill had stained my gown. "Oh, good *heavens!*" I gasped. A large white smear disfigured the front of my dress.

Mr. Inglebright, balancing a plate in each hand, turned to see what had upset me. His mouth dropped open at the sight of the strange-looking stain on my bodice. "My word! How did you do *that?*"

For a moment I didn't know how to answer. The stain looked more like paint than ratafia. Then I remembered. "The *paint!*" I muttered, agonized, and I stared in horror at the palm of my left glove. "I forgot about the paint."

"What paint?"

"On my g-glove . . ."

"You *painted* your *gloves?*" He blinked at me for a moment in disbelief and then emitted an ear-deafening guffaw. "That's the most ridiculous pass I've ever heard tell of. Painted gloves! And you say you're not an eccentric?"

As if his first guffaw was not enough, he now indulged in a paroxysm of laughter which caused several people standing nearby to gape at us. But I was too infuriated to let their stares bother me. "So you find this an amusing pass, do you?" I demanded, teeth clenched tightly.

He could only shake his head helplessly, the laughter rumbling through his chest. It was all he could do to keep the plates in his hands from tilting and spilling their contents on the floor. When his laughter had subsided to a mere chortle, he caught his breath and offered me a plate. "Here, take this supper before I drop the plate. I don't think I've ever laughed so much—"

I took the plate from him. "If stains on clothing amuse you so, let's hear you laugh at *this!*" I said, and I emptied the contents of my plate upon his head.

A gasp sounded from the people nearby. Henry Inglebright, frozen in chagrin, stood staring at me as bits of food slipped from his head to his nose, his shoulders or the floor.

"Young woman, are you *mad?*" a dowager standing nearby exclaimed in shocked tones.

I was painfully aware of the horrified expression on the faces of the growing circle of gawkers who surrounded us, but their patent disapproval only angered me more. Did it occur to *no one* that I might have had provocation for what I'd done? As a result of this additional resentment, I snatched the second plate from Inglebright's nerveless hand and added its contents to the remnants still remaining on his head.

"You're *worse* than eccentric," he yelped. "You're touched in your upper works, that's what you are!"

"*Am* I indeed? Then you will not be greatly surprised when I add the final touch to my decoration of your head." And before anyone could guess what I was about, I speedily dipped the ladle into the punch bowl and emptied the reddish liquid on top of all the rest. "There! Let's hear you laugh away *those* stains!"

"You cracked-brained vixen!" Inglebright shouted, wiping punch from his face.

"Miss *Saunders! Really!*" Dory Gilbart burst through the crowd and ran up to Inglebright with cries of sympathy. "Oh, poor *dear* Henry! Are you all right?"

"Yes, I suppose . . . confound it, just *look* at this shirt-front—!" he sputtered, brushing pieces of candied turnip from his shoulder and removing a sprig of watercress from behind his ear.

"Don't worry about that," she told him soothingly. "We'll just go along to Colin's room and get you a clean one."

She took his arm and began to lead him through the crowd but not before she looked over her shoulder at me and threw me a look of angry reproach.

I saw that look echoed in every face as I blundered my way through the crowd. My cheeks burned, and my eyes stung. Not one person seemed to care that Inglebright had humiliated and insulted me. I had not behaved like a lady, and that was all that mattered to them. Everyone I passed turned away from me in embarrassment. No one seemed to want to have anything to do with me.

I ran through the drawing room and into the hallway, which was blessedly deserted. From the entryway came the chimes of a clock. I counted ten. *Dash it all,* I thought unhappily, *I have to remain here for an hour and a half before Trewin comes for me.* Well, I would *not* return to the party, that much was certain. I looked down the length of the empty hallway. Somewhere along its length there had to be an unoccupied room. I would find it and hide myself within until my carriage came. Until then, I knew I would find myself fully occupied . . . in crying.

Chapter Seven

THE FIRST DOOR I tried opened upon a deserted room. It seemed to be the library, for it was too large to be a sitting room, and there were a small number of books arrayed upon the shelves that lined one wall. Whatever the room was, it contained a pair of high-backed chairs which had been placed before the fireplace, the farthest of which I approached. Turning it so that its back faced in the direction of the doorway, I seated myself in it, safe from the prying eyes of any chance intruder.

The tears which had been lurking just below the surface began to fall. In abject misery, I removed my gloves and dabbed away at the stain on my bodice. My eye fell on the roses tucked into my sash. The recollection of Oliver's presentation of them earlier that evening made my throat burn, and I gently removed the nosegay and pressed the blooms to my nose, my tears falling even more profusely. At that moment I heard the doorknob turn.

I started in fright. I had no wish to—I couldn't—face anyone in my condition. Quickly, I tucked my skirts and my legs under me and tried not to breathe.

"If I don't sit down for a moment or two," someone said from the doorway, "I shall collapse before this disastrous evening ends." I recognized the imperious tones of Lady Gilbart.

"Take the armchair near the window," came the voice of her daughter, Eliza, "and I'll push up the ottoman for your feet."

While they settled themselves into their chairs, I tried to find the courage to show myself. But I hesitated, and, meanwhile, her ladyship went on with her complaints. "Was there ever," she asked in a voice that trembled with annoyance, "a more vexing series of calamities? This sudden downpour of rain is the very last straw!"

"It *is* too bad the weather changed so abruptly," Eliza said soothingly, "but the footmen were very quick to move the tables inside. Nothing was spoilt."

"Nothing spoilt? The whole party is spoilt! It's been one long catastrophe! If nothing else, the evening was destoyed by the scene created by that bizzare Saunders chit. Everyone's whispering about it. It's quite ruined everything."

I tried to pull myself to my feet, but Lady Gilbart's words had made it almost impossible for me to reveal myself. Although I didn't wish to remain in the room eavesdropping (knowing quite well that the eavesdropper never hears good of herself—I'd already heard myself called bizarre), I couldn't seem to move. I told myself that the longer I hesitated, the more awkward it would be for me to make my presence known. But my eyes were red, my dress stained and my spirit shattered. I lacked the courage to bring further attention to myself and embarrassment to the two ladies on the other side of the room. Instead of standing and speaking up, I tensed every muscle into frozen motionlessness and prayed silently that I would not be discovered.

In the meantime, Eliza Gilbart was trying to reassure her mother about the success of her party. "You are making too much of it," she said in her soft-voiced way. "The dance floor is now full, the buffet continues to attract a throng and, if I'm any judge, everyone is enjoying the affair."

"Really, Eliza, you're so determinedly optimistic that sometimes you make me wish to scream. You'll tell me next that you expect the bird in the cuckoo clock to lay eggs! Are you trying to pretend that this party *isn't* a disaster?"

"Of course it isn't. Giving people something to whisper about doesn't lessen their enjoyment. And even Henry Inglebright is recovering his good spirits. I went to check on him in Colin's room, and I found Dory flirting with him shamelessly. Colin and Laura were there, too, and I believe that the dramatic events of the evening only increased their pleasure in participating in what seems to them a scene of delicious intimacy. All four were getting on famously."

I had to cover my mouth to keep from groaning. It was the last straw that I should have done something to help Colin "get on famously" with Laura Inglebright.

Lady Gilbart apparently had little interest in Henry Inglebright's state of mind. "At least you're willing to admit that the scene on the terrace was dramatic," she muttered sullenly.

"Yes, I admit that. Speaking of the drama, I can't help wondering where Miss Saunders has hidden herself. The poor child must be dreadfully upset."

"Poor child? She's a wretched little *cat,* and I don't care *where* she's gone. Has no one ever taught her how to go on? She shall never be invited to set foot in *this* house again, I promise you that!"

As if I would, even if you did *ask me!* was my mental rejoinder.

"Now, Mama," the gentle Eliza said, "you're being unfair. After all, we don't know what Henry might have done to the girl to upset her so."

My heart swelled with gratitude. There was at least *one* person in the world who gave a thought to my position.

But her mother would not be softened. "I don't care *what* Henry did. There is no possible excuse for the Saunders chit to have behaved so intemperately. I really can not imagine what it was that Colin saw in the creature. Thank goodness pretty little Laura's caught his fancy. If Colin must take up with a young woman at this early age, she's preferable to Anne Saunders by far! But the worst of it all is that our chances of ever making the acquaintance of Lord Fleming are now ruined. I suppose you realize *that,* don't you?"

"Please, Mama, I don't wish to speak about—"

"Naturally you don't. You *never* wish to speak about matters that are of real concern. Do you think I arranged this affair to provide entertainment for Dory and Colin and the rest of the children? You may think again, my love. The only reason I went to the trouble of holding this party was to give you the opportunity to make Fleming's acquaintance."

"You are being excessively foolish, Mama. Everyone knows the man is a confirmed bachelor. I don't see why you concocted a scheme so unlikely to bear fruit. If your reason really *was* to attract Fleming, you must have taken leave of your usual good sense."

"Eliza, I don't understand you at all! About everything in the world you maintain a highly optimistic view, but when it comes to your*self*, you see nothing but the worst. Why is it so hard for you to admit that you could easily attract a gentleman like Lord Fleming. I've been told that, some years ago, Fleming was pursuing Harriet Worthing, and Lady Jersey says that she was in many ways your *double*. She was fair, intelligent, sensibly restrained in manner, well-read and modest. You are, if anything, more graceful and pretty. Why then could *you* not attract him?"

"Mama, this conversation is silly. Fleming didn't *wed* Harriet Worthing, did he?"

"No, you're right about that. She let him escape her somehow. But you—"

"I haven't shown any particular ability to attract gentlemen who are much *less* slippery, so why do you insist that Lord Fleming would fall into my lap?"

"The only reason you haven't yet attracted a husband is because you haven't tried. If only you'd put a bit of *enthusiasm* into your dealings—"

"Enough, Mama. I sometimes think I'm not suited for marriage at all. I don't seem to be able to work up sufficient interest—"

"Nonsense! Every woman is suited for marriage. You *must* be! Do you want to end your days on the shelf? I'm not suggesting that Lord Fleming is the only prospect, however. Even here in Cornwall there are other possibilities. What did you think of Mr. Penrose?"

"The gentleman with the triple chins? Really, Mama—"

"Yes, I know. Hardly the answer to a maiden's prayer." Lady Gilbart gave another of her lusty sighs. "Every one of Cornwall's bachelors seems either to be doddering or under twenty. Dash it all, I had such high hopes of Lord Fleming."

"Don't fall into the dismals over it, Mama. I shall pass the summer here quite happily without having to trouble my head over callers and swains."

"Well, I *am* in the dismals. If that peculiar chit had not destroyed everything, we still might have hopes of meeting her guardian. Why did a man like Lord Fleming take it on himself to raise so eccentric a brat?"

"Please, Mama, you are being unkind. Miss Saunders is not really so strange a child as you seem to think."

"Isn't she? With that wild hair, those piercing eyes, that boyish manner and that sharp tongue—to say nothing of her dreadful temper—I'd like to know what else to call her."

I felt the blood draining from my face. Was I really as freakish as Lady Gilbart described me?

Eliza jumped to my defense by suggesting, "You might call her an original," but her mild compliment could not ease the pain which her mother's judgment inflicted on my soul.

"Ha!" her mother sneered. "She's an original, all right, though I wouldn't consider that appellation to be particularly complimentary."

"Nevertheless, Mama, some might find it so. And it may very well be that the girl's ways reflect her upbringing. Perhaps Lord Fleming is as eccentric as his ward. In any case, we don't know him and are not likely to learn any more than we do now, so this conversation is too speculative to be sensible. We should return to the party, shouldn't we? Our absence will be noted if we stay away much longer."

"Yes, you're right. Help me up, my love, there's a dear. Good heavens, that's a dreadful thought."

"What's a dreadful thought?"

I could hear them crossing to the door. Lady Gilbart sighed again before answering her daughter. "That Lord Fleming might be an eccentric himself. I don't think it possible. Lady Jersey and all the others who knew him when he lived in London, before the old earl died, speak most highly of him."

"But that was *years* ago. He may have changed considerably since."

They opened the door. "If he *has* turned eccentric, my dear," Lady Gilbart said from the hallway, "then perhaps it's just as well we won't meet him."

"Hush, Mama," her daughter cautioned, "we don't want anyone to hear—"

The door closed again and I was alone.

The sense of relief which I should have felt at having escaped

detection did not come. I was too shaken by a cruel vision—
a glimpse of myself which Lady Gilbart had supplied. I could
suddenly see with her eyes the strange configuration of appearance and manner which I presented to the world—a creature so wild-eyed, impulsive and unmannerly as to be "bizarre."
When I'd suggested to Colin at our first meeting that he'd
looked at me as if I were a *lusus naturae*, I'd only been joking.
But perhaps I really *was!*

A freak of nature! This startling glimpse of myself was a
blow of enormous proportions. I suddenly understood that in
some subtle, essential way—undetectable to me but quite plain
to sophisticated Londoners' eyes—I was distorted, twisted,
deformed. I found myself trembling with self-loathing. Shaken
and bewildered, I rose from the chair like a sleepwalker and,
clutching my gloves and my precious roses, stumbled out into
the hallway and out the front door.

Rain was pelting down in sheets, but I barely noticed it.
Instinct alone turned my feet toward home. Without paying
heed to my surroundings I stumbled through fields, climbed
stiles, sped over footpaths and circled trees until I'd traversed
the four miles of terrain that separated Nancarrow from Pentargon. Somewhere on a muddy lane I lost a shoe. Once I
tripped over the root of a tree and fell on my face. Running
blindly across our south lawn, I stumbled and fell on my knees,
ripping the hem of my gown. But I had only the vaguest awareness of any of this.

I sped across the lawns and through the kitchen gardens and
ran into the kitchen door. My chest heaved as I strove for air
in great, gasping breaths, but I dashed up the back stairs without
pausing. I was relieved to find the hallways dark and deserted,
and without a moment's hesitation I headed like a homing
pigeon for the destination which my instincts had chosen from
the first—Oliver's study.

From halfway down the hall I could see a thin beam of light
shining beneath his door. He was awake and waiting for me,
as I knew he would be. Without so much as a pause for a
knock, I burst in on him. He sat at his desk writing a letter in
the light of his prized Argand oil lamp, but he looked up at
once at the sound of the door, his expression eager and a smile
about to dawn on his lips. At the sight of me, however, his
face froze and a look of alarm flashed into his eyes. I realized

for the first time what I sight I must have been. Wet strands of hair hung over my face, raindrops dripping from the ends. My dress was muddy, torn and soaked through. My face must have been ghastly white and streaked with dirt. It must have taken iron control for him not to have gasped aloud.

Belatedly aware of my shocking appearance, I hesitated in the doorway. He rose from his chair, came round the desk and crossed the room in three strides. Without a word he held out his arms. I tumbled into them. "Anne, my dear, are you hurt?" he asked tensely.

I tried to speak but burst into sobs instead. All I could do was shake my head.

"You're soaked to the skin!" he exclaimed. "Didn't you come home with Trewin?"

Again I tried to answer, but I was too choked with sobs. I was shaking from head to toe and trying desperately to take in air in short, shallow, almost hiccoughing gulps.

Oliver lifted me in his arms and carried me from the room. "There, there," he murmured, "don't try to talk. Everything will be made right, whatever it is, I promise you."

He carried me up the stairs, shouting for Miss Gribbin as he climbed them. By the time we'd arrived at my bedroom door, Miss Gribbin and Mrs. Trewin were following anxiously behind him. "My heavens, what's *happened?*" Miss Gribbin cried out when Oliver laid me on the bed and she got a glimpse of me.

"Don't pelt her with questions, woman," Oliver barked. "Just strip those wet things from her back and make her dry and warm. I'll be right back."

I was immediately engulfed in waves of tender solicitude. Both Miss Gribbin and Mrs. Trewin murmured and clucked and emitted bleats of sympathy as they towelled my hair and gingerly removed my clothing. Under their soothing ministrations my sobbing diminished, and Mrs. Trewin, unable to contain herself, soon blurted out a question despite his lordship's order. "The carriage baan't overturned, be it, chiel? Ye ain't 'ad an accident, have 'ee?"

"Hush, Mrs. Trewin," Miss Gribbin whispered over my head as she gently slipped a clean flannel nightdress over me, "you know his lordship said to leave the girl be."

"It's all right," I said, lying back against the pillows. "I'm feeling much better. There was no accident, Mrs. Trewin."

Mrs. Trewin expelled a relieved breath as she drew a coverlet over me.

"But didn't the carriage come for you?" Miss Gribbin asked, completely puzzled. "Trewin set out shortly after eleven, just as arranged."

I felt drained and numb. "I didn't wait for him," I explained, closing my eyes. "I walked home."

"*Walked?* In this downpour? Why on earth—?"

Miss Gribbin stopped speaking abruptly as a knock sounded at the door. She admitted Oliver, who came in carrying a milky liquid in a tall glass. With a movement of his head, he indicated to the women that they were to leave us. Obediently, without a word of remonstrance or an exchange of looks, they withdrew and closed the door behind them.

"Here," he said, giving me the glass. "Drink it down."

I took a sip and made a face. "It's as bad as ratafia. What is it?"

"Warm milk laced with brandy. Drink it. You must be chilled through."

I did as he bid me and found the warm liquid surprisingly comforting.

"So they gave you ratafia, eh? If that's the sort of refreshment they offered it couldn't have been much of a party." He took the empty glass, placed it on my nightstand and seated himself on the edge of the bed. "But a drink of ratafia, unpleasant as it is, would scarcely have caused such an outpouring of emotion. Do you wish to tell me what happened tonight?"

I lowered my eyes to the counterpane, hesitating. "I . . . I . . ."

I could feel his eyes searching my face. "It's all right, my dear. You needn't speak if you don't wish to. Shall I send in Miss Gribbin instead? Would you rather talk to her?"

I shook my head and grasped his arm. "No, no. P-Please stay."

His hand tightened on mine. "I only want to know . . ." He paused and looked closely at me. "If anyone has hurt you, I—"

"Oh, Oliver," I cried, throwing my arms about his neck and burying my face in his shoulder, "I'm so m-miserable! If I ask you s-something . . . something tremendously important . . . will you p-promise to tell me the truth?"

"Yes, if I know it," he said, stroking my head gently as he had done once before.

I lifted my head from his shoulder so that I could watch his face. "The *absolute* truth? No evasions or platitudes or . . . or gammon?"

"Now, girl, when have I ever given you platitudes or gammon? Or evaded any question you've asked?"

"Never, that I can remember. But I . . . I've never asked you a question like this."

"Well, I've given my word, so ask away."

I pulled away from him and leaned back against the pillows, keeping my eyes fixed on his. "Am I a . . . a *lusus naturae?*"

"What?" He blinked at me as if he'd never heard the phrase.

"You know. A f-freak of—"

"I know what the words mean, you goose. I just don't understand the question. Surely you must know that you are, in every way that I can see, a healthy, normal young woman with two eyes, a nose in the right place, ten fingers and ten toes—"

"I do know that," I snapped impatiently. "I mean, am I odd, peculiar . . . bizarre?"

"Bizarre?" His brows snapped together in puzzled concentration. "I'm afraid I still don't understand. Did someone call you bizarre?"

I nodded.

His amazement was rather comforting. "But why? Did you do something shocking, you vixen?"

"Yes, I did. But it was more than just that." I took a shivery breath and let out the whole story.

He laughed aloud when I related the incident at the buffet table, but by the time I'd repeated what I'd heard Lady Gilbart say about me (I very carefully had omitted all the references she'd made to himself), his expression showed tightly controlled fury. "That woman ought to be *horsewhipped!*" he snapped, getting up and pacing about the room. "Bizarre, indeed!" His hands clenched into fists as he strode from the foot of my bed to the window and back again. "I'd rather be a bizarre freak than a conformable sheep! Lady Gilbart seems to be nothing more than a jingle-brained goosecap whose tastes and ideas are dictated by the whims of the *ton.*"

"But . . . you're saying, then, that I . . . I *am* a *lusus naturae,*" I mumbled, crestfallen.

He stopped in his tracks and swung about to face me. "I'm saying nothing of the sort!" He strode to the bed, leaned over and seized me by the arms. "You asked for the truth, didn't you? Well, you shall have it. A *lusus naturae* is a creature deformed by some natural error—a mistake—a pathetic distortion of some sort. The phrase has *nothing whatever* to do with you! But nature also creates an occasional *rara avis*. Since you seem so attached to Latin phrases, attach yourself to that one. It refers to a bird of rare individuality, unusual color or the ability to fly higher than the rest. That phrase, my dear, is much more applicable to you. You're a *rara avis*. Remember it!"

My eyes opened wide. *"Am* I, Oliver? Really?"

"Yes, really."

"But . . . I suppose people may find a *rara avis* rather bizarre, might they not?"

"Only because of her uncommon individuality. The common birds in the flock feel confusion and envy when confronted with uniqueness and may therefore react to the *rara avis* in unkind ways. But there isn't one of them who wouldn't want to change places with her."

I looked up at him suspiciously. "Is that true?"

"Are you questioning my veracity, ma'am?"

"I want very much to believe you, but—"

"But—?"

"Doesn't Burton say in your precious *Anatomy of Melancholy* that *all our own geese are swans?"*

He rubbed his beard thoughtfully. "Yes, I suppose I could be guilty of *some* predisposition in your favor. But I'm not besotted, as a real parent might have been. I'm only your guardian, after all. You can have full confidence in my objectivity in this matter."

"Oh, Oliver, I wish I could believe—"

His eyebrows rose in exaggerated offense, and he dropped his hold on me. "You can believe me or not, as you wish," he said, starting for the door. "I've said all I intend to say on the subject."

"Well, if I'm such a *rara avis,"* I challenged, "why did Colin drop me like a hot coal as soon as Laura Inglebright came along?"

He turned and smiled at me, a hint of affection in his eyes. "Because, you greenhead, your Colin is nothing more than a callow youth. He hasn't the sense to see that you've not yet learned to preen your feathers. But just wait, my dear. In a very few years, your color will be so bright and you'll fly so high that fools like Colin Gilbart and Henry Inglebright will be dazzled."

"Oh, *Oliver!*" I breathed, completely overwhelmed. "Do you *mean* it?"

"See here, Miss, I am becoming quite tired of hearing your repeated doubts about the credibility of my word. I never say anything I don't mean."

Two tears spilled over and ran down my cheeks. "Th-Thank you, Oliver. I f-feel ever so much b-better now."

"Good. Then I'll bid you goodnight."

"Of course, I don't much care about dazzling the likes of Colin and his *poseur* of a friend. It's enough to know that I *could* do it if I wished."

"A very sensible attitude. Goodnight, my dear."

"Although one can't help wondering . . ."

He gave a patient sigh. "Yes?"

". . . how one goes about *learning* how to preen one's feathers."

Oliver made a wry face and stroked his beard again. "I admit that you've asked the very question I hoped you wouldn't. I don't know the answer to that one. I had intended to go to my study and ponder on it. If you'll be good enough to cease your chatter and give me leave to withdraw, I shall attempt to find an answer."

"You'll think about it? About how I'm to learn?"

"Just so. Is it goodnight, then?"

"Yes. *Do* think hard, Oliver. I should like to learn, even if I never choose to fly anywhere else." I blew him a kiss. "You have my leave to withdraw, sir. Goodnight."

He went to the door. "Goodnight, you goose," he said with a wave.

"Oliver, wait."

He turned impatiently. "Now, what?"

"Who was Harriet Worthing?"

His eyebrows rose. "Harriet *Worthing?* Good God, where did you hear of *her?*"

"Someone mentioned her name. Was she a . . . a *particular* friend of yours?"

"I suppose you might say that. But it was a very long time ago. Why do you ask?"

"I just wondered."

"Nothing worth wondering about. She was a young woman with quiet charm whom I knew in London. I think she married a French marquis and went to live on the continent. Does that satisfy your curiosity?"

"Did you mind?"

"Mind what?"

"Her marrying a French marquis?"

He looked at me in complete puzzlement. "Why should I mind? It was no business of mine. See here, Miss, if you persist in babbling on about inconsequential matters, you'll keep me from thinking about our more important concerns. So, for the last time, goodnight, my girl."

After he left, I leaned toward the nightstand to pinch out the candle. My eye fell on the remnants of a nosegay of rust-red roses. *Rosa rubiginasa.* They were crushed, faded, spackled with mud and darkening with decay around the edges of the petals. But they were a token of affection from Oliver. My own Oliver. I lifted them from the table and held them to my cheek, sighing with relief and happiness. What did I care for young men, for parties, for all the nonsense I'd submitted to this evening when right here in my own home was the one person in the world I truly loved?

I snuggled into the pillows. He's said I was a *rara avis.* If only I could learn to preen my feathers, I could be dazzling. *Dazzling!* That was Oliver's very word. I was dizzy with the joy of it. He'd not used that word to describe anyone else that I'd ever heard of . . . not Mrs. Longmuir, not any of the village girls, not Harriet Worthing, not even Mama. He'd used it only for me. With that one word he'd taken what had been the worst evening of my life and turned it completely around.

Suddenly, with the kind of clarity that one feels in a moment of brilliant insight, I knew what I wanted for my future. It didn't matter any more that Colin had lost interest in me. It didn't matter what Henry Inglebright thought of me. I cared nothing about dazzling any young man in the whole world. Ever.

But if one day I could dazzle Oliver himself, that would be wonderful indeed.

Chapter Eight

THE NEXT DAY Lady Gilbart called at Pentargon on the pretext of returning the shawl I'd left behind the night before. Trewin came to the greenhouse where Oliver and I were working to announce her presence, but Oliver refused to see her. I chortled to myself in satisfaction. I knew why she'd really come—she wanted to make Oliver's acquaintance so that she could attempt to arrange a match between him and her elder daughter. Eda's shawl had only been an excuse. But to my delight Oliver would not bother to greet her. Whether his reason was his annoyance with her for having upset me the evening before or his unwillingness to interrupt his botanical activities to endure a social call, I couldn't say. But whatever his reason, I was gleeful. If Lady Gilbart wanted to marry off her daughter, she'd have to look elsewhere.

My elevated spirits did not outlast the day. By nightfall I felt peculiarly heavy-headed. Miss Gribbin put an anxious hand to my forehead and shook her head. She put me to bed, a frown creasing her brow. The next morning I didn't feel much better, but I tried to get up. Miss Gribbin, however, would not hear of it. By the end of the day it was plain that I was feverish. I shivered despite the warmth of my room, my eyes burned, and every muscle in my body seemed to ache.

The next day it became clear to everyone in the household but me that I was very ill. The doctor was sent for, and he— as well as all the others in the house—bent over me and examined me with worried faces. But by that time I was aware of very little that occurred.

I learned later that I came very near death's door, an infection of the throat having spread to my lungs, but in my stuporous state I had no apprehension of my danger. I was sometimes delerious, sometimes comatose, and almost always unaware of my surroundings. They say that my semi-conscious state lasted for almost a fortnight, but I had no sense of the passage of time. Sometimes I woke and found Miss Gribbin looking down at me with frightened eyes. Sometimes it was Oliver watching over me. Once I even believed I saw Eliza Gilbart sitting beside my bed, but I told myself I was dreaming.

One night, feeling hot and dry, I threw off my covers and sat up. Sitting beside my bed, as erect and stiff-lipped as I remembered her, was my grandmother. "Good Lord!" I croaked. "I must be dying."

"No, no, you're not dying," came Oliver's voice, and I felt myself being gently urged back on my pillows and covered to the neck. I closed my eyes and let sleep overtake me. *My grandmother,* I thought, *must be another hallucination.*

When I began to recover, I discovered that neither Eliza Gilbart nor my grandmother had been an hallucination. They both had been present at my bedside for many hours.

I soon learned that much had changed during my illness. For one thing, the relationship between our household and Nancarrow had completely altered. Eliza Gilbart related the events to me. The change began, she told me, the moment Trewin had come to call for me on the night of the party. When the Gilbart's butler had been unable to find me, Eliza and her mother helped to search through the house, but nothing of me was found save my shawl. She and her mother then realized that I had walked home in the rain. They were instantly struck with guilt. That a guest of theirs should have been so unhappy in their home that she'd run off without waiting for proper transport was a blow that filled them with shame. Lady Gilbart had come to Pentargon the very next day to ask Lord Fleming's pardon for having permitted such an incident to occur. But when Lord Fleming had refused to see her, she'd given up and withdrawn. "After all," she'd said to Eliza, "I tried my best."

But when word had trickled back to Nancarrow that I was ill, their sense of guilt redoubled. Eliza and her mother called again, this time carrying with them a number of nostrums, medications, fruit juices and emollients of herbs and powders. This time Oliver admitted them, glad of any assistance to bring me back to health. Since then, the entire Gilbart family had been daily callers, their concern for my health almost as great as that of the inhabitants of Pentargon. Miss Gribbin told me how great an effort the ladies of Nancarrow had expended in my behalf.

It was Oliver who told me how my grandmother came to be at my bedside. On the night of the party, after he'd soothed my disturbed spirit, he'd sat down in his study to solve the vexing problem of my future. If I was to learn to "preen my feathers," something would have to be done. Unfamiliar with the methods of rearing young ladies, Oliver had written a letter to my grandmother requesting her advice.

He'd expected a response by letter. Instead, on the day when my illness was at its peak of severity—when everyone in the household was benumbed with worry and fatigue—a carriage drew up at the door, and Trewin came running up to the sickroom to announce the arrival from London of Lady Marietta Saunders. Oliver, completely startled, had dashed downstairs at once and explained that matters had changed since he'd written and that I was too ill to see her.

My grandmother, guessing from Oliver's strained face the severity of my illness, insisted on being helped upstairs to the sickroom. With the assistance of her cane and her ever-present Mrs. Panniers, she climbed the stairs. She entered the sickroom leaning as heavily on her cane as ever, but after taking one look at my ravaged face she'd thrust it aside, thrown off her bonnet and joined the others in nursing me back to health. Everyone in the household was awed by her energy and determination. She and Oliver were the strongest of the sickroom aides, taking the night vigils so that the others might sleep.

My recovery brought relief and jubilation to the hearts of all the inhabitants of Pentargon and Nancarrow, but not to me. I felt as if I'd gone to sleep in one world and awakened in another. I found that I was no longer living in contented solitutide with Oliver. Not only did Grandmamma and her companion seem to be entrenched in our lives, but I was subjected to daily calls from the Gilbarts as well. Although I was grateful for the interest and concern they all had shown, I longed with all my heart for a return to our former situation.

As the summer passed and I grew stronger, my longing for our erstwhile solitude grew stronger, too. My grandmother was constantly present, making caustic comments on our way of life, on my devotion to Oliver's botanical experiments, on my shockingly boyish mannerisms and on the slovenliness of the household. In additon, the Gilbarts called every day, Grandmamma and Lady Gilbart becoming fast friends, Colin returning to his fascination with me in the absence of Laura Inglebright or any other pretty creature to divert him, and Dory (having forgiven me for my "cruelty" to Henry Inglebright, although she was still enamored of him) finding me to be "a very interesting individual despite your eccentricities." Eliza called, too, but not as frequently as the others. When she came, I noticed that Oliver was always there to welcome her, and they often took long walks in the gardens by themselves.

I was wild with jealousy, but I could not dislike Eliza Gilbart. She was invariably kind, sensitive and sympathetic to my moods, intelligent in her comments, sensible in her advice and always restrained and unobtrusive. I could not forget, either, her kind assessment of my character the night of the party when everyone else had condemned me out of hand. I couldn't blame Oliver for showing her the admiration and respect she richly deserved. But if he fell in love with her, I knew I would die.

Fortunately for my peace of mind, the weeks passed without a noticeable increase in her visits to Pentargon or a sign of any particular intimacy developing between them. And as August drew to a close, I began to hope that Oliver and I would soon be able to return to our former way of life: Grandmamma announced that she would be returning to London by the month's end, and Lady Gilbart remarked that she and her family would do likewise. "We never intended to remain in Cornwall beyond July," she explained, "but it has been so pleasant here that we all agreed to stay another month."

I was delighted. *By fall,* I told myself, *everything will be back to its normal state, and Oliver and I will be alone again.*

But I was about to learn that my life would never again return to what it had been before. On a hot afternoon in late August, after Lady Gilbart, Dory and Colin had made their daily call and Grandmamma had gone upstairs for what she

liked to call her "siesta," Oliver asked me into his study and
waved me to a chair. "I've been giving some thought to your
future, Anne," he said without preamble, "and I think it's time
we talked about it."

"My future? I don't see why we have to talk about *that*."
I stretched my legs out before me and put my hands behind
my head in the pose of relaxation which he often assumed.
"I've already made my plans."

His right eyebrow lifted in amusement. "Have you indeed?
Then perhaps you'd better tell me what they are."

"Tell you?" I blinked at him, a bit startled. I hadn't expected
the question. Uneasily, I sat erect, folding my hands primly in
my lap and lowering my eyes. "No, I can't. I'm not... not
ready to tell you yet."

"Not ready?"

"No." I flicked him a quick look. "I assure you, Oliver,
that you will be fully informed as soon as... that is, in due
course."

"In due course?"

"Yes."

"Thank you, ma'am," he said drily. "It's very kind of you.
When do you think you'll be 'ready' to let me know?"

I frowned. I could recognize Oliver's disdain when I heard
it. "I don't know. It's... hard to say."

"A week, do you think? A year? Two? Five?"

My fingers clenched. I couldn't tell him—at least not yet—
that my plans were all bound up with him. They were very
simple, really. I intended to go on just as we were until I'd
matured enough to win his heart. Then we would marry and
spend the rest of our days together. There was so much that
we would share—I would help him with his botanical experiments, we would ride together, study and read together, perhaps even travel to distant places and see the strange and
wonderful sights of the world hand in hand. But I couldn't tell
him all this now. Not now, while he still thought of me as a
child, an eccentric, bizzare sixteen-year-old who knew nothing
of life and love. "I don't know," I answered lamely.

"Then, since you can't tell me your plans, will you do me
the favor of listening to mine?"

"Yes, Oliver, if you wish me to, but it seems a waste of
time, since mine are quite definite."

"Oh, are they?" The mockery in his voice was too slight for me to find offensive. "I hope they are not too definite to permit you to consider what I have in mind for you. After all, you did ask me, did you not, to think about how you're to learn to 'preen your feathers'?"

"Oh, yes!" I looked up at him with renewed interest. "Is *that* what you wish to talk about?"

"Yes, it is. That's why I wrote to your grandmother, and that's why she made the prodigious effort of traveling this great distance. We both realized that you've reached the stage where a change must be made. I knew that I was not capable of teaching you what you need to learn, and obviously Miss Gribbin is not much better qualified than I. So your grandmother and I have been discussing the problem. And we've consulted with Lady Gilbart and Eliza as well."

"Eliza Gilbart? You discussed me with *her?*"

"Yes." He looked up at me curiously. "Why not?"

I shrugged and fixed my eyes on the buckle of my shoe. "No reason, I only wondered why you sought the advice of a young, unmarried lady on such a . . . a matter."

"She's young and unmarried, true, but she has been out, she tells me, for five years, and she seems to me to be more sensible than most."

I cast a sidelong glance at him. "Do you like her, Oliver?"

"Yes, very much," he said matter-of-factly. "Don't you?"

I was certainly no expert on matters of the heart, but there seemed to me to be nothing of *amour* in Oliver's blunt response. "Yes," I said with relief and perfect sincerity, "I do."

"Then you'll be pleased to learn that she agrees whole-heartedly with the solution which your grandmother and I have found for the problem of your education."

"You've found a solution? What is it? Am I to have a new governess? You won't send Miss Gribbin away, will you? You couldn't possibly let her go, you know, for she hasn't anyone in the world to—"

"Must you jabber away about nonsequiturs? You will *not* have a new governess, nor have I the slightest intention of letting Miss Gribbin go. In fact, she will accompany you when you go off to school. We've decided, you see, to send you to school with Dory in the fall."

My mouth dropped open. "Send me to . . . to *school?*"

"Yes. That is our plan."

"*Where? What* school?" My heart was pounding with a sudden, terrifying alarm.

"I believe it is called the Finchlow Academy for Young Ladies. It's in Bloomsbury."

"Bloomsbury! But that's ... *London!*"

His eyes fell away from my horror-stricken gaze. "Yes, the outskirts. It will make it convenient for you to be able to pay frequent weekend visits to your grandmother, or to go home with Dory to the Gilbart town house."

I was stricken speechless. His words struck my brain with dire presentiments of disaster. He was *sending me away!*

After a long moment of silence, during which he didn't lift his eyes from the paperknife he unwittingly turned in his fingers, he spoke again. "I know it must be a blow to realize that you'll be leaving Pentargon, which you've no doubt grown fond of during the—"

"Grown *fond* of!" I cried out in outrage. "I've thought of it as my *home!*" I jumped up from my chair and ran to his desk to confront him. "My home! And now you ... you callously propose to take it away from me!"

"I propose nothing of the sort. Pentargon will always be your home, and you may return to it whenever you wish."

"Well, I wish not to leave it at all. So there!"

"Anne, my dear, try not to be childish. You said yourself that you wanted to learn to—"

"—to preen my feathers. Yes, I did say that. But if it means leaving home, I don't want it after all."

"Nonsense. You must learn to live in the world, and you cannot learn that in this secluded backwater."

"Then I don't care to learn it at all. I won't go!"

Oliver got up and walked round his desk. I thought he'd pick me up bodily and drop me out in the corridor in a weeping heap, as he was wont to do to end an argumentative scene. Instead, he lifted my chin and smiled down at me gently. "Don't pout, child. You'll feel much better once you've thought the matter through."

"No, I won't," I cried, throwing my arms about his waist and hiding my face in his chest. "Please don't make me go!"

"I don't wish to compel you against your will," he said, stroking my hair. "I'm not an ogre. But you see, my dear, neither can I permit you to waste your life away. You must grow up and find your place in the world. One must make sacrifices to gain one's ends, you know. You *do* wish to become a polished, refined, presentable young woman, don't you?"

I turned my face up to his, my eyes beginning to fill. I didn't care about becoming polished and refined. I didn't care about any of it. There was only one place in the world I wanted to fill. But in order to fill it, *he* had to find me presentable. *One must make sacrifices to gain one's ends.* If I was ever to win his love as a woman, I had to go away to school and learn to be a proper lady. "How l-long will I have to b-be away?" I asked.

"Until your come-out, I expect," he said, taking my arms from around him and turning away. "Two years."

"Two years!" The ground seemed to give way beneath me, and I stumbled back to my chair. "I'll *die!*"

"You won't die," Oliver muttered from the window where he stood staring out at the lawns, darkly green under the late-summer sun. "In a month you'll scarcely remember Pentargon at all."

"Won't I?" I wouldn't deign to contradict him. He should have known me better than that. "Will you remember *me?*" I asked pathetically.

He turned slowly from the window to stare at me, his mouth curved in a slight smile. "Remember you? You, my rarest of rare birds? All the days of my life, I promise you."

I left him then, for I was unable to say anything more. His last words, uttered with a combination of sadness and self-mockery, rang in my ears, and I wanted to be alone to savor them, to press them so deeply into my memory that they would stay with me—with every inflection intact—throughout the two long years to come.

Chapter Nine

THE MISSES FINCHLOW were two elderly ladies of breeding whom impoverishment had pushed into the profession of educating the young daughters of wealthy Londoners. They had turned their large house in Bloomsbury into a school for gentlewomen. Twenty-three young ladies between the ages of fifteen and eighteen occupied the six bedrooms on the third floor, studied in the classrooms and the music room on the second, and dined and received visitors on the first. Every hour of the day was marked by the ringing of a brass bell. The bell wakened us at six, summoned us for prayers in the small sanctuary at seven, called us for breakfast at eight and marked the rest of the day into hourly periods of study. These "studies" (which the Misses Finchlow and their additional staff of two taught in classes of no more than six students at a time) included Deportment At Public And Private Functions; Posture And Carriage; Forms of Speech And Proper Address; Dancing For The Ballroom; Music For The Voice; Instrumental Instruction (in the Harp or the PianoForte); French Grammar And Usage; Sketching And Watercoloring; and Stitching And Fine Embroidery.

We dined at seven in a large downstairs room whose walls

were lined with forbidding portraits of the Finchlow ancestors, and then were given one hour for "informal group discourse" before falling, exhausted, into bed at ten.

The entire course of study seemed ridiculous to me. Not one of the subjects had any use in the life I later intended to lead. Dory, who had attended the school for eight months during the previous year, tried to prove to me that these matters were of the gravest importance. "How will we ever get on in society," she asked reasonably, "if we can't tell a fish fork from a salad, serve tea to a gentleman caller, or make a proper bow to the Regent?"

"I don't know if I wish to 'get on' in society at all," I muttered irritably.

Dory was patient with me during those early weeks at school, guiding me through the days with friendly sympathy. She could see that, underneath my outward contempt for my surroundings, homesickness sat upon my spirit like a shroud. I had been torn completely from all attachment to my former life—even Miss Gribbin, for whom there was no accommodation at the school, had had to remain behind in Cornwall. The lessons seemed pointless, silly and dull, the girls appeared to be insipid dolts, and the months seemed to stretch ahead of me like an eternity of emptiness.

But during the second month of my stay, Eliza came to the school to pay us a visit. She had attended the Finchlow school herself and was greeted by the headmistresses with eager embraces. With one month of "study" behind me, I observed her appearance and movements with new eyes. She looked taller and slimmer than I remembered, and she was dressed in a most alluring walking-dress of green muslin with a flat, disc-like straw hat secured to her head with a wide green ribbon and tied beneath her chin with a rakish bow. Her step was neither the "Mince" nor the "Bounce-and-Stride" (the latter phrase being the description Miss Felicity Finchlow used for mine), but she seemed to glide across the floor in an assured, graceful flow of motion. Her voice was low and melodious, her laugh trilled, and her eyes sparkled with animation as the girls and the teachers clustered round her.

The Misses Finchlow beamed with pride and pointed out to some of the new pupils (myself among them) how excellently high she held her head, how gracefully she used her hands when speaking, and how delicately she lowered herself into her chair. "Do you see," Miss Felicity asked me, "how the mastery of our techniques results in ladylike perfection? Take note, Miss Saunders, of the *gentilesse* which is possible when one studies with the proper seriousness."

I had already, you see, become the despair of the teaching staff. My skills at the Pianoforte were sadly deficient, I walked like a tomboy, I spoke far too loudly, my views were arrogant, and I laughed like a hoyden. "But," Miss Charity Finchlow whispered to me comfortingly, "there is every hope that, in two years, you, too, will excite admiration when you enter a room. If you work very, very hard at it, of course."

Eliza Gilbart's mastery of the *accoutrements* of gentility was indeed impressive. If I could learn to glide across the floor with such aplomb, if I could carry on my head so breathtaking a hat with such nonchalance, if I could tame my laugh to such incredible melodiousness, perhaps I might achieve my secret goal.

That day marked a change in my attitude. I threw myself into the task of acquiring the petty little techniques of social intercourse with as much enthusiasm as I could muster. The lessons never ceased to appear to me to be superficial and often ridiculous, but I made up my mind to master them. Only at night, when we girls went up to our bedrooms and the teachers retired to theirs, did I give vent to my antagonism. I entertained large groups of girls into the wee hours by mimicking the voices and mannerisms of all our instructresses, indulging in lengthy parodies of the day's lectures. The girls giggled and whooped and, on occasion, screeched so loudly at my performances that Miss Felicity was sometimes awakened. She would burst into the room, an avenging fury in a pink swansdown robe and curl-rags, vowing to give us nothing but bread and water for the rest of the week. When the girls had flown out of the room, their white flannel nightdresses flapping behind them, she would fix me with a glowering eye, sigh helplessly, threaten to write a stinging letter to my guardian and predict that I was quite unlikely ever to come to any good. By the next day, however, the incident would be completely forgotten and all would proceed as before.

My letters to Oliver were infrequent, for I didn't wish to reveal by any slip of the pen or the emotions how very much I missed him. I wrote careful, polite, insignificant notes with boring bits of news, like: *Miss Colclough, our Drawing Mis-*

tress, instructed us today in the manner of making Chinese ink drawings. Mine would have very pretty if I hadn't blotted the ink right in the center. Or: Dory has come down with the sniffles and has been seen by a doctor, but she hasn't any fever. She is quite disappointed. She had hoped to develop a severe Inflammation of the Lungs so that she would be sent home for a month of cossetting, good eating and late sleeping.

Oliver's letters to me were even worse. There was never a personal word in them. He never once said he missed me or gave me a hint of what his feelings were in my absence. Once a month I received a two-page missive in which he made a routine inquiry after my health and my progress in my studies and then described in detail the results of his latest experiment, like the development of the *Cydonia oblonga* since he'd transplanted the saplings out of doors. I began to think of his letters as my Monthly Botanical Report.

By the time I saw him again, a year and a half had passed by. Napoleon had been defeated at Waterloo, Lord Byron had left England forever, and I had grown up.

Chapter Ten

BY CHRISTMAS OF 1816, time and eighteen months under the tutelage of the Misses Finchlow had made an effect. I had grown two inches, I'd acquired some polish in manner and voice, and I could attend a party or appear among the members of the *ton* without embarrassment. Dory and I had become intimate friends, and she, even more than the teachers at the school, was responsible for my progress. She helped me to choose my clothes, watched my behavior with a critical eye and pointed out all my *faux pas* with affectionate frankness.

My hair had been a major obstacle in my attempt to transform myself into a lady, its wild incorrigibility defying all my attempts to restrain and to force it into some semblance of style. Even Dory (who, despite a tendency to plumpness brought about by her insatiable appetite for cake and bonbons, was the most stylish girl in school) could not seem to devise a coiffure which would keep its arrangement for longer than an hour. "There's nothing for it, Anne, my love," she said after months of diligent struggle, "but to cut if off."

"Cut it *off?*" I exclaimed, horrified. "I couldn't. Is it stylish to go about looking like a shorn sheep?"

"You won't look like a shorn sheep, I promise. I'll leave

little ringlets all over your head, in the manner of Caro Lamb. It will be *distinctive*."

"But I don't want to be distinctive. I want to be..." I looked at myself in the tiny mirror which the Misses Finchlow deemed adequate to the needs of four vain girls and frowned at my *retroussé* nose, my still-brown complexion sprinkled with freckles and my unmanageable mane of red hair.

"What do you want to be?" Dory prodded.

"Elegant," was my prompt response.

"Ha!" She pushed me down in a chair with a scornful toss of her elegant curls. "You're asking for the moon. Distinctive, my dear, is the very best you can expect. Now, hand me those scissors, hold your head still and turn away from the mirror. I don't want to hear a word from you until I've done."

The result of Dory's barbering was perhaps not distinctive, but it was a decided improvement over what had been. I looked taller and less tumultuous. My face seemed less pointed and urchin-like and more womanly rounded. And best of all, my hair always looked stylishly tousled rather than unkempt. Dory had done well.

The year before, during my first Christmas at the Academy, I had hoped to be given permission to return to Pentargon for the holiday season, but my grandmother had demanded my attendance at her festivities in Mount Street, saying that there would not be time for me to make the long journey to Cornwall and still manage to return in time for the reopening of school. This year at Christmastime, knowing that permission would again be withheld for the same reason, I didn't bother to make the request. I accepted my fate with more equanimity than I'd been able to summon up the year before, for I knew that spring was not far off. My come-out would be held in May, and after that, my long exile would be over. Meanwhile, I tried to look forward to the pleasures the holidays in London would offer me.

Dory had made a number of exciting holiday plans. Even though I'd moved in with Grandmamma for the fortnight during which school was "out," the Gilbart carriage came for me almost every day to bring me to Dory's side. We went shopping together at the Pantheon Bazaar; we visited the museum to see the famous Elgin Marbles; and, on a particularly enjoyable night, we were escorted by Colin and Henry Inglebright (who still held a weak grasp on Dory's affections) to the theater at

Drury Lane to see *Twelfth Night*. The young men had come down from Oxford for the holidays, and the four of us, released from the drudgery of school, made a very merry time of it.

Lady Gilbart had decreed that it would not be appropriate for us to attend many balls or parties until our presentation-season had officially begun in the spring. Even the famous Almack's was out-of-bounds for young ladies who had not yet been presented. But we had one exciting *fête* to anticipate—a New Year's reception being held by Lord and Lady Gilbart. It promised to be what Dory gleefully described as a "dreadful squeeze," and we were to be present, Lady Gilbart deciding that an afternoon party in her own home would not be an improper festivity for Dory and me to attend. We looked forward to the occasion with excitement, for we intended to use the opportunity to test our newly learned techniques for flirting.

Grandmamma bought me a new gown for the Gilbart reception. It was a white lustring underdress cut low across the shoulders and covered with a half-robe of pale blue gauze. The gauze floated in undulant billows when I moved and made me feel more graceful than I'd felt in my life. I wore no adornments in my hair, but Grandmamma gave me a string of pearls to wear at the neck. This time, I knew, I would not look odd.

When Grandmamma and I were ushered into Gilbart House by one of their white-and-gold-clad footmen, my heart beat with nervous dread, the horrible recollection of the party in Cornwall having popped painfully into my mind. But from the first moment, I could feel that everything was different: Lady Gilbart and Eliza greeted me with the affectionate warmth of old friends; Colin handed me an empty glass and whispered, "Just *pretend* to be drinking. That way you can't spill anything;" Henry Inglebright, who had long since forgotten his anger at me and treated me with indifference, kept out of my way; and Dory slipped an arm about my waist and assured me that I looked "almost elegant."

For a while I had a wonderful time. Several young men eyed me longingly from across the room, three made cakes of themselves trying to arrange introductions, and one, having coaxed Colin to make him known to me, declared himself to be instantly and permanently smitten. I moved through the crowd, making sure that my step was a glide, my head was elegantly erect and my smile was properly "pleasant but not effusive." Then something happened that ruined the day completely—across the room I caught sight of Sir Averil Luton.

I had completely forgotten his existence, but the sight of him brought every detail of our past association flooding back to me. My mother's last lover! He had changed remarkably little in the years since I'd seen him. There seemed to be a touch more grey in his hair, a bit more jowl on his face, but no other change was evident. As I stared across the room at him, a strange series of images flashed quickly across my inner eye—my mother throwing her arms round his neck as she greeted him at the door . . . my mother and he engaged in their last and most vicious quarrel . . . his hat and cane resting in their familiar place on the chair near the front door of my mother's York Place house . . . the cramped tightness of his handwriting on the note he sent to me the day she died.

My spirits plummeted. Why had he made an appearance here when I had been finding the afternoon so enjoyable? Why had my mother's past risen up to haunt me at just this time?

Sir Averil's eyes, sweeping the room, suddenly met mine, and they seemed to widen in puzzlement. I quickly turned away, hoping he hadn't recognized me. The last thing in the world I wanted was to be forced to speak to him.

I started across the room to make my way to another part of the house, but I'd barely gone halfway to the door when a smiling, eager-eyed Sir Averil caught up with me. "Little Anne Saunders!" he exclaimed loudly enough to cause several guests standing nearby to turn their heads. "What a delight to lay these old eyes on you after all these years! You *do* remember me, don't you?"

I met his eyes, my own expression as cold and aloof as I could make it. "How do you do, Sir Averil?"

His eyes raked over me, slowly sweeping over every line and curve of my body with a lewd appreciation. I felt my color rise in revulsion. "You've grown into most admirable womanhood, my dear," he murmured, taking my arm and firmly maneuvering me out of the press of people and into a somewhat secluded corner. "Your mother would have been proud—you are every inch perfection. Where *have* you been hiding yourself for the past . . . let me see . . . how long has it been. Four years? Or is it five?"

I pulled my arm from his grasp. "I was not aware that I'd been hiding."

"Perhaps not, but you most assuredly have not been here

in town, for if you had, I'd have discovered you long before this."

"But why, sir? Have you been searching for me?"

"No, I haven't, but—" He stopped himself, grinned down at me with what I could only describe as a leer and then went on. "But I certainly *should* have."

He said the words in an oily, suggestive tone, as if the words had a particular and meaningful significance, but I couldn't fathom them. "What can you mean?" I asked in bewilderment. "Why should you have searched for me?"

"Because, my dear, you seem to be a treasure. One that's been buried away somewhere. And what does one do about a buried treasure but search for it. Except that when I last saw you, I had no idea that such riches were stored up in you."

"You are speaking in riddles, sir," I said in disgust, catching enough of his meaning to discern its fulsomeness, "and I'm afraid I'm too busy to stand here trying to solve them." I turned quickly and began to walk away.

He caught my arm again. "You mustn't go yet. After all, I'm an old...er...friend of the family. One whom you haven't seen in years. And I've not yet learned where you've come from and where you're staying."

"I don't believe, sir, that my whereabouts are of any real interest to you. If you'll excuse me—"

"They are of *enormous* interest to me," he said, his grip on my arm tightening. "In fact, I must speak to you. In private. Come across the hall, my dear. I believe the sitting room is deserted."

I held back, hesitating. I wanted very much to break his hold on me and run away. I had no idea of what he had in mind or even of what subject he wished to speak, but I knew enough to understand that I wouldn't be pleased by anything he said. However, my training at the Finchlow Academy had taught me that breaking away and running off would be both childish and *gauche*. There had to be a more ladylike method of handling matters.

My mind ranged over the various alternatives. I must admit that the first idea that occurred to me was to tell him that I wanted first to go to the buffet for a drink of punch so that, when he bent over the table to fill the cup, I could push his head into the bowl. But I reminded myself that I'd outgrown the tendency toward such hoydenish behavior, and I pushed the temptation aside. But there were other alternatives which I'd learned in my eighteen months as a student of mannerly behavior. Surely one of the techniques I'd learned would serve me now.

I remembered quite clearly the lessons in Deportment when the subject of dealing with "Importunate Gentlemen" had been discussed. Three courses of action had been suggested: first, one fixed the miscreant with an icy stare and begged to be excused; second, one pretended to feel faint; and third, one screamed for help. I didn't believe that the first technique would work with the self-assured Sir Averil. The second and third would call embarrassing attention to me. Eyebrows would be raised, and people would stare and whisper. I would hate it.

Thus far this afternoon I had behaved like a pattern-card of virtue. Everything I'd done had been performed with unexceptional propriety. I had no desire to spoil the impression I'd thus far made. Reluctantly, therefore, and filled with a mound of misgivings, I let Sir Averil lead me out of the room and across the hall.

He did not attempt to close the sitting-room door, which relieved some of my tension, but he led me to the sofa on the far side of the room. He took a place so close beside me that I was forced to inch awkwardly away. "You can have no idea how much you've changed," he said into my ear. "You quite take my breath away."

"You are exaggerating, sir," I said with asperity. "I can feel your breath quite plainly on my ear." I knew I was being rude, but I was disgusted with myself for having been so easily maneuvered into this position.

He was not offended but merely laughed appreciatively. "Why, you're a *charmer!* I like your spirit. Why on earth have I heard nothing of you before this?"

"You keep making the same foolish remark, Sir Averil. Why do you insist on believing that my presence in London should be bruited about in your circles?"

"I told you. Because you're a rare treasure. Has no one ever told you so before?"

"Perhaps. But what has that to say to the question at hand?"

"When a new beauty shows her face in town, I am always among the first to know. I've heard nothing of you, and *you,* my girl, are a new-blooming *rose.*"

"You are mixing your metaphors, sir. First a treasure and

then a rose. What next will you be likening me to, do you think?"

He laughed again, brushing my cheek lightly with his fingers. "I suspect I shall find many more metaphors for you before long," he murmured.

I was feeling increasingly uncomfortable. "I wish you will not fondle me," I said, moving aside again. "Please say what you have to say quickly, sir. I am expected elsewhere."

He moved closer, his expression growing serious. "I must know, my dear... who is your protector?"

"My protector? I don't know what you mean. I have a guardian, of course. Is that whom you're asking about?"

"Guardian? No, of course not. Why would I—?" He stared at me closely. "Are you really such a little innocent?"

"I must be, for I don't understand you at all."

His eyes narrowed with suspicion. "Don't play coy games with me, Anne. You are your mother's daughter, after all. And you're no longer a child. Why, you must be eighteen or nineteen years old by this time."

"I am not yet eighteen, sir, though I am my mother's daughter. And as my mother's daughter, I do not intend to play games with you, coy or otherwise. I know too well the cost of them. Please tell me what it is you want of me and let me go."

"You are not giving me any encouragement, are you? But your strategem of cool reluctance is very effective... it only increases your value in my eyes. Very well, then, my dear, since you desire blunt speaking, let me proceed without round-aboutation. I'll even weaken my bargaining position by admitting that you've stirred my blood more than anyone has done before in so brief a meeting. Much more than your mother ever did, I'll add. You have something of her in your looks, yes... but there's something more... something especially provocative in you. I realize that this is a large commitment on very short acquaintance, but if it is true that you really are free of any prior... er... constraints, the gentlemen of this world won't permit you to be free for long, if I'm a judge. Therefore I must act quickly. Let me be the one to take care of you, my dear. You can count on every luxury life can offer. There is nothing you could ask for that I would hesitate a moment to supply."

I stared at him in amazement. *Bargaining position...?*

Large commitment...? Prior constraints...? Every luxury...? What was he *saying?* "I don't think I understand you, sir. Take *care* of me? Are you offering, after all these years, to be my *guardian?*"

He smiled. "I believe you are too old to need me in such a capacity, are you not? Besides, your grandmother must have taken that position years ago."

"She did not, but that is quite beside the point. I'm confused, sir. If you were not offering to become my guardian, I don't see what—? Good *heavens*, you can't be ... offering to ... to *marry* me!"

He gave a loud, snorting laugh. "What an amusing little vixen you are, my love. Life with you promises to be a thorough delight. Since you know quite well that I already have a wife, you must certainly have guessed that I wish to be your protector."

"Protect—?" I began, confused. Then his meaning burst on me with a blinding flash. *"Good God!"* I gasped, feeling the blood drain from my face. He was offering me a *carte blanche*. "You're suggesting that I take my mother's place as your *mistress!*"

"Are you really so surprised, my dear, or is this part of your game? Surely I'm not the first to ask—"

I slapped him smartly across the face, the blood pounding in my ears. Then, as he gaped at me, stunned, I got to my feet. "You *are* the first," I said through clenched teeth. "And the last! And if you *ever* dare to say such words to me again, I shall send for my guardian. When *he* has dealt with you, you'll learn the *real* meaning of the word protector!"

I turned on my heel and stalked out of the room, slamming the door behind me. Once alone, I began to tremble, my body shivering from top to toe. How *dared* he! What had made him believe that I would be receptive to so vile a suggestion? Had I done something, said something, behaved in some way that suggested I was that sort of female? Was there some mark on me that a knowing man could recognize ... a mark announcing that I was a potential courtesan? Some secret look in my eye? A way of walking? A curl to my lip? Or was it merely that I was my mother's daughter?

Was I never to be free of the curse of my heritage? My brain reeled in agony. I was in no condition to return to the festivities. Before I could return to my former equanimity I had to find some answers to the questions that whirled in my head.

But I had not forgotten the chaos I'd caused when I'd last run from a party without taking proper leave. Therefore I beckoned to a footman stationed near the front door. "Please convey a message to my grandmother, Lady Marietta Saunders," I requested. "I think you'll find her in one of the card rooms. Tell her that I have the headache and have taken the carriage home. I shall send it right back for her. And ask her, if you please, to convey my regrets to Lady Gilbart."

As soon as I arrived at Grandmamma's house, I evaded the quizzical looks of the butler, Hewes, and the clucking questions of Mrs. Panniers. She followed me all the way up to my room in her attempt to discover what was amiss, but I closed my door on her.

I waited with my ear to the door until I heard her footsteps disappearing down the hall. Then I hurriedly took from under my bed the large bandbox which I'd brought with me from school. I crammed it full of as many warm clothes as it could hold. I stripped off my lovely gown, put on a traveling dress of thick worsted, and I sat down at my dressing table to count the few guineas I had remaining from the pin money which Grandmamma had given me for the holidays. It made a very small pile. I prayed fervently that the amount would be sufficient for four days of travel.

I scribbled a hasty note to Grandmamma, telling her not to worry, and propped it up on my pillow. Then, covering myself with my warmest cloak, I pocketed my coins, picked up my bandbox and tiptoed from the room.

There was only one place in the world where I could go for help, and I was on my way to it.

Chapter Eleven

I RAN OUT of funds at Exeter and could not convince the owner of the livery stable to supply me with a coach and driver to take me the rest of the way on credit. "'Tain't that I disbelieve 'ee, Miss," he said, "but I ain't ne'er seed no ward of a earl what was travelin' cross the country wi'out so much as a maid with 'er."

But I am nothing if not intrepid, and I made my way to Pentargon on the backs of hay wagons, donkey carts, a mail stage making its way between Okehampton and Launceston (whose driver let me climb up on the box beside him out of pity) and shank's mare.

I arrived at Pentargon on the afternoon of the sixth day of my journey, footsore, weary, hungry and bedraggled. Since no one in the household had any expectation of a visitor, there was no one hanging about in the front hall when I arrived. Gratefully I stowed my bandbox inside the door, slipped out again and ran all the way round the castle to the greenhouses.

He was sitting at the far end of the west building, closely examining a wilted-looking mulberry shoot. I stood in the open doorway for a long time, watching him study the underside of the leaves through a magnifying glass and make notations in the ledger book. "Trouble with your *Morus Nigra?*" I asked after a while.

He seemed to freeze for a moment, the hand holding the magnifying glass poised in the air. Then he turned slowly and stared at me. "Yes," he said, blinking as if he didn't trust his eyes, "I'm afraid my *Moraceae* have succumbed to a parasitic infestation. What the devil are you doing here?"

I gave a shivery laugh. "Is that how you greet me after eighteen long months?"

He carefully placed the glass on the table, got to his feet and took three steps in my direction. "Anne!" he said hoarsely, the glow in his eyes unmistakable even at that distance, and held out his arms.

I flew down the narrow aisle, my cloak bruising some of the seedlings that lined the edges, and threw myself upon him. "Oh, Oliver, my dearest, I am *home!*"

I could feel his arms tighten about me. I think we were both trembling. I clutched him about the neck and pressed my face into his shoulder. This was where I'd always wanted to be... where I *belonged*.

I could have remained there in his embrace forever, but he soon released me, took my arms from round his neck, tilted my face up and studied it carefully. "You've cut your hair," he remarked with a kind of sadness.

"Don't you like it?"

"No. It reminds me painfully that you're growing up."

"Yes, and about time, too. You'll like me better grown up. Just wait and see."

"I like you well enough already." His voice was gruff, with a touch of anger that I thought was directed more at himself than at me. I didn't understand his mood, but I knew with heart-lifting certainty that he'd been more than glad to see me. He dropped his hand from my chin, stepped back and looked me over. "Good Lord! You're as bedraggled as a stray cat in the rain. Have you *walked* from London?"

I laughed. "Only the last few miles. Are you very put out with me for coming home like this?"

"I suppose I should be. You've embroiled yourself in some dreadful scrape, no doubt, and expect me to pull you out of it. But never mind it now. Come into the house. You're probably exhausted and starved. We'll have plenty of time to talk when you've been cleaned, fed and rested."

He put an arm about my shoulders, and we strolled in companionable silence back to the house, my heart at ease for the first time in many months.

No sooner did I set foot in the door when I heard Trewin shout, "'Ere she is!" He had seen my bandbox at the door and set the whole household searching for me. I was almost immediately surrounded by Mrs. Trewin, Mabyn and Miss Gribbin, all of them exclaiming words of affectionate welcome and all of them trying to embrace me at once.

As soon as the greetings and explanations had been made (Oliver declaring firmly that I'd come home for a brief visit only), Miss Gribbin, looking over my bedraggled costume and streaked face with dismay, ordered Mabyn to fill a tub for me, and she and Mrs. Trewin each took an arm to lead me off to my room. I looked back over my shoulder at Oliver in helpless appeal, but he merely shrugged and mouthed the word "later."

It was not until dinnertime (and then not until he'd ordered Trewin to leave the port and make himself scarce) that we found ourselves alone again. Oliver filled a goblet from the decanter Trewin had left at his elbow, lifted it and stared abstractedly at the light of the candles shining through the dark red liquid. But his eyes were not seeing the candle-glow, nor were his thoughts on the wine. It was as if he were bracing himself for a blow. "Now, my girl," he said, expelling a long breath, "let's have it. You must have been hard pressed to have run off from your grandmother's without protection or adequate funds. What's happened? Have you got yourself betrothed to a bounder?"

"*Betrothed?*" I snorted at the ridiculous suggestion. "Of course not."

I thought he seemed relieved. "Then what *have* you done?"

I couldn't keep my eyes on his face while relating the humiliating story of my encounter with Sir Averil, so I picked up an apple and began to pare it with exaggerated care while I spoke. He listened to my tale without interruption. But when I'd concluded, I glanced up and found him staring straight ahead of him, his face tight and his lips white-edged. His fingers tightened on the stem of the wine goblet until, suddenly, the stem snapped from the bowl. He let out a low curse as the bowl of the glass rolled off and fell, spilling its liquid over the white cloth.

"You've cut yourself," I cried in alarm.

"No, no," he said impatiently, tossing aside the broken remnant still in his hand. "I'm not scratched." He peered at me closely. "See here, Anne, I hope you're not unduly disturbed by that incident. Luton is an arrogant fool, and his behavior is indeed iniquitous. But your response was just what I would have wished, and your behavior above reproach. There is not the slightest need for you to upset yourself over this, I assure you."

"But I *am* upset, Oliver. More than I can tell you."

"Why? Luton's the one who should be upset, not you. And when I've finished with him, he will be. His behavior only illustrates his own depravity; it in no way reflects on you."

I felt my lips begin to tremble. "Perhaps it does."

He frowned. "That's ridiculous. How could it reflect on you?"

"Because..." I lowered my eyes. "...he would n-never have asked such a thing of D-Dory... or Eliza... would he?"

His head came up sharply. "*Anne!* That's—!" His brows knit in sudden concern, and I could *feel* him studying my face even though I'd averted my eyes again. After a moment he rose to his feet. "Let's get away from this debauched-looking table. Come to the library."

I followed him meekly down the hall. He shut the library doors after us and motioned me to the sofa. Then, standing over me with his arms akimbo and his expression forbidding, he demanded to know what maggot had got into my head. "Were you suggesting to me that there is something about you that *attracts* the kind of proposition Luton offered you?"

I nodded dumbly.

"What is going on in that shatter-brained head of yours? What sort of thing do you imagine it can be? A symbol on your forehead like the mark of Cain?"

I burst into tears. "I don't know. Is th-there something in my glance? Or the way I walk? Or the sw-swing of my hips?"

"Don't be a fool!" He sat down beside me and took me in his arms. "I've told you before, and I'll tell you again, there is nothing whatever wrong with you. I suppose that Luton's intimacy with your mother may have been at the root of his miscalculation of your character, but miscalculation it was— and a very stupid one at that."

"Really?" I asked tearfully, pulling out his pocket handkerchief and blowing into it. "Do you mean that no other gentlemen are likely to . . . to make me . . . er . . . ?"

"Offers of a similar nature?" He laughed wryly and rubbed his cheek against my hair. "I wish I could give you that assurance, my dear, but I'm afraid there are many men in this world who behave stupidly where a beautiful woman is concerned. It's the price you must pay for being the *rara avis* that you are. But all you need do, when they insist on behaving stupidly, is just as you did with Luton. The word will soon spread that you're not a lady to be trifled with."

I burrowed into his shoulder, letting myself be comforted by his words and his closeness, just as I had always been before in times of great distress. "Am I, Oliver?" I mumbled into his shoulder.

"Are you what? Not a lady to be trifled with?"

"Am I a beautiful woman?"

For a moment there was a pause. "The young men of London must surely have given you the answer to that question by this time," he said, withdrawing his arms.

I sat up and brushed a fallen curl from my forehead. "I know that some men find me so. Do you?"

He turned his head away. "All fathers find their daughters beautiful, I imagine."

I had no intention of letting the matter drop. "You're not my father," I said distinctly.

"Don't quibble, Miss." He got up abruptly and went to the fire. "And don't fish for compliments, either. It doesn't become you," He gazed down into the flames, his face hidden from me. "Go up to bed now, and don't give another thought to the despicable Sir Averil. I shall deal with him."

"Deal with him? What do you mean?"

"Never mind. Just go up to bed."

"But it's not yet ten. I want to stay here with you, Oliver. I'm no longer a child, you know."

"I'm very well aware of that." He came back to the sofa, pulled me to my feet, turned me around and, with hands on my shoulder, propelled me before him to the door. It was a new way of ending a discussion in place of his erstwhile habit of lifting me under his arm and depositing me on the floor outside his door. "You need your sleep. You'll have to rise before dawn tomorrow to begin your journey back to school."

"I'm not going back to school," I told him as he marched me to the stairs. "I've quite decided that."

"Oh, *have* you now? Then you may *un*decide it at once. You *are* going back. You will finish the term, you will have your come-out, and you will become the most sought-after young lady in all of London."

"I don't want to be sought-after, don't you know that?" Despite my objection to the early bedtime, I took the first stair. "There's only one thing I want, and for that I don't need any more schooling . . . or a come-out."

"And what is that, may I ask?"

I turned on the step to face him. "I want to stay here, Oliver. Always."

He had to look up just a little to meet my eyes. "You're being very childish, you know, my dear. Eventually, everyone has to grow up and leave the house of one's parents. One should not try to cling to childhood forever."

I shook my head, smiling down at him with the self-confidence brought on by my superior knowledge of my intentions and by my superior position on the step above him. "I don't want to remain for any childish reason," I said, placing my hands lightly on his shoulders. "My reason is quite mature. I want to *marry* you."

His face froze with shock. Then he dropped his eyes. "Don't be so silly," he said brusquely.

I understood the tone. I had sprung this upon him without warning, and his first reaction had been to dismiss the subject by a quick denigration of its importance. But I'd embarked on it, and I would not permit him to turn it aside so easily. I locked my hands tightly behind his neck. "Why is it silly, Oliver? I love you."

He winced. Then he gently removed my hands from about his neck. "Of course you do. All little girls want to wed their fathers. But you should long since have outgrown—"

"Dash it all, you're *not* my father! Why do you keep saying it?"

"Because for almost five years I've *been* your father. And I'm certainly old enough—"

"No, you're not! Besides, I've thought about *that* possibility, you know."

"What possibility?" he asked, confused.

"That you might be my father. My *real* father."

His expression hardened. "Your father was Reginald Saunders. Why should you question that fact?"

"Because even Grandmamma questioned it. 'We were never sure that you were his issue,' she once said."

"She should have been strangled!" he muttered savagely.

"Oh, I've long since ceased to care about who my father was, so long as I was sure it wasn't *you*. But you told me you were sixteen when you met my mother. And I was born a year later. Even my mother wouldn't have seduced a sixteen-year-old youth, would she?"

"She wouldn't, and she didn't!" he snapped. "And I very much dislike this entire conversation. It's extremely unbecoming in a young lady of your years to indulge in such speculations."

"I know. But I don't care if it is unbecoming. I don't care to be a lady." I replaced my arms round his neck. "I only want to be your wife."

"Release this stranglehold you insist on taking on my neck, Miss. You are speaking utter nonsense. I'm your *guardian*... and a cousin to boot. And thus not to be considered a candidate for the position as your husband."

I didn't move but merely tightened my hold on him. "You're not my *legal* guardian, you know. Grandmamma says she never legally relinquished her guardianship of me. And I know of many cousins—in closer consanguinity that we—who have wed. A marriage between us would be completely acceptable in the legalities." I grinned down at him. "You see, I've thought of everything. There's no reason, my love, why you can't be my husband."

"There are *dozens* of reasons!" Firmly removing my hands again, he sat down on the stairs and drew me down beside him. "There are so many reasons that the suggestion is untenable. You must see that."

"What reasons?"

"For one thing, my dear, you don't know the first thing about love between a man and a woman. What you feel for me is a daughter's love for her father."

"*You are not my father!*" I cried in chagrin. "I know better than you what I feel."

"How can you be sure of what you feel? You've not yet met a young man who's courted you properly."

"Yes, I have. There was Colin—"

"Puppy love."

"Yes. I suppose so, but—"

"Listen to me, Anne. I came into your life in a time of terrible loneliness and pain, and I became the father you didn't have but desperately needed. You are understandably grateful, of course—"

"Grateful! Do you think it's merely gratitude which makes me yearn to be with you all the time? To wish to talk with you, work with you, spend my life with you?"

"I don't deny that we've developed a bond of close affection, but it's a far cry from the feeling that should exist between a man and a woman who intend to wed."

"Do you mean the way you and Harriet Worthing cared about each other?" I asked curiously.

"Harriet Worthing?" He blinked at me as if I'd startled him by an irrelevancy. "No, I don't mean that at all." With a gesture, he dismissed the subject and turned his mind back to the present. He lifted my chin and said with avuncular sincerity, "Just wait until a proper young man crosses your path—in a year or two from now. You'll tumble into love as quickly as the tight buds of the *Delphinium ajacis* open in the spring sunshine. And then you'll realized how naive—"

I couldn't bear to listen. *"Stop* it! It will never occur as you say, never! What you're trying to tell me, in this roundabout fashion, is that *you* don't love *me!*

"Of *course* I love—"

"No, don't *say* it! I won't hear you say it in that disgusting, fatherly way! You know I don't mean that sort of love."

"That is the only way I *can* love you, Anne. Anything else would be misusing my position—"

I put my hands over my ears. I didn't want to hear any more. To him I was still the child under his care. Was there no way to make him see that our relationship—which had changed so completely for me—could change for him as well? How could I make him accept the idea that we were a man and a woman who belonged together in a new way?

He took my hands from my ears and held them in his. "Please try to understand, my little one. I am too much your elder, too much your parent, too much an old bachelor to take this scene you're playing seriously. I've had too much experience in the ways of females to believe that you know your own heart at such an early age. You have a great deal to learn."

Not as much as you think, I thought bitterly. I knew enough.

I'd learned years ago. On the subject of *amour* I was very precocious. How could I show him?

Abruptly, I wrenched my hands from his grasp and flung them round his neck again, this time throwing myself upon his chest. Before he realized what I was about, I pressed my lips to his. For a moment he resisted, stiffening and reaching up to pull my arms away. But I clung fast, pressing myself against him, winding my arms about him like vines of the *Hedera helix* twisting themselves round a treetrunk. I felt rather than heard him groan, and soon his hands slipped down over my back, pulling me close and closer until I could scarcely breathe. My blood sang in my ear, pounded in my temples and coursed through my body giving off bursts of tingling fireworks as it flowed. I was filled with a dizzying joy . . . and an overwhelming terror. I knew I had acted badly—quite like the trollop my grandmother expected me to become—and I wondered how Oliver would react when he'd recovered his equilibrium. But I'd proved one thing which, try as he might, he could never henceforth deny: that his response was not fatherly.

When he released me, he stared at me for a long while with eyes distended and chest heaving. "Very well, you brazen wench," he muttered when he caught his breath, "you take the trick." He stood up and turned his back on me. "What do you think you've accomplished by it, eh? What have you proved? That I am as capable of depravity as your friend Luton?"

I was beset with fearful misgivings, but I managed to toss my head and give him a spirited retort. "I accomplished just what I meant to do—to prove to you that you needn't persist in dealing with me in that false, fatherly manner."

He wheeled about. "But I *will* persist in it, despite this temporary aberration. You are my ward and nothing more! And if you don't choose to remain my ward, this house can no longer be your home."

"*Oliver!*" His words struck at my chest with the impact of an arrow. I slowly rose to my feet, my hands held out as if to ward off any other assault. "You don't really mean—"

"I do mean it. I'm only a poor mortal, my girl, not a saint. And you are becoming too much for me to handle."

I gaped at him, aghast. What was happening here? I suddenly had the feeling that the ground was slipping away from me. What had I done? With that foolish, impetuous embrace, had I severed my connection with the one person in the world I cared about? I couldn't permit such a severing to come to pass. "I . . . I'm sorry, Oliver," I whispered humbly. "Please forgive me. I should never have—"

"No, you shouldn't," he cut in furiously. Angry with himself, he seemed to find satisfaction in lashing out at me. "Nor should you ever do such a thing again! To *anyone*."

"What did you say?" I could hardly believe my ears. How could he say such a thing? How could he even *think* that I would ever throw myself at anyone else? "What do you mean by that?" I demanded, glaring up at him.

"You know very well what I mean. I realize you are young and inexperienced, but you're not a simpleton. You can't go about doing or saying whatever comes into your head in that free-and-easy style of yours."

I felt myself stiffening in every muscle. "Free-and-easy style?" I echoed, appalled.

"Yes. Good God, girl, if you'd thrown yourself at Luton as you did at me just now, I couldn't have blamed him for suggesting what he did."

"Are you hinting that I *might* have done it with Sir Averil . . . or anyone else?" My stomach was tightening in a growing fury.

Oliver, his emotions also off-balance, didn't seem to notice how close we were coming to the edge of a precipice. "I'm not hinting anything. I'm only trying to point out—"

"It sounded to me as if that was *just* what you were hinting at," I insisted, icily cold.

"I'm only trying to point out," he repeated, glaring at me, "that you might be tempted to behave as impetuously in some future circumstance as you did tonight, and that the gentleman involved might not have the moral rectitude—"

"To suggest that I might misbehave in that way in the future, with some other gentleman, is worse than anything you've ever said to me," I accused, my voice choked with tears. "You *do* think I'm a b-born trollop, just like Grandmamma does, don't you!"

His head came up sharply. "Don't be an idiot!"

"You *do*, or you'd never have s-said such a thing to me!"

We stared at each other as if we each could not believe this sort of altercation could have been exchanged between us.

"Anne, you can't think I—" he began.

But I was too bruised to listen. I wanted only to strike out at him. "I *do* think it. Once I was naive enough to believe that you were different from other men. I thought you were the one person in the world who understood me and cared for me. But you're cruel and . . . and *hypocritical*, just like all the rest!"

Taken aback by my vehemence, he whitened. "Anne, I—"

"No! Don't bother to say anything. I d-don't want to hear it!" I felt my tears rush to the surface. My world seemed to be crashing down about my ears, but I didn't even try to save myself. Heedlessly, I rushed on into calamity. "You all pretend to be such *fine gentlemen!*" I ranted. "All of you! You take lovers, you steal kisses in dark corners, you make overtures of all sorts to innocent, unsuspecting females, and you indulge in all sorts of *amour,* but if we . . . *I* . . . dare to make the slightest gesture of . . . of affection, you think I'm a . . . a harlot!"

"Damnation, girl, I never said—!"

"You didn't have to say the words. The implication was quite clear. But don't trouble yourself about me any more, your lordship. Perhaps my grandmother's house is the b-best place for me after all." I turned and started to run up the stairs, my tears flowing unchecked. "She may not think any m-more of me than you do," I flung back over my shoulder, "but at least she's not a *hypocritical m-male!*"

"Confound you, girl, *wait!*" He took the stairs three at a time and caught up with me at the turning. He grasped my arm and pulled me about so that I fell back against the bannister. "Why are you trying to twist my words? I meant only to warn you that men will begin to find you a very difficult creature to resist."

I dashed the tears from my cheeks with furious pride. "Am I indeed? *You* seem to be able to resist me easily enough!"

"Do you think this is *easy?*" He gripped both my arms tightly and shook me in wrathful helplessness. "I don't even know how to *speak* to you anymore."

"That's because there's n-nothing left to say."

He stared at me a moment before releasing me and turning away. "You're right. Let's make an end to this foolishness. Go up to bed. We'll talk about plans tomorrow, when we're calmer."

"We shall not talk tomorrow at all, for I intend to be gone," I said with all the dignity I could summon, and I walked on up the stairs.

I didn't leave my room again until the next morning. I don't know how Oliver spent that dreadful night, but I spent it in the most bitter weeping of my life.

Chapter Twelve

MISS GRIBBIN WOKE me the next morning. Since I had fallen asleep only a short while before, my mind did not immediately grasp the significance of her unaccustomed air of tension. "I'm to go back with you," she explained, reading my confusion in my eyes. "To London! Lord Fleming is sending us back in his town coach. You'd better hurry, my love, for Jacka will bring it round by eight."

Slowly I became aware that she was already attired in her traveling gown and had even put her bonnet on. She bustled about the room in half-distracted, half-purposeful excitement, readying my dress, repacking my bandbox and keeping a nervous eye on my dreamlike progress in rising from my bed. I felt thickheaded and numb. I moved about the room like a sleepwalker, following Miss Gribbin's instructions with mindless exactitude. I performed my ablutions, dressed, brushed my hair and donned my outer garments all without awareness of what I was doing, and I followed her down the stairs and across the hallway to the breakfast room without having a conscious thought or feeling.

Mabyn served us breakfast, her eyes flitting from my face to Miss Gribbin's with surreptitious intensity, like the visitor at a sickbed looking anxiously from the patient to the doctor but unable to speak of her concerns while the patient remains conscious. I didn't understand the strained atmosphere of the breakfast room, but my mind was unwilling to exert itself to find an answer. The fog-like blanket that seemed to have benumbed my brain and my emotions was soothing; it seemed to cushion me against the cold reality of the revelations of the night before, and I didn't want to brush it away.

I swallowed some tea but ate nothing. When the clock in the hallway struck eight, Miss Gribbin got up and hurried me to the front door. Mrs. Trewin stood just inside, waiting to bid me goodbye. Her hands were tightly clenched at her breast and her brow furrowed. Trewin stood beside her, looking equally worried. A small, separate uninvolved compartment of my mind clicked into awareness, and I wondered if they'd all heard some part—or all—of the scene which Oliver and I had enacted on the stairway those few hours before. That would explain the unwarranted apprehension in their manner. But I didn't care if they'd heard us or not. I didn't seem to care about anything.

Mabyn brought my cloak, which she'd carefully cleaned and pressed, and threw it over me. Then they each bid me a rather funereal goodbye, and I started down the stone steps to the waiting coach. That same, uninvolved compartment of my mind continued to function in its detached, precise fashion, recording the impressions made by my senses without stirring any emotion. I saw the horses pawing at the ground, their breaths rising like clouds in the cold morning air. I saw Jacka stowing my bandbox and Miss Gribbin's well-worn trunk on top of the carriage and lashing them down securely with a length of rope. I saw Miss Gribbin adjust her bonnet as Trewin ran down the steps to help her aboard.

Only that one little part of my brain seemed to be functioning, ticking away like a mantel clock that had somehow been left in a deserted forest. *You are departing*, it declared in short, exact, toneless syllables, its rhythm as steady and dispassionate as a metronome. *You are leaving Pentargon, perhaps forever. You are walking down the steps. You may never mount them again. Mrs. Trewin is watching. And Mabyn. And Jacka. But not Oliver. Oliver is not here. Jacka is looking at you in a strange way. He's waiting to hand you up, but you've stopped on the third step and are not moving. You are looking around . . . for Oliver. But Oliver is not here. Oliver is nowhere in sight.*

I felt another little compartment of my mind blink itself awake, and then another, and suddenly every cell in my brain began to tingle with energy. What was the *matter* with me? Had I been bereft of my *senses?* How could I leave Pentargon like this? How could I go away while this terrible rift between Oliver and me remained unmended? How could I leave without the assurance that I would be permitted to return?

A rush of feeling swept through me like a gust of wind through the open sides of an unused summerhouse, and it blew away all vestiges of fog and cobweb, all remnants of the numbness that had clogged my brain. I whirled about and went flying up the steps. I flung myself through the still-open door, rushed by the gaping Mrs. Trewin and the wide-eyed Mabyn and dashed down the hall. *"Oliver!"* I shouted like a hysteric; and I burst into his study.

The room was deserted. I came to a stop just inside the doorway, suddenly arrested by indecision. Where had he gone? The breakfast room? The greenhouses? The stables? I turned around to begin a search, but my way was blocked by Trewin who stood watching me from the doorway. "'E's gone, Miss Anne. Galloped off afore seven. Said 'e won't back 'til nightfall. Said for 'ee t' set off wi'out 'im."

The pain of the night before returned in full measure. "Are you sure?" I asked stupidly.

He merely nodded, and after throwing me a troubled look, he led the way back to the entrance hall. Once more I nodded goodbye to Mrs. Trewin and Mabyn, and once more I descended the steps. Jacka opened the coach door and handed me up. Too quickly for words, before I'd even leaned back against the squabs, I felt the carriage begin to move. We were rolling down the drive. I fought the instinct to turn to the rear window and watch the castle disappear into the morning mist. What was the use? I would only weep. The pain of my departure was keen enough without that.

We rode for almost an hour in silence, my eyes fixed on the grim winter landscape that passed in monotonous inevitability outside my window and Miss Gribbin's eyes fixed on me. Then she cleared her throat. When she did it again, I realized she wanted my attention. I turned to her with raised brows. "Is something amiss, Miss Gribbin?"

She reached into her reticule and withdrew a folded, sealed document. Biting her underlip worriedly, she handed it to me. "It's from his lordship," she said in an awed whisper. "He said to give it to you when we'd passed Launceston."

My heart stopped beating, but I managed to thank her as I took the letter and turned it over in my hand. My name was scrawled across the face in Oliver's familiar, slanted letters. I broke the seal, my fingers shaking, but before I unfolded the sheet, I turned to the window so that Miss Gribbin would not be able to see my face as I read.

A quick glance told me that the letter was not long, and its brevity did not offer much hope that my circumstances would be improved by reading it. Nevertheless, my pulse began to race as my eyes flew over the words:

My dearest girl,

I hope the morning light has brought some clarity to your mind as it has to mine. In that clarity I see that I would be a greater fool than I already seem to myself if I add to the foolishness of last night's row by dwelling upon it further. The whole incident is best forgotten. It should be the future with which we concern ourselves, not the past. And that future presages a change in our way of life.

Difficult as it will be for both of us to face, our lives must now take separate paths. However satisfying was my guardianship of your girlhood years, that guardianship is now inadequate. I am not the proper mentor to guide a lovely young woman—which is what you suddenly have become—into adulthood. That tesk would be better handled by your grandmother and Lady Gilbart, both of whom have (since the summer of your illness) repeatedly expressed their eagerness to take charge of you. If their guardianship does not please you, keep in mind that in all likelihood it will be of brief duration. Shortly after you are introduced to society, my dear, you will find yourself betrothed and embarked on a life of your own. You are certain to find that life happier and more fulfilling than anything you've experienced in the past. That is why I must now be cruel and compel you to take the road that leads to such a destiny.

I have often wondered if the tree weeps when it must

shed its blossoms to make way for the fruit. But, tears or no, the time of the fruit must come.

One thing more. I have never thought of you as anything but the bright, pure, sparkling, unique creature that you are. Believe that. Yours, etc., Oliver.

The paper shook in my hand. *I have often wondered if the tree weeps* . . . that couldn't have been written by a man who didn't care. My heart swelled in tenderness for him. He cared for me, that much was clear. And for a moment it was all that I wished to know. The tone of the letter was a balm to my wounded spirit. But before I would permit myself to feel even the beginnings of hope, I read the letter again.

That first ray of hope immediately faded. He might care for me, but the real meaning of his words was that he was sending me away from him. However gently he'd said it, the message was clear. He wanted me to go out into the world and find myself a husband. A new life at the end of a path that diverged from his. And there was no indication—not a word or a sign—of any desire on his part for my return. No, the letter had not revealed his love—at least not the love I wanted. He'd cared for the child I was, not the woman I would be. He had been charmed by the blossom . . . but he'd left the fruit for someone else.

"Is . . . anything wrong?" Miss Gribbin asked timidly.

"Wrong?" I gritted my teeth in anger—at him, at my grandmother, at my mother, at her lovers, at all men young and old, and at everything and everyone who had brought me to this place of utter loneliness and devastation. "Why do you think something's wrong?"

"The letter . . ." She threw me a frightened look. "You read it so . . . avidly. With such . . . intensity . . ."

I crushed it in my fingers. "It was nothing," I said dully. "Just . . . words."

She kept her eyes on my face, her mouth pursed in an expression of heartfelt concern. "Just words? I don't know what you mean."

"I mean that there's nothing in this of any import. Just penscratches on a piece of paper. Nothing that's written here will change our lives a jot." And I tossed the crumpled wad into the far corner of the carriage.

Later, however, when the incessant rocking of the carriage

had lulled her to sleep, I inched over to the other side of my seat and picked up the crumpled ball of paper. I smoothed it out on my lap and read it once again. With no one's eyes on me, I permitted a few tears to fall. Then I tenderly folded the wrinkled sheet and tucked it into the bosom of my dress.

They were only words on a sheet of paper . . . and they changed nothing. But they were all I had left of him.

Chapter Thirteen

"A COME-OUT IS not a simple thing, you know," Grandmamma said from her bed. Though it was past noon, she had not yet bothered to rise and dress for the day. She was leaning back against a mountain of pillows and bolsters, a lorgnette perched on her nose, her hair hanging over her shoulders in two thin braids, and a tray on her lap littered with cards and envelopes. "In fact," she countinued, "it is a ritual of unbelievable complexity. You will be expected to shine not only at your own presentation ball but at all of the others."

"Ugh!" I grunted from the window where I was perched on the seat, dividing my attention between Grandmamma and the view of her garden through the depressing spring rain which seemed to have been falling for days. "I'm beginning to be sorry I ever agreed to—"

"You never *did* agree to it, my love," Grandmamma said calmly, peering closely at an invitation card as if she were inspecting a forgery. "You were given no choice in the matter."

"Yes, you're right there. How many balls shall I have to smile through?"

"Who can say? I shall choose only the most advantageous,

you can be sure of that. The Pressbury's ball is a must, for they have three eligible sons, each of whom has several eligible friends. But I think you can skip the Leemings'. He is only a baron, and she can be considered nothing better than shabby-genteel."

"The whole business seems nothing better than shabby-genteel to me. Just ostentation and snobbery."

Grandmamma didn't even bother to take offense. She had grown accustomed to my sour tongue during the past two months and no longer took any notice.

Miss Gribbin and I had moved in with her on our return from Cornwall, although I had shortly thereafter returned to the Finchlow Academy for the conclusion of my studies there. Dory and I had, only a week ago, been certified by the Misses Finchlow as ready to make our bows in society. (If the dear ladies had reservations about *my* readiness—and I'm convinced they did, for since my return from Cornwall I'd been more truculent and rebellious than before—they refrained from expressing their misgivings about me aloud. They were, no doubt, relieved to be rid of me.) They had held a "graduation ceremony" for the nine pupils in the school who had reached the age of eighteen, at which parents and relations were invited to partake of punch and cakes and listen to Miss Felicity expound at length on our promising futures while Miss Charity flittered about the drawing room pressing the guests to take "a teeny-weeny bit more" of the cake. Grandmamma, who had attended the ceremony in company with Lord and Lady Gilbart, Colin and Eliza, had kissed me affectionately at its conclusion and presented me with a pair of pearl earrings. I'd also received a leather-bound keepsake album from the Gilbarts to celebrate the occasion.

Dory and I had exchanged identical gold bracelets, as a sign of our undying affection for each other, and although the jewelry was not very costly, we both agreed that the bracelets were our most precious gifts. I, however, kept looking for something from Pentargon to show that Oliver still thought of me. But nothing had come that day nor in the week since.

With school behind me, I'd returned to Grandmamma's house. She immediately set about—with enormous zest and energy—to running my life. I was about to be presented to the polite world, and she (in company with Lady Gilbart) had determined to see that I was properly launched. She set Miss

Gribbin the task of acting as secretary, she told Mrs. Panniers to assist as my abigail and hairdresser, and she herself took on the tasks of arranging my appointments, deciding on my schedule, choosing my clothes and supervising my every waking moment.

I did as I was told, although nothing kept me from expressing my scorn of the entire business. I didn't care how I spent my days. Grandmamma, Lady Gilbart, Eliza and even Dory might believe that I would soon find someone to love and wed, but I knew better. I despised all men and intended to marry none of them. If even the best of them could hurt me so, what could I expect from the rest? I determined never to permit myself to be hurt again. Instead, I would do the hurting. If any man should be foolish enough to attempt intimacy with me—intimacy of any sort at all—he would soon learn the pain of rejection. My path would be strewn with the fallen bodies of men whose hearts I had slain. I quite looked forward to the fray.

Grandmamma, of course, had no idea of what was in my mind. She serenely went on studying the invitation cards and letters, smiling over some and raising a disparaging eyebrow over others. "The cheek of Mrs. Frobisher sending you a card! As if I would permit you to attend her rout. Her husband is nothing but a tufthunter!"

I merely shrugged. I cared nothing for the gradations of the social heirarchy which everyone of the *ton* considered so important. As far as the invitations were concerned, Grandmamma was welcome to do as she liked.

"I know what you're thinking," Grandmamma said placidly, "but you're quite wrong. Where you're seen and in whose company you spend your time is of enormous importance. The entire idea of a come-out is to present the novice to the polite world so that she may become known by the proper people and recognized by her peers. If one appears in the wrong places or—" She paused and stared at a letter, her eyes lighting. "Ah!" she cried, holding it up like a flag of triumph. "Here's what I've been waiting for. The Princess Esterhazy has sent you a voucher for Almack's."

I grunted again. "You make it sound like a medal of distinction."

"It is, my dear, it is. You are very lucky to get it, considering . . ."

I stiffened. "Considering who my mother was, is that what you were going to say?"

She raised her eyes from the note to stare at me in mild reproval. "Really, my child, must you climb on your high ropes at every possible opportunity? Your mother was who she was, and you may as well learn to face that fact with equanimity. It is a blemish, but you are not the only young woman who has to compensate for blemishes. Look at Lydia Pressbury who is always breaking out in spots. Or Cynthia Harcourt who has such a dreadful stutter. Even your friend Dory, whose lineage is impeccable and whose fortune is considerable, will have to overcome the disadvantage of her tendency to acquire fat."

"There's nothing wrong with Dory's figure. I find it perfectly charming."

"I admire your loyalty, my dear. Nevertheless, she is too plump. As for your 'blemish,' it is certainly nothing that need trouble us. Your grandmother, I am please to say, has sufficiently potent force in society to overcome any adverse effects which your mother's reputation may cast on you, so you needn't worry."

"I *don't* worry. I don't care *what* society thinks of my mother or of me. They are nothing but gossips and hypocrites, all of them."

Grandmamma continued to sort through the cards, notes and messages with serene concentration. My rebelliousness disturbed her not a whit. "As I was saying earlier," she proceeded, resuming her lecture on the nature of come-outs as if nothing had in interrupted her train of thought, "there are not only the presentation balls and the dances at Almack's on Wednesday evenings, but there are the galas, the rout-parties, the luncheons and teas and receptions, the dinner dances and all sorts of *fêtes* and festivities to which you will be invited—"

"Good heavens, what an infernal bore."

"—and they, too, must be carefully screened. I shall choose only those occasions in which there is some definite advantage for you."

"I don't see why you bother. Why don't you just stand me up on a platform in the middle of St. James Square, invite all the eligibles and sell me to the highest bidder?"

"Don't be vulgar." She threw back the edge of her bed-cape in a gesture of disdain. "The purpose of all this activity is not, need I remind you, to find you a rich husband. Do you think your grandmother is some Hans Town dowager searching for a title and a fortune? The granddaughter of Lady Marietta Saunders has no reason to connive in that way. My object, you little idiot, is to see you settled and happy."

"I won't find happiness that way," I mumbled, turning back to the window and the rain.

"You have no way of knowing *where* your happiness may lie." I heard her put aside the tray of letters. "Call Mrs. Panniers for me, my love, and ask her to come and help me to dress. I think I should like to take you shopping today."

I turned to gaze at her in wonder. In the years since I'd first left for Cornwall, she'd grown thinner and her skin more translucent. She had declared, those six long years ago, that having me with her would be too much for her. Now, older and undoubtedly more frail, she'd taken me in and thrown herself into making plans for my social season. Even though she would not be accompanying me to all the social affairs which I'd have to attend (she'd arranged for Lady Gilbart or Eliza to do that), she insisted on overseeing everything else. She and she alone would make the decisions on what I should wear, what functions I should attend and what gentlemen I should give permission to call on me. Even today, in this steady downpour, she seemed eager to embark on a shopping trip. How could she manage all this at her age?

I walked to the door to do her bidding, but I paused before putting my hand on the knob. "Why are you doing all this, Grandmamma?" I found myself asking.

"Doing what?" came the surprised response.

I turned to face her. "Why have you suddenly taken this interest in me and my future?"

"What a strange question. You're my granddaughter."

I walked back to the foot of the bed. "But I was your granddaughter when Mama died, yet you didn't take me then. What has changed?"

Her eyes fell. "I didn't think I could handle a child," she said, toying with the satin bow at the neck of her bed-cape. "Besides, I thought you'd be better off growing up in Cornwall than in London."

"You don't say!" I declared, cold with scorn and disbelief. "Better off, you say? Your reason had nothing whatever to do with your conviction that I was a potential little harlot?"

Her eyes flew up to mine, shocked. Then her eyebrows rose

haughtily. "I never had any such conviction."

"You *said* it! In just those words."

"I *never*—!"

"I *heard* you, Grandmamma. You said it to Oliver, on the day of Mama's funeral."

"Oh, *that.*" She made a dismissive gesture with one bony hand. "That was only for a . . . a purpose."

"What purpose?"

"Because . . ." She frowned at me in annoyance. "Really, Anne, must we speak of these matters now? If I don't get dressed at once, we shan't get to the milliner's before three, and that will hardly give you time to change for tonight's musicale at Lord Lithgow's."

"I don't care. This is more important than the milliner's."

"You have a strange sense of priorities. A new hat is by far—! Oh, very well. You needn't look at me in that *lugubrious* way. There's no mystery about it. My purpose in saying those dreadful things to Oliver was to goad him. I didn't think he would agree to take you unless I angered him enough to feel protective of you. It was simply a ruse."

"A *ruse!*" My knees gave way, and I sank down upon the bed. "Good heavens!"

"What's the matter? You couldn't have believed I *meant* such a dreadful thing!"

"Why couldn't I? If you expected *Oliver* to believe it, why wouldn't you expect me to do the same?"

"Well, you weren't supposed to hear it."

I leaned my forehead on the bedpost. "But I did hear it, you see. I heard every word."

"Are you telling me that you've believed, all these years, that I think you have bad blood in you?" She threw aside the covers, swung herself off the bed and padded up to me, her bare feet, veined and bluish-white, sticking out pathetically from beneath the hem of her nightdress. "Look here, my dear. Here at my face. Don't you know that you mean more to me than anyone on earth? How could you believe—?"

I could only gape at her. "I? Even . . . *then?*"

She sat down beside me. "From the moment you were born," She put an unsteady hand to my hair. "I took one look at you in your swaddling clothes . . . with your dreadful red hair and those shrewd, knowing eyes . . . and I knew you were something extraordinary. Something...I don't know quite how to describe it—"

"I know," I said, half tearful and half mocking. "A *rara avis.*"

"Yes, exactly. I could have had you taken from your mother and brought to me when Reginald died, but I could see how much she loved you. I knew she needed you more than I did. I've always been...strong."

"But why, later, did you want Oliver to take me? If you're so strong, you could have managed—"

The hand that had been smoothing my hair ceased. She threw me a quick, measuring glance before looking away. "I had my reasons." She folded her hands in her lap and stared at them a long while before going on. "You're not trying to tell me that you were *unhappy* with Oliver, are you?"

"No. I was not unhappy with Oliver."

"Then why all these questions?"

"I simply want to understand my...situation. You say you care for me, yet you shunted me off to Oliver. Oliver says he cares for me, yet he shunted me off to you. Is it any wonder I'm confused?"

"No, I suppose not. Your life has not been easy, I admit. And this moving you about from pillar to post must seem puzzling. But perhaps, before long, you may be able to understand better what I—" She stopped herself, as if she wanted to prevent herself from saying too much. "Don't think about the past, my love. Try to concentrate on the present. However wrong I may have been about my part of your upbringing, I meant it all for the best. The truth is, my dear, that my whole life has been brightened by having you here with me at last. Knowing that may be of comfort to you...perhaps even comfort enough to bring us close. You have always, since you were a little girl, held me off from you. Now, perhaps..."

Her pale blue eyes, showing a surprising vulnerability in the strong, lined face, watched me closely. I wanted to say something reassuring and loving to her—something to the effect that I *was* comforted by learning of her affection for me...that I would be happy living here with her...that I would, all at once, become a close and loving granddaughter. But I could not. Too many bitter memories intruded themselves between us, memories too real and too clear to be easily banished. I looked down at my folded hands and said nothing.

She waited for a long while, but when a response from me did not come, she sighed and patted my hands fondly. "Well, one cannot order up feelings as one does three-minute eggs. Let's give it time. Go along, now, girl, and call Mrs. Panniers. If we hurry, we may still have time to visit the milliner's this afternoon."

I got up and went to the door. But just before leaving, I looked back and caught a glimpse of her, still seated on the edge of the bed, surreptitiously brushing a tear from her cheek. Nothing she'd said moved me so much as that brief glimpse.

I went down the hall feeling somewhat healed, as if a plaster had been placed on a raw wound of my spirit. My grandmother had not meant those awful things she'd said those many years ago. Even though I'd thought I'd long since come to terms with those words I'd overheard . . . even though I'd long ago told myself I would never follow in my mother's footsteps . . . it had been depressing to think that my grandmother had believed I was condemned to do so. Now I knew this was not true, and I was consoled by it.

When I returned to Grandmamma's bedroom to say that Mrs. Panniers would be following shortly, I found her sitting at her dressing table, unplaiting her long grey braids. "By the way, Anne," she said, watching me in her mirror, "have you heard that he's come back to town?"

"Who's come?"

"Oliver."

My heart did a sudden lurch in my breast. "Oliver?" I echoed stupidly. "When?"

"A few days ago. He's staying at the Fenton. He's planning to remain in town long enough to attend your ball."

"Oh." I felt suddenly uncomfortable under her intense scrutiny. "I . . . how did you learn of it?"

"He called here. Last night, while you were at the Gilbarts'."

"You've *seen* him?" I stared at her reflection in the glass, my feelings a mass of confusion. "How is he? Why didn't he wait to see me? You knew I'd be home by ten."

"He has other things to do, you know. He has many friends in town and all sorts of business matters to see to."

"Yes, I suppose so. Did he . . . ask for me?"

"Of course. I told him you were doing splendidly."

"Did he say . . . ? Is he coming back?"

She shrugged. "I don't know. One of these days, I expect. And you're bound to run into him here and there."

I was stung with disappointment. "You mean he didn't even . . . make arrangements to c-call on me?"

She busied herself with her hair. "*Call* on you?" She put a handful of hairpins in her mouth. "Why should he call on you?" she mumbled, her words irritatingly indistinct. "He'll surely see you at your ball, and that's all that counts."

I turned back to the door blindly. The ball was more than a fortnight away. "Yes, of course," I said bitterly as I closed the door behind me, "my ball. That's all that counts."

Chapter Fourteen

THAT EVENING, AS soon as I entered Lord Lithgow's music room in the company of Dory and Lady Gilbart, I searched among the faces of the huge crowd for a glimpse of Oliver. Over a hundred chairs had been set up in rows so that Lord Lithgow's guests could enjoy the program of chamber music (performed by the Concert of Ancient Music, a society of musicians of noble birth and amateurish talent) in comfort. Most of the guests were already seated, but Oliver was not among them.

I took my seat next to Dory, folded my hands in my lap and tried to lose myself in the music, but my spirit was too depressed and the music too uninspiring. My mind niggled away at the subject of Oliver in, much the same way that a tongue worries a loose tooth. *How could he,* I asked myself over and over, *have been in London for over a week without having made a real attempt to see me?* The answer was obvious: he was avoiding me. And the only reason I could find for that avoidance was that he no longer wished to entangle himself in my life. He'd responded to Grandmamma's invitation to attend my ball because to refuse would be to reveal to the world that we were estranged. He *had* to attend the ball, if only to prevent raised eyebrows. But that was all that was required of him, and it was probably all he intended to do for me.

It was a crushing blow. If Oliver could be so near and yet not make any effort to see me, our estrangement was deeper and more permanent than I had imagined. I tried to find comfort by reviewing in my mind the precious phrases of his letter (which was at this moment tucked into the bodice of my gown)—phrases like: *lovely young woman*, and *bright, pure, sparkling creature that you are*—which during the past four months had brought some balm to my bruised soul. But this time they failed to console me.

I tried to tell myself that it was time for me to learn to accept the inevitable . . . to admit to myself that Oliver was no longer a part of my life. But I couldn't accept the finality of it. My dreams refused to die, and thus my pain did not lessen. My spirit would take no comfort—not from the music, not from the nearness of my friends, and not from the prospect of the social whirl ahead of me.

That prospect of the social whirl, I realized, would be dramatically affected by Oliver's presence in town. Everywhere I went I would be watching for him. I would find myself crushed, as I was tonight, by his absence or (perhaps worse) terrified into incoherence if I should come upon him without preparation. How was I to face the next fortnight with any sort of composure?

By the time intermission was announced, I had not only failed to find a solution to my dilemma but I'd convinced myself that no solution existed. Dory, unaware of my emotional turmoil and delighted at the prospect of a half hour's respite from the boredom of the music, jumped to her feet and pulled me to mine. "Let's take a walk through the adjoining rooms," she whispered eagerly. "We'll look over the eligibles first and then see what there is to eat."

I roused myself by sheer force of will and followed her and Lady Gilbart out of the room. Buffet tables had been set up in all of the adjoining rooms, their surfaces covered with the usual punch bowls and platters of pastries, sweetmeats and assorted delicacies. Lady Gilbart, with an admonition to her daughter to eat nothing more than one fish-cake and a glass of negus, "for you will not wish to put on any more weight before the ball, my love. You surely will not want Madame Virelle to let your ball gown out again," she wandered off to gossip with her friends.

Dory made a face behind her mother's back and began immediately to heap a plate with banana cream tarts, almond-paste cakes and French nougats. "I hardly see a man about who's under the age of forty," she muttered, nibbling on a tart and holding her plate out to me.

"Perhaps we should wander about in one of the other rooms," I suggested, rejecting the pastries but trying to smile with some semblance of enthusiasm.

"These banana creams are *divine!* Why won't you take one?"

"I'm not very hungry. And you'd better put that plate down before your mother comes back, or she'll—"

"Goodness!" Dory was staring at something past my shoulder. "Who's that coming toward us? He looks as if his coach had been overturned."

I turned round and looked directly into the nervous eyes of Sir Averil Luton.

"Good evening, Miss Saunders," he said, rigidly formal. "I've come here tonight especially to seek you out."

I took a step backward and grasped Dory's hand. "I'm afraid my friend and I were . . . were just leaving," I improvised.

His eyes dropped to Dory's loaded plate. "Surely you were not leaving until your friend has finished her repast."

I flushed in frustration. "She just said she's had enough, didn't you, Dory?"

"Yes, I did," Dory said promptly, feeling the urgency of my grasp. "I don't believe we've met, sir, have we?"

"Oh, I beg your pardon," I muttered awkwardly. "Dory, this is Sir Averil Luton, a . . . a friend of my . . . the family. Sir Averil, my friend, Miss Dorothea Gilbart."

They made their bows, Dory's eyes sweeping over his face curiously. And indeed, he made a strange appearance. His face looked terrible. The skin around his left eye, although covered with a thick film of flesh-colored *maquillage*, looked badly discolored. There was a large plaster over a wound on his right cheek, and his upper lip was swollen and badly split. Nevertheless, his dress was impeccable, his hair neatly combed back from his brow and his manner polite and restrained. "I hope, Miss Gilbart, that you will permit me a few moments conversation with your friend. I have a message which I've given my word to deliver at the earliest opportunity."

I clutched Dory's hand even tighter. "We are really pressed for time, sir. Could you not write the message down and send it to my grandmother's house? I am certain to receive it by morning."

Sir Averil frowned. "But what I have to say will take a moment only." His tone was so different from the leering manner of his last conversation with me that I sensed he was truly attempting to be reassuring. "If you would just come with me to the corner of the room—right over there—your friend could keep you in plain sight."

It seemed more expedient to acquiesce than to stand there arguing with him. "Don't go away," I hissed to Dory, and I put my hand on Sir Averil's arm.

As soon as we were out of earshot I turned on him. "I hope you're not going to renew the subject of our last conversation," I warned. "Miss Gilbart's mother is close at hand—"

"You needn't be alarmed. I have no such intention. I've come only to make my most sincere apologies for that earlier conversation," he said quietly.

I was taken by surprise. "Apologies?"

"Yes. It has been...er...rather forcibly brought to my attention that, in bringing up the subject which engaged us during our last meeting, I had badly misjudged you." He put his fingers meaningfully on his bruised cheek. "Your guardian has made me see the error of my ways, and...er...he very pointedly suggested that I ask your pardon."

I was astounded. "My guardian? Are you speaking of Lord Fleming?"

"Indeed I am, Miss Saunders. I should have trusted your word when you told me that you were well protected. You are fortunate to have so convincing and so...er...powerful a person to look after you."

I was stricken almost speechless. "Thank you," I breathed in stupefaction.

"That is the gist of what I have to say. Except, of course, that you have my assurance that I will never speak to you on such a subject again."

I nodded and turned away. But before I had gone two steps, he called my name. "One thing more, Miss Saunders," he said, coming up to me again. "Will you inform his lordship that I've expressed my deepest regrets? And will you do it soon? I shouldn't enjoy receiving another...er..." He put a hand gingerly on his swollen lip. "...another visit from him."

"I'll tell him if...when I see him," I said.

He made his bow and quickly disappeared into the crowd. I stared after him, my mind whirling. Evidently Oliver had sought him out as soon as he'd arrived in London and had made his disapproval clear by landing Sir Averil what pugilists like to call a "proper facer." Oliver *had* said something to me in Cornwall about "dealing with Luton," but I'd forgotten all about it.

But Oliver had evidently not forgotten. Did that mean he still thought of me? Did it mean that I should permit myself to hope again?

Dory came up behind me. "What was *that* all about?" she asked. "Is anything amiss?"

"No, nothing worth speaking of," I assured her. "I think the musicians are ready to resume. We'd better return to our seats."

I felt Dory's eyes on me during the remainder of the concert, and I was very much afraid that she would persist in questioning me about Sir Averil, but when the music ended, something occurred which took my meeting with Sir Averil out of her mind. She was introduced to Lord Dawes.

It was hard to believe that Theodoric Dawes could interest a lively, spirited, lusty young creature like Dory, but I could see at once that she was taken with him. It was Lord Lithgow himself who brought the young man to meet us. "My cousin Theo," he said in his overly hearty manner, "has been admiring you lovely ladies from afar. He says that you are both the prettiest chits in the room. Well, speak up, fellow! Tell them it's true!"

Lord Dawes said nothing. He merely fixed his eyes on Dory's face with a strange intensity. The silence was uncomfortable, and Dory, embarrassed, giggled awkwardly.

Lord Lithgow glared at his cousin in disgust. "Well, at least make your bow, you clunch," he muttered, and, turning his back to his cousin, he winked at us. "The strong, silent sort, my cousin Theo," he told us with a grin and promptly wandered off.

The three of us were left standing together in mortifying discomfort. Lord Dawes stared at Dory, Dory stared at her shoes and I watched them both without knowing how to ease the strain. After a moment, Dory peeped up at her admirer. "Did you *really* say to your cousin that we were the prettiest chits in the room?" she asked boldly.

"I said 'young ladies,' not 'chits.' My cousin Lithgow is not very accurate."

"You, sir," I ventured, "are not very accurate yourself. I see at least three ladies here who would be considered prettier that either of us."

"The only judge of beauty, Miss Saunders," Lord Dawes responded with solemn deliberation, "is the taste of the observer."

"You're quite right, Lord Dawes," Dory said, smiling at him warmly. "Therefore we shall happily accept your compliment as being sincere."

"Thank you, ma'am," he said with another of his stiff bows. "I am *always* sincere."

I looked at them in some amazement. I couldn't easily adjust to Dory's obvious attraction to the fellow. What did Dory, who was always frivolous and gay, see in this sober-sided, dour-faced fellow who was as tall, thin and angular as she was small, soft and rounded? Nevertheless, I was delighted. There was something about the awkward Lord Dawes that I liked. And since I'd never really recovered from my early distaste for Henry Inglebright, I could only hope that a rival for Dory's hand had appeared.

By the time we gathered at the Gilbart domicile the next evening, preparatory to departing for the Pressburys' gala in Berkeley Square, Dory had become so absorbed in her new romance that she had no recollection of Sir Averil or the strange encounter at the buffet at Lord Lithgow's. Theodoric Dawes had called on her that afternoon and taken her for a drive in the park. "He is as solemn as an owl and spoke in nothing but epigrams," she told me in a whisper before her parents came down to escort us to the dance, "but I like him very well. Tell me honestly, Anne, do you think I'm silly to think he's ... attractive?"

"I think he looks like a hungry crow and sounds like a scholar," I grinned, slipping an affectionate arm about her waist, "and you're not in the *least* silly to be attracted. He's worth ten of a certain other of your swains whose name I shall not mention but who's considered by the world to be so very handsome and charming."

"I know what you mean," Dory said thoughtfully. "Lord Dawes is, as he himself claimed, *sincere,* while Henry is . . ."

"Affected," I supplied promptly.

Dory gave her trilling laugh. "Won't Henry be *livid* if he finds himself ousted by a—how did you put it?—a *scholarly crow?*"

She was still laughing when we climbed into the carriage behind her mother and father. There was an air of excitement in the carriage which I wished I could share. The Pressburys' daughter's presentation this evening was to be a grand affair, and Lady Gilbart had spoken of nothing else for days. She only hoped that our own ball would turn out to be as great a squeeze. *(Our* ball—at which Dory and I were to be launched together— was to be held under the joint sponsorship of the Gilbarts and my grandmother, and was to be held at Gilbart House. Two hundred cards had already been sent out for the affair, and Grandmamma had ordered the finest crystal, plate, flowers and champagne that were available in London. She'd also hired an army of cooks and servants to supplement Lady Gilbart's already large kitchen staff. Dory and I had already been fitted into our gowns, which we agreed were luxurious beyond our dreams. If the Pressburys could outdo all this, I would be very much surprised.)

Lady Gilbart was convinced that the Pressburys would fill their rooms with young "eligibles," and she and my grandmother had both stressed the importance to Dory and me of acquiring a retinue of admirers before our own ball would be held. "It is not only that from that retinue will come your serious suitors," Lady Gilbart instructed, "but it will provide enough admirers to fill your dance-cards at all the social events and give evidence to the world that you are sought-after and popular. Nothing so attracts a gentleman, my dear, as the knowledge that a lady is desired by other men."

(Dory and I had exchanged amused glances during this monologue, for Lady Gilbart's words were an echo of those we'd been hearing from Miss Felicity Finchlow for two years.)

Actually, Dory had already acquired a considerable "retinue." Henry Inglebright was a faithful and persistent caller, two or three other young men had also taken to paying morning calls on her, and now there was Lord Dawes as well. As for me, I was not without admirers of my own. Two or three youths, not much older than myself, followed me about with sickening persistence, but since I found it difficult to tell one from the other, I paid them little notice. Colin sometimes escorted me to an evening gala, but I had, by this time, become more his friend than his *innamorata*. Colin had long since tired of the pretty Miss Inglebright and had gone on to an amazing assortment of new flirts. Every week, it seemed to me, he became enchanted with a new female, and I was always greatly entertained by his accounts of his most recent amatory adventures. But I could always count on him to sign my dance-card and to keep me from standing alone at parties.

But all of these pre-nuptial games failed to engage my spirit. They were somewhat diverting, I admit, but they had little to do with what I really considered important—my life in Cornwall. I knew that the chances of my returning there to live became more remote with each passing day, and that it behooved me to grasp the present with more enthusiasm and make more realistic plans for my future, but I couldn't seem to be able to take myself in hand.

Even now, sitting beside Lord Gilbart in the carriage, listening to him joke about the certainty of our coming home "the new belles of London," I felt no sense of anticipation or excitement. I was aware only of a dull feeling of dread—dread that Oliver would not be there this evening, and dread that he would be.

He was not. I ascertained that during the first half hour after our arrival, and I steeled myself for a long, tedious evening. I was shaken out of my lethargy by the onslaught of all three Pressbury brothers, each importuning me for the first dance. They were all handsome, lively young fellows, and I was kept mildly amused by their loud, boisterous rivalry for my hand. This rivalry brought me to the notice of many other young men in the room and, just as Lady Gilbart and Miss Finchlow had predicted, they seemed to find me desirable because of the notice of the others. *Men!* I said to myself in disdain as I permitted one after the other to lead me onto the dance floor.

The evening was drawing to a close when "Toddy" Pressbury introduced me to a gentleman I'd taken notice of earlier. He was older than most of the "eligibles," looking close to thirty, but the magnificent cut of his coat, the perfection of the intricate fold of his neckcloth and the air of self-assurance with which he looked over the crowd had drawn my notice. This fellow was every inch a Corinthian. "Miss Saunders," Toddy said, "this is Sidney Owen, Lord Mowberly, who had compelled me by force to make you known to him. You must take no particular notice of him, however, for he is a notorious rake and will undoubtedly try to make you forget all the rest of us."

"Go away, Toddy, like a good fellow," Mowberly murmured, his eyes flicking over me appreciatively. "Can't you see she's forgotten you already?"

"Are you indeed a rake?" I asked when Toddy had obediently toddled off.

"Yes, I am. I'm surprised you haven't heard of me already and been warned."

"I'm afraid I'm rather new to the social scene, sir," I said, "but I should think it is not an epithet to boast about."

He took my arm and began moving toward the dance floor. "Does it frighten you, my dear, to learn of my shocking reputation?" he asked condescendingly.

"Not at all," I retorted boldly. "I intend to become a bit of a rake myself."

He stopped in his tracks, "Do you indeed?" He grinned at me, his smile brilliant and his eyes glowing. "Is that a challenge, ma'am?"

"Yes, I suppose it is."

"Then be warned, my dear. I am not known in my set as Master-Hand Mowberly for nothing?"

"Master-Hand? What does that mean?"

"It means, my little innocent, that I've good hands with horses and with ladies as well. There are not many females who've come away from an encounter with me unscarred."

"You don't frighten me, Sir Master-Hand. There are few gentlemen who've encountered *me* on whom I haven't left a mark."

"Is that so?" he laughed. "I would be impressed, except that since you're a mere child, I surmise that the arena of those battles must have been the playground."

"Perhaps so," I acknowledged, "but I'm now of age and quite ready to test my mettle. Beware, sir, of the youthful challenger. We make up in vigor and zest what you older fighters have in experience."

He grinned down at me again, put an arm about my waist and, in perfect time to the music, swung me into a set. "Then the battle is joined. We shall see, my dear, what we shall see."

Later that evening, Dory drew me into a private corner and

whispered to me excitedly, "Do you know with whom you've been dancing so frequently this evening? Master-Hand Mowberly!"

"Is that something to be remarked upon?" I asked curiously.

"Of *course* it is! You've stood up with him three times! He rarely asks a lady more than once unless he means to court her. Eliza says he's supposed to be *devastating!*"

"Good heavens, what a word. *Why?*"

"For one thing, he's the *Compleat* Corinthian—handy with his fives, with his horses, with everything. And a devil with the ladies, you know. Never has he been even *close* to being leg-shackled. They say his trail is literally *littered* with broken hearts."

"What fustian! He seemed quite ordinary to me. But his name—Mowberly. I know I've heard it somewhere. . . ."

"Of course you've heard it. What have I been *telling* you? He's *notorious!*"

I shook my head. "No, I don't mean recently. Somewhere in the past. . . ."

But I couldn't remember. Dory and I returned to the crowd, but I did not see Lord Mowberly again that evening. Just when I'd decided to refuse him any more dances that evening, he'd decided not to ask. *He plays the game well,* I admitted to myself ruefully.

In the coach going home that night, Lady Gilbart complimented me on my success. "You were quite the most sought-after girl in the room," she said with pride, "and your conduct was, I'm glad to say, almost completely above reproach. But for the next time, my love, please remember that two dances are more than enough to permit any one suitor. And keep a wary eye on Lord Mowberly. I'm told that he's never been broken to the bridle, and if a gentleman is not the marrying sort, you may as well not waste your time with him."

I assured her that Mowberly was the last man in the world I'd care to wed, but once home in my bed I found myself dwelling on his name. Where had I heard it before?

I fell asleep before I'd found an answer, but later, in the darkest part of the night just before the hall clock struck five, I awakened from a deep sleep with a sudden start. I sat up blinking, some words of my grandmother's—uttered six years before—ringing in my ears: *Mowberly wouldn't give her his name, though she'd given him her best years . . .*

Suddenly there in the darkness it all became clear. Mowberly had been my mother's first *amour*. Not *this* Mowberly, of course, but his father. It had been his father who'd won my mother's affection during her marriage to Reginald Saunders, my father. Then, when my father had died, and poor Mama had expected her lover to wed her, he'd refused. I could almost picture the pathetic scene, the elder Lord Mowberly laughing at her with his brilliant smile and telling her with caustic self-assurance that "not many ladies have come away from an encounter with me unscarred." Thus had my mother been set on the course which led to her downfall.

Mowberly came to call on me the next day, and I agreed to ride with him in his high-wheeled phaeton. He was in excellent spirits and unsparing in his compliments on my appearance and charm. After enduring a half hour of his practiced badinage, I remarked with elaborate casualness, "Did you know, sir, that your father and my mother were acquainted?"

He threw me a startled, quizzical look. "Yes, but I didn't think . . . that is, you could not yet have been born."

"I heard of it spoken of, later. How *is* your father these days?"

"My father, my dear Miss Saunders, has long since gone to his reward."

To a properly suitable reward, I hope, I said to myself grimly.

Mowberly was tending to his horses with necessary concentration, for the traffic in the park was, as usual at this hour of the afternoon, congested. But a somewhat lecherous smile curled the corners of his mouth and a look of calculation lit his eye. I was not much surprised when he said softly, "I hope, Miss Saunders, that you and I may become as good . . . friends . . . as I've heard your mother and my father were."

I contained my fury and managed to turn to the son-and-heir of the man who'd ruined my mother with my most enticing smile. *"Were* they good friends?" I asked innocently.

He smiled broadly. "The best."

"How interesting. But as to a friendship between *us,* my lord, it is much too soon to say. As you said to me last evening, we shall see what we shall see."

He turned his eyes back to his horses, giving me the opportunity to study his face from the corner of my eye. I seethed with fury. Never before had I seen a man who so perfectly

fitted my notion of a cad. The arrogance of Henry Inglebright—
and even that of Sir Averil—was nothing compared to the self-
love and conceit I saw in the face beside me. Never before had
I encountered a gentleman who seemed so deserving of a set-
down. And I, with my memories of my mother and my aversion
toward the male sex so strongly fixed in me, was the very
person to administer that set-down.

That night I didn't permit myself to think of Oliver, as I
usually did just before sleep overtook me. Instead, I dwelled
on my new purpose in life. My despair over Oliver remained
unchanged, but my life seemed suddenly to have a new zest.
I felt stimulated, challenged and enlivened. I had a *purpose*—
to wreak a devastating revenge on the overweening, presump-
tuous Lord Mowberly—and it didn't seem to trouble me at all
that the purpose was completely wicked.

Chapter Fifteen

I DID SEE Oliver before the come-out ball, but only once. It was at a dance held by a close friend of Lady Gilbart's, the Countess Satterleigh. It had been a rather unexciting evening, despite the luxury of the surroundings. The Countess possessed one of London's most awe-inspiring mansions, with a ballroom that held several hundred revelers without crowding, a dining room which could seat thirty-six, three large drawing rooms, and a terrace which crossed the entire width of the house at the back. For me, however, there had been little cause for excitement. Lord Mowberly had not yet made an appearance (a Corinthian of his note was not likely to present himself at a social event until very late and then not stay above half an hour—in order to impress upon the world the extent of his popularity and the necessity for him to make appearances at no less than three affairs in one night), and my dance-card had been filled by a number of gentlemen who interested me not at all: my host, Colin, one of the Pressbury sons and the three young gentlemen who made up my "retinue."

I'd just completed an energetic dance with one of my admirers who had become so enlivened by my company that he'd whirled me about the floor with too much enthusiasm. I had therefore excused myself as soon as the dance had ended and made my way toward the doors which led to the balcony. I needed nothing so much as a breath of fresh air. I was about to step over the threshold when I came face-to-face with Oliver. At first I didn't know him, and I was about to pass him by without a second glance when he grinned at me. "Anne—?" he asked, his right eyebrow cocked curiously.

"*Oliver!*" I gasped. "I didn't...! I hardly...! Good God! What's happened to your *beard?*"

His grin changed to an embarrassed smile, and he rubbed his chin ruefully. "I didn't wish to look the eccentric while staying in town. Do I appear as naked as I feel?"

It was all I could do to restrain myself from throwing myself into his arms. "No, of course not. I just didn't recognize you at first. You look...wonderful."

And he did. His clean-shaven face looked younger and less formidably intellectual. To me he had always seemed imposingly beautiful in appearance, but I hadn't thought of him as actually handsome by fashionable standards. Now, however, I could see how impressive he really was. With his hair trimmed and brushed into the *Brutus* and his well-cut evening clothes emphasizing his strong, shapely legs and broad shoulders, he was by any standards one of the best-looking men in the crowd.

"You look wonderful, too," he said, his eyes searching my face intently. "Quite grown up."

I felt myself color. I wondered what he *really* thought of my ridiculously low-cut gown and the blacking on my lashes that the Misses Finchlow insisted was necessary to bring out the brightness of a young woman's eyes. "It's what you wanted, isn't it?" I asked petulantly. "The time of the fruit?"

His smile faded. "Let's not stand here in the doorway. If you were going out for a breath of air, perhaps you'll let me join you. Or have you a young swain lurking in the shadows waiting to keep a tryst?"

"Of course you may join me," I said curtly, crossing the threshold without waiting to take his arm. "And I *don't make trysts!*"

He followed me out to the cool gloom of the terrace. "Don't be so deucedly brittle-tempered. I meant nothing significant by that remark. Why are you on the defensive?"

I wheeled around. "Why haven't you come to see me in all

this time? Grandmamma says you've been in London for a
fortnight!"

"I thought it would be best to stay away. You, I know, are
very busy with your parties and your presentation . . . and I had
various preoccupations of my own."

I threw him a look of disgust and strode across the terrace
to the balustrade. Looking over the darkened city garden (so
unimpressive when compared to the expanse of lawn and woods
which greeted the eye from the terrace at Pentargon), I felt my
throat constrict. He came up behind me and put a comforting
hand on my arm. I shook it off. "If it had been I who'd come
to town," I said in a choked voice, "I would have c-come to
you at once."

"I know," he said softly. "But you mustn't believe I don't
think of you. I've even brought you a present. Something to
wear with your presentation gown. I have it with me, so if you
wish you may have it right now."

It was like someone trying to placate a spoiled child with
a sweet. But I couldn't resist it. "Oh yes," I breathed, turning
eagerly, "please!"

He reached into his waistcoat pocket and withdrew a small
package wrapped with masculine carelessness in soft, thin paper. He handed it to me with a tentative smile. I almost burst
with eagerness as I unwrapped it. Inside the folded paper lay
an oval locket on an ornate gold chain. The locket, too, was
gold, intricately etched with leaves and curlicues to form the
letter P. "It was my mother's," he explained. "The P is for
Pentargon, of course. My father gave it to her when he first
brought her to the castle."

"It's *beautiful!*" I said, quite moved. It meant more to me
than the lovely pearls Grandmamma had so generously be-
stowed on me. This was the sort of gift, I imagined, that a
man saved for his bride. What did it mean that Oliver had
offered it to me?"

I fumbled with the tiny catch at the locket's edge. "Is there
something within?"

He put his hand over mine. "Yes, there is, but don't bother
about it now. It's quite dark out here. Put the bauble in your
reticule and look at it at your leisure in the privacy of your
room. For now, I think a young man is waiting in the doorway
to claim your hand."

I looked up. It was only one of the trio of undistinguishable

admirers who always dogged by footsteps. "It's Mr. Ludbrooke," I said with a sigh of frustration. "I've promised him
the next dance. But I can put him off. Will *you* dance with
me, Oliver?"

"No, my dear, I won't. Go along and give Mr. Ludbrooke
his turn." And in his usual, forthright style, he turned me about
and propelled me physically in the direction he wanted me to
take.

With teeth-gritting reluctance, I did what he ordered. I danced
with all the gentlemen who'd signed my card, I went down to
dinner on Colin's arm (as I had agreed to do earlier), and I
behaved with perfect propriety. But when, near the end of the
evening, I saw Oliver dancing a waltz with Eliza Gilbart, I
wanted to stamp my foot in frustration. How had Eliza prevailed
when I had not?

Dory and I were not yet permitted to dance the waltz (the
night of our ball would be the first time we would be allowed
to do so), and we were forced to stand on the sidelines watching
the fortunate couples circling the floor. Oliver and Eliza were
the most eye-catching pair thus engaged. She looked as slim
and pliable as a willow (I wondered if Oliver had told her she
reminded him of a *Salix babylonica*) in her green Florentine
silk gown, and he amazed me with the assurance and grace
with which he executed the turns of the complicated dance. I
envied Eliza so much that I was startled by the strength of it.
I envied her her loveliness, her air of dignity, her age and her
place in Oliver's arms. If only she were not so kind and a
generous friend, I would gladly have hated her.

Then, across the room, I saw Mowberly enter, and a mis-
chievous impulse leaped into my head. Without a word, I left
Dory's side and walked round the dance floor to meet him.
"Waltz with me," I ordered without even waiting for his greeting.

His eyebrows rose. "Tonight? You know you shouldn't—"

"Hurry, you cawker," I hissed, "or it shall have ended before
we've had a chance!"

With a shrug of amusement, he took my arm and led me
on the floor. "Lady Gilbart will be reading you the riot act for
this, my girl," he murmured in my ear as he slipped his arm
about my waist and whirled me out among the dancers.

For a few seconds I regretted my hasty action. Never before
had a man held me so in public. And although Dory and I had

practiced the steps of the waltz in the privacy of her drawing room for many hours, this was the first time I'd executed the steps on a real dance floor within a man's arms. I felt wicked, exposed, and very like the lightskirt I was once afraid I would become.

But the rythm of our movements was invigorating, the music drummed in my ears and my feet seemed to fly across the floor with an ease I had not expected, and soon I forgot my embarrassment. I surrendered myself to the music and the pressure of my partner's arm and permitted myself the luxury of sheer enjoyment.

After three or four swings about the floor, my surroundings became sharper than a blur to my eyes, and I was able to catch glimpses of faces around me. Once I caught sight of Dory watching me wide-eyed, her mouth forming a perfect little "O" of shock. Then I had a glimpse of a horrified Lady Gilbart; the gossips must have sped like lightning to the card room to have roused her so promptly to her feet and out to the edge of the dance floor. I could almost imagine a cloud of cards trailing in her stormy wake. And at last I managed to catch a look at Oliver's face. It was to catch his attention that I'd maneuvered myself into this position in the first place. My glimpse of him was more than satisfactory. He had looked away from his partner, and his eyes were following me with an inscrutable intensity. That he was surprised was unmistakable, but what else he felt could not be discerned. Was he—as I'd hoped— as envious of my partner as I was of his?

As Mowberly and I swept by him, I heard him ask Eliza, "Who on *earth*—?"

I bubbled inside with wicked glee. I hoped he was livid. Perhaps next time he'd think twice before refusing to stand up with me. *I shall win you yet, Oliver Fleming,* I promised myself as Mowberly whirled me into the final spin.

Of course, as soon as the dance ended, reality asserted itself with a vengeance. Lady Gilbart whisked me out of the ballroom before I could even properly thank my partner. She herded her daughter Dory and me out the door with such dispatch that I found myself in the coach before I realized that I'd lost the opportunity to say goodnight to Oliver. She didn't even send to the card room for Lord Gilbart to escort us home. She was beside herself with fury. "I could scarcely believe my *eyes!*" she expostulated loudly, her hands waving about in helpless frustration. "Have you learned *nothing* in your years at the Academy? Have you no sense of propriety at all? Did you not think of the *result* of such behavior, or how it would reflect on Lady Marietta and even on *myself*? And D*ory!* Didn't you even think of *Dory?* With the two of you being presented together, everything you do is certain to be associated with her! I can't *believe* it of you. On the eve of your presentation, to make yourself the subject of gossip and disparagement! How can you have *done* it?"

I could only hang my head and say nothing. But Dory came to my defense by telling her mother not to make so much of it. "It was only a little waltz," she pointed out loyally. "It's not as if she were caught kissing Lord Mowberly behind a potted palm—"

"Good *God!* I should hope *not,* indeed!"

"But that's just how they discovered Miss Leeming just a month ago, remember? She was kissing the odious Lord Potterfield almost in public view . . . and, as far as I know, *her* come-out was unaffected by it."

Her mother cast Dory a look of utter contempt. "Let us not discuss ridiculous extremes. You can hardly consider Anne in the same breath as Miss Leeming. The Leemings are nothing but *parvenus.* What can one expect of them but shocking behavior of that sort? One does *not,* however, expect indecorous conduct from the granddaughter of Lady Marietta Saunders! Tonight's little escapade will be bruited about all over town by morning."

"Are you suggesting, Lady Gilbart," I asked incredulously, "that the success of our ball will be affected by my dancing a waltz without permission? That people will send their regrets and not *come?*"

"No, I don't mean that, exactly. I don't mean to imply that matters are as bad as *that,* But you will be spoken of in whispers, and your reputation will be damaged. They'll say that you're headstrong and wild, and I wouldn't be at all surprised if Mr. Ludbrooke's mother advises him to withdraw from his pursuit of you."

"If that's the worst that comes of it," I said with a disparaging laugh, "it will have been worth it."

Lady Gilbart glared. "Anne Saunders, you are *incorrigible!* I hope you'll be able to laugh when your *grandmother* hears of this. And hear of it she will, for I intend to make her a full report in the morning. Don't look at me that way, Dory, as if I were a tale-bearing traitor. You know perfectly well that Anne has become like a daughter to me. But I've said from the first that she's willfull and impulsive and . . . and . . ."

"Bizarre," I supplied.

"Well, I wouldn't say bizarre, exactly . . ."

"You said it once, when I emptied the punch bowl over Henry Inglebright."

"Did I?" She threw a troubled glance in my direction, her anger suddenly subsiding. "I shouldn't have said such a thing. A bit of high spirits is certainly not bizarre in a lively young woman. But, my love, you *can't* go about in society saying and doing whatever comes into your head. Do you *want* people to speak of you was wild and headstrong and unbridled?"

I didn't care *how* people spoke of me, but I didn't say that to Lady Gilbart. I made a polite apology and withdrew to the corner of the coach. It was best, I decided, to let the subject drop. I was bound to hear a great deal more of it when my grandmother learned what I'd done. In the meantime I wanted to think about the incident for myself. There was only one thing about my behavior which concerned me, and that was what Oliver thought of it.

Had *he* found me wild, headstrong and unbridled? Had he been horrified at my behavior? Was it possible that I hadn't made him jealous at all but had only succeeded in making myself odious in his eyes?

What was the matter with me? Why did I always manage to behave in so reprehensible a fashion? I'd come to London to attend school for the purpose of learning to be a lady—the sort of lady who'd make a proper wife for a man of Oliver's nobility and dignity. A lady . . . like Eliza Gilbart. Instead, I'd thrown myself at him in Cornwall and probably disgusted him by my conduct tonight. Would Eliza have ever done what I had done? What had made me think that Oliver would admire my making a spectacle of myself on the dance floor?

He was probably ashamed of me. That possibility, more than all Lady Gilbarts' accusations, made me sorry for what I'd done. I was overwhelmed with humiliation. I suddenly saw myself as tawdry and vulgar, and I became so downcast that when the carriage drew up to my grandmother's door and I bid a choked goodnight to Dory and her mother, they could hear the distress in my voice. "Don't make so much of Mama's scold," Dory murmured solicitously, pressing my hand. "It'll all pass over and be forgotten before the week is out."

"Yes, my love," Lady Gilbart agreed, her heart softening at my downcast aspect, "there's no use dwelling on the incident. If you've learned your lesson, some good may come of all this."

But I went up to my room unconsoled. If Oliver despised me, there was no good to come of it that I could see.

Miss Gribbin, waiting up to help me undress, could see at once that something had occurred to distress me. But she didn't prod me with questions. She merely began to undo the buttons at the back of my gown. I wanted to ease her mind by making some lighthearted allusions to the evening's adventures, so I searched my memory for some small detail with which to regale her and which would give no hint of my scandalous conduct at the evening's end. It was then that I remembered the evening's most momentous occurrence: Oliver had given me a gift! The *locket!* I hadn't yet seen what was *inside* it!

My impatience to look at it was almost painful, but I couldn't do so with Miss Gribbin's eyes on me. I didn't want any witness when I faced the contents of the locket, for it might prove to be a moment of some significance. Whatever it was that he'd chosen to put inside, he must surely have given the matter some thought. Of course, he could have chosen almost anything— a lock of his hair, a lock of mine, a miniature painting, a lucky coin, a cryptic message or one bearing words of affection— *anything*. But the choice would have meaning . . . and perhaps a very special meaning for me and my future.

Forcing myself into an outward calm, I ordered Miss Gribbin to go to bed. Overriding her objections by employing Oliver's technique (propelling her firmly to the door and shutting it behind her), I was soon alone. I lit the branch of candles on my dressing table and withdrew from my reticule the little packet.

I sat down at my dressing table, my breath thrumming in my throat. What *had* he put inside? Before opening it, I made a kind of bargain with myself. *If it is something positive and loving—like a lock of his hair—then I can still have hope,* I reasoned. *But if it is something impersonal and fatherly—like the tooth I'd lost when I fell from my horse during my first year at Pentargon, or a pressed blossom of the* Belamcanda chinesis *which he'd crossbred with such pride—then I must face the truth and tell myself that he doesn't care for me . . . and give up all hope of him.*

I opened the paper. The gold oval glittered enticingly in the candlelight. I held my breath as my fingers struggled awkwardly with the tiny catch. But in a moment I realized that the catch needed only to be pressed inward, for when I accidentally did so the lid sprang open. What it revealed made me cry out in both disappointment and gratitude. If Oliver's choice had any symbolic meaning, however, it was too ambiguous for me to interpret. It could have meant ánything, from a loving sensitivity to a gentle, warning reproach. For he'd placed into the gold oval frame a tiny ivory miniature of my mother.

Chapter Sixteen

LADY GILBART, IN spite of having softened toward me at the last minute the night before, was true to her word and gave Grandmamma a full report of my misbehavior the next morning. I was not surprised. I was quite ready when Mrs. Panniers came to my room and told me frigidly that Lady Marietta wanted to see me at once.

Wearing an expression of chastened humility, I presented myself to her in her bedroom where she sat, queenlike, among her pillows. "So you have done it again," she said calmly. "Set us all on our heads."

"You don't seem to be at all discomposed, Grandmamma," I couldn't help remarking.

"Nor do you. Nevertheless, your behavior was completely reprehensible. What made you do it, eh?"

"I wanted to waltz, that was all. It was an...impulse."

"That, of course, is the very worst sort of excuse. Since when does a young lady do as she 'wants' whenever she wants to? You knew, did you not, that a lady, even one who has been out for some time, cannot indulge in waltzing without the express permission of some responsible chaperone?"

"Yes, I knew that."

"I was quite sure you did, since I seem to remember mentioning it to you myself. Then your action was a deliberate flaunting of convention, was it not?"

"Yes, I suppose it was."

She raised an eyebrow. "Is that all you'll say for yourself? That you cared not a rap for the conventions of society?"

"I didn't *think* about the conventions of society. I only thought about the dancing. But it's a rather silly convention, is it not?"

"Silly or not, it is one of the rules by which we live. The doyens of English society do not require your approval of their precepts. You came in a moment ago with an air of what I took to be sincere regret, but now I see that it was a mere pretense."

"No, it wasn't, Grandmamma. I *am* sorry for what I've done, truly."

"Hmmmmph. You'd better be. Another such display, and the mamas of all the eligibles'll be warning their sons to give you a wide berth."

"Much I care for that!" I muttered under my breath.

But she heard me. "You'd *better* care for it, Miss Hoity-Toity! If you don't watch yourself, you'll lose your reputation, and everyone will begin to remember who and what your mother was."

"Let them!" I said, putting up my chin.

She shook her head. "Do you want to be tarred with the same brush? Use your head, girl. What am I doing all this *for?*"

I looked her in the eye. "You're doing it to get me properly wed and off your hands. But I've warned you from the first that I had no interest in wedlock."

"You'll be interested enough when the right man comes along. Just make sure you don't ruin your chance by getting yourself a reputation for being fast."

"Does indulging in a mere little waltz mean I'm fast?" I asked in disgust.

"No, not quite. But the tale the gossips make of it will plant a seed. Don't water that seed with a second display of that sort. I want your word that you'll refrain from any other act of wanton impulse."

"You have it, Grandmamma." But then, a recollection of my determination to wreak revenge on Mowberly flashed into my mind, and I quickly added an amendment to my promise. "That is, at least until the come-out ball."

Her eyes narrowed shrewdly. "Why only until then? What deviltry are you brewing, young lady?"

"Nothing at all."

"You mean you won't tell me." She shook her head in helpless disapproval. "I knew I would have trouble with you. Knew it from the first. See here, Anne Saunders, I give you fair warning. Whatever it is you've taken into your head to do, you'd better not do it until *after* the ball is over. If you spoil your come-out in any way, you will face my wrath!"

"I promise, Grandmamma. There's not the least need to fall into a taking."

"I hope not." She shifted her position so that she sat up straight. "Now that we've concluded *that* business, pick up my bed-tray over there and set it down here on my lap. The tea is probably revolting luke warm, but sit down and have a cup with me."

I placed the tray over her legs. "If it's truly undrinkable, Grandmamma, let me fetch you another pot."

"No, it will do. Tell me, my love, what is that thing about your neck which you've been fondling all morning?"

"It's a locket. Oliver gave it to me for my presentation."

The hand holding the upraised teapot ceased its motion. "Oliver? You've *seen* him?"

"Yes, last night at Countess Satterleigh's. Didn't Lady Gilbart tell you he was there?"

She turned her attention back to her pouring. "No, she didn't. So you got a chance to speak to him at last. Are you pleased with the bauble?"

"Oh, yes! Very pleased. Don't you think it's lovely?"

She looked up at it with a measuring eye. "Quite. I remember seeing it round his mother's neck. She was inordinately fond of it. Carried her husband's likeness inside, as I recall. Is it still there?"

"No. Look!" I removed the chain from round my neck, undid the clasp and held the locket out to her.

She put down the teapot, took the locket and reached over to her night table for her lorgnette. "Your mother, eh?" She peered at it closely. "An amazing likeness. This must be the ivory that Reginald had commissioned. Thomas Phillips painted it the year they were married. She was a lovely creature, wasn't she? I wonder where Oliver came by it."

"I don't know." I took the locket back and studied the miniature again. The woman who stared back at me was heart-wrenchingly youthful and innocent of aspect, her eyes wide and sparkling with hope for the future. It was difficult for me to remember the changes in that face that the next decade had wrought. "But it was good of Oliver to find it for me, don't you think? I've never seen a likeness of Mama in the years before . . . before I was born."

"Yes," Grandmamma agreed, picking up a teacup and offering it to me, "it's a lovely gift. Oliver, who seems so often to have his mind only on his studies or his botanical experiments, can sometimes be surprisingly thoughtful."

"Did you know him well, Grandmamma, when he was young?"

"Oliver? Of course I did. He was my brother's son, after all. He was always a bright, thoughtful sort of boy. With that quiet sense of humor that never failed to startle me. I was always enormously fond of him. Wouldn't have put you in his charge if I weren't."

I stirred my tea absently. "I've always wondered . . . why he never married and had children of his own."

I felt her eyes on my face, but I didn't look up. She was silent for a few moments, and I could hear the rattle of her cup being placed in its saucer. "Your cousin is a confirmed bachelor," she said, "although he came close to it once or twice. I recall a Miss . . . Miss . . ."

"Harriet Worthing?" I offered quickly.

She gaped at me. "That's the one. Wherever did *you* learn of her?"

"I overheard someone speak of her. Did you know her?"

"Only slightly. Tall, willowy girl, I remember, with a soft, deliberate manner of speech. I thought at the time that she'd manage to ensnare him, but he slipped away from her net in the nick of time."

"Why do you say it that way? Didn't you wish him to wed?"

"Yes, of course. We all did—the whole family. But his mother and I were secretly agreed that Harriet Worthing was too proper, too self-contained, too . . . lacking in spontaneity for a man like Oliver."

"How strange. I thought you *liked* young women to be

proper and self-contained. You certainly don't encourage spontaneity in *me*."

Her eyes flicked up at me and then down to her cup. "There are degrees, you know. One needn't go to extremes of propriety, just as one needn't go to extremes of spontaneity."

"I see. So it was Oliver who broke with her?"

"There was no break, for there had been no betrothal. Oliver simply lost interest. I believe that his father died at about that time, and he left London to see to the estate. He became so engrossed in the Cornwall property and his botanical interests that he never returned to town again for more than brief visits."

"Do you think it possible that you are mistaken? That Oliver never married because Miss Worthing ran off with her French marquis and broke his heart?"

"No, I don't, for it seems to me that she did not marry until two or three years later. No, my love, a more likely explanation of Oliver's escape from wedlock is that, as I said, he's a bachelor at heart."

I met her eyes over my cup, and it seemed to me that there was a strange glint in them. Were her words a challenge to me? Did she wish me to argue with her? I lowered my cup. "No man is a bachelor at heart when he's faced with a woman of sufficient resolve," I said pompously.

Grandmamma snorted. "To find a woman with sufficient resolve to break through your cousin Oliver's defenses would be a miracle."

And with that depressing analysis as her last comment on the subject, my grandmother turned her attention to other things.

For the next few days, the arrangements for the come-out ball took precedence over everything else. Grandmamma's household seemed to be in a flurry of activity as Mrs. Panniers and Miss Gribben rushed about readying every item of clothing we would need for the grand occasion. At the Gilbart house it was even worse. A host of servants were engaged in emptying the downstairs rooms of furniture, polishing the chandeliers and windows, waxing the floors and woodwork and hanging all sorts of festoons and banners from the rafters. Dory and I laughed at it all when we could speak together in the privacy of her bedchamber. We alone were aware of how unnecessary the whole affair would be. She had already made up her mind to accept the hand of Lord Dawes as soon as he found the courage to declare himself; and I had no intention of wedding anyone. What need, therefore, for us to be introduced to the Marriage Mart in this ostentatious fashion?

Since we knew it was useless—and far too late—to make any attempt to convince the Gilbarts and my grandmother to cancel the affair, Dory and I agreed that we might just as well make the best of it. "After all," Dory said, "we shall be in our best looks..."

"...in our best gowns," I added.

"...and the object of all eyes. It would be foolish to permit ourselves to be bored by it all."

"I know." I stretched out on her chaise and stared up at the ceiling. "But how can we help but be bored? We've attended a dozen such balls in the past month. Will this one be more interesting than the others just because it's being held in our honor? Once we've received all the guests (which is the greatest bore in itself), we shall have to do just what we've done all those other times—dance with the nodcocks who've signed our cards."

"That's true." Dory slumped down upon her bed, discouraged. "How very disheartening. To think that our very own ball is nothing more than...than..."

"...a gigantic anti-climax."

"Yes, dash it all!" She turned her soft eyes on my face appealingly. "Anne, you've always been ingenious at turning boring affairs into surprises. Can't you think of something?"

"If you're hoping I shall spill champagne all over my gown or push someone's head into the punch bowl for your entertainment, you may think again. I promised Grandmamma I would be on my very best behavior."

She drew herself up in offense. "I wouldn't *dream* of suggesting anything so abominable. Push someone's head into the punch bowl, indeed!" The corners of her lips twitched. "Besides, having already done something very like it, you would not wish to repeat yourself."

"Then it was wicked of you to even try to set my mind in that direction."

"I didn't mean it, truly. You mustn't even *think* of doing anything indecorous. Isn't there something else—?"

"Anything *decorous* is bound, by definition, to be dull."

She sighed. "Yes, I suppose that's true."

"Unless—" I sat up, suddenly inspired. "Unless we made a *game* of the affair."

Her eyes brightened. "What sort of game?"

"I don't know. If we each set ourselves a goal of some sort—something difficult to achieve—and then we tried all through the evening to achieve it."

"What what sort of goal have you in mind?"

"Let me think. What if you pledged to eat no more than three pastries for the evening?"

"Oh, pooh! Who cares for that? If I couldn't eat pastries, there'd be nothing left for me to *enjoy*, except the two dance I'm permitted to have with Lord Dawes."

I grinned. "Dawes! Dory, that's *it!* Your goal could be to inveigle Lord Dawes to offer for you before, say, eleven-fifteen."

"Anne!" A beatific smile lit her face. "What a superb idea! That is indeed a challenge. It would make the evening most exciting. Do you think there's a *chance*—?" But doubt clouded her eyes. "No, no. It's too impossible. He'd never come through. He shall offer for me one day, I wager, but not for months and months. He's not the hasty sort. Why, in all the afternoons I've ridden out with him, and through all the *tête-à-têtes* I've permitted him since the evening we met, he's never said anything more personal than 'Please permit me to hold this umbrella for you, Miss Gilbart, for I shall not need it. In your company I find myself more affected by *inner* than outer weather.'"

"Did he really say that?" I giggled. "He is marvelous! But why do you despair, Dory? I find that a most encouraging remark."

"Yes, I suppose it is, but it's hardly a declaration of love. This week he held an umbrella for me; next month he may take my hand; next year he may even lift it to his lips. Lord Dawes may be in many ways exemplary, but one could never describe him as dashing. I believe our courtship will be a very protracted affair."

She sounded so doleful that I tried very hard not to laugh. "But, Dory, I understand that *most* gentlemen are slow to declare themselves. They must be *encouraged* a little."

She stared at me speculatively, turning the matter over in her mind. Soon her eyes began to dance. "Yes, why not? If I wait for *him* to take the initiative, I may soon find myself an old maid at my last prayers. I'll *do* it, Anne. I'll play your game. If I haven't managed it by eleven-fifteen, it won't be for lack of trying."

"Good girl!" We grinned at each other mischievously. The come-out ball was beginning to excite us at last.

"But what about you?" Dory asked after a moment. "You must have a goal, too, so that we may compete against each other. The one who achieves her objective first becomes the winner."

"I've already decided on my goal. I shall try for an offer from Mowberly."

Her face fell. *"Mowberly!* You don't mean it."

"Why do you say that? Of course I mean it."

"Anne! You haven't—! *Please* don't say that you've tumbled into *love* for him!"

"Don't be silly. I'm incapable of tumbling into love, didn't you know that?"

She tossed her head disdainfully. "I know that's what you always *claim*, but I can't believe it. You'll fall in love one day, just like every other female I've ever met."

"No, I won't. I'm . . . immune. Have been from childhood. I've always found that most men aren't worth a second look."

"Most men, perhaps, but that doesn't mean *all*. And if you're so immune, why do you want to attach Mowberly?"

"I have my reasons."

Her brow knit worriedly. "He's not the sort who'll take kindly to being trifled with, my dear. I hope you're not playing with fire."

I laughed. "If I'm immune, how can I be burned?"

"I don't know. But Mowberly is at least ten years your senior and very knowing in matters of the heart. You, my dear, despite your declarations of sophistication and immunity, are nothing but a green girl. I've heard it said that green wood makes a hot fire."

"But you *wanted* me to think of a way to enliven the ball, didn't you? What can be more enlivening than a little playing about with fire?"

"We needn't make the game so enlivening that it's positively *dangerous*, need we?" She turned her large, pleading gaze on me. "Can't I dissuade you from toying about with Mowberly, love?"

"No, Dory, you can't. But you needn't worry. I can see no danger in it at all."

She rose from the bed and stood over me, shaking her head. "Do you know something strange? I suddenly believe that Mama was right about you. You *are* incorrigible." She frowned down at me for a moment longer and then her irrepressible smile broke out again. "But, confound it, you *have* managed to inject an atmosphere of excitement into the affair. I'm suddenly impatient for the night to arrive—in fact, you could say I'm almost *agog!*"

Chapter Seventeen

THE NIGHT ARRIVED, as all nights must, in its due course. By that time I'd already realized that the evening would be exciting even without my infusion of the artificial stimulation of the "game." I'd realized it as soon as I'd slipped my white brocaded-taffeta gown over my head.

Grandmamma (resplendent in a new gown of Argyle purple, a festive change from her omnipresent black lace) and I arrived at the Gilbarts' early so that we would be on hand to welcome the first guests. Dory, dressed in a white gown similar to mine, looked charming with her blonde hair held back tightly at the top of her head by a diamond clip and her bouncy curls falling below. She had also been given the Gilbart diamond pendant to wear about her neck, and she found it difficult to keep from putting a hand to her throat to touch the magnificent gem. (Grandmamma had urged me to wear her diamond necklace for the occasion, but I had chosen instead to wear my locket. Though Grandmamma had put up a strong battle, I had the feeling she did not really mind losing it. The locket was quite lovely enough. Grandmamma wore the diamonds herself.)

My short curly hair had no need of clips of ornamentation, so the only other decoration I wore was a small circlet of interlaced roses on my wrist. A few floral offerings had been delivered to our house that afternoon: Mr. Ludbrooke had sent a bouquet of tiny pink roses of the *muscosa* variety, Lord Mowberly had sent a nosegay of lovely camellias, and Oliver must have sent all the way to Cornwall for some of his *rubiginasae*. He'd probably had Trewin send a potted shrub, from which a half-dozen blood-red blooms must have been cut this very day and shaped into the wristlet I now wore.

Each of my three floral offerings had been accompanied by a note. Mr. Ludbrooke had written: *If you carry these tonight, you'll be carrying my heart.* The message was typical of the man himself—strongly emotional but making little sense. Lord Mowberly's message, on the other hand, was completely calculating. He'd written:

> *Tied at throat or thrust in breast,*
> *These shall lie where I would rest.*

He would undoubtedly be chagrined to learn that his fragrant and undcubtedly expensive blooms were lying, not on my breast, but back home on my commode.

Oliver's note simply read: *Try not to be too dazzling.*

The first guests arrived in a thin trickle, but soon they began to crowd the entrance and the hall, seeming to arrive in one great body. It was indeed a tremendous squeeze. Dory and I acknowledged to each other that the evening was exciting already. Almost before we knew it, the party was in full swing.

Dory, partnered by her father, led the procession of dancers onto the floor. I followed on Oliver's arm, my heart beating expectantly. But it was a very sedate waltz, completely approved and completely proper. He held me at arm's length, said only that I was in my best looks, and as soon as I had made my polite thanks, the dance was over. He did not approach me again for a single dance.

I was passed from hand to hand as every "eligible" in the room took his turn with me. I saw Dory stand up twice with her Lord Dawes before Lord Mowberly had approached me once. It looked very much as if the "game" would be hers.

After supper, however, Mowberly came to my side. "Lead me away from this mob," he whispered. "I haven't been able to snatch a word with you all evening."

"The 'mob' won't keep me from hearing what you have to say right here," I countered archly.

"Don't be missish," he insisted, taking my arm in a tight grip. "Isn't there a sitting room somewhere..."

The thought crossed my mind that I might yet win my game, and I led him down the hall to the little sitting room at the back of the house. There, as soon as we were seated side by side on the sofa, he began his attack. "Whose blooms are those on your wrist?" he demanded.

"I'm not at all sure you have a right to ask me that," I said in mock offense.

"Have I not? Are you going to pretend that I am nothing to you?"

"You are becoming a very good friend. But friendship does not entitle you to—"

"Friendship?" His lips twisted into a sneer. "I've made it clear from the first moment we met that it was not friendship I was seeking."

"Oh? Then what was it?"

"Don't play the innocent, my girl. You acknowledged as bluntly as I did that we would be embarking on quite another sort of relationship. Now, *tell* me—what knight has tied his colors to your wrist?"

"I have no recollection of discussing our 'relationship' at all, my lord. And as for my knight, he will remain—as far as you're concerned—no more than an unknown admirer."

To my surprise, he laughed. "So *that's* your little ruse. You think to capture me by *jealousy*. It's the most obvious of all the devices of romance, you little idiot, and the one most commonly tried. I warned you I was not a novice in this game."

"You flatter yourself, my lord. When I tied these roses to my wrist, I didn't think of you at all."

He leaned back against the arm of the sofa and surveyed me through narrowed eyes. "Didn't you? What an excellent player you are, my sweet. Completely enticing, I assure you. Were I younger and less experienced, I would no doubt be grovelling at your feet. But I understand you well, and I know that your words are false ... as false as the suggestion that the donor of those flowers is someone who interests you more that I do. Shall I guess who gave them to you? It was your grandmother, was it not?"

"No, it was not. And, my lord, I am not enjoying this

guessing game. I came here with you because you said you wished to speak to me. If the subject of this conversation is only to be the identity of the gentleman who gave me these roses, then it's pointless to continue. Good evening, my lord."

I got up and started for the door. He waited until I'd almost completely crossed the room before he stirred. But when he realized that I did not intend to pause, he leaped up and crossed the room in three strides. He gripped my arm and whirled me about. "You *are* a devil!" he muttered, pulling me against him. "A red-headed, tantalizing little devil. But, hang it all, I can't get you out of my mind." With a practiced assurance, he held me tightly, pressing one hand on my back and turning my head up with the other. Before I could cry out, I found myself being hotly kissed.

I won't deny that I found myself responding to the embrace at first. He was handsome and dashing, and I knew it was something of an achievement to have won his attention. My heart beat rather wildly in my throat as I sagged against him, helpless to do anything else. But after a few moments, I remembered another embrace—one which had begun rather awkwardly and at my own instigation, but which had grown increasingly more thrilling as it had progressed. This one became less so the longer he held me. In fact, it began to make me feel uncomfortable. It suggested the sort of embrace in which I'd seen my mother indulge. It suggested *amour*.

I felt myself shudder, and I began to push at his chest. How could I make him release me? I wondered. But just when I began to feel frightened and desperate, the door opened. "Anne, are you here? Some of the guests—Good *God!*" It was Oliver.

Mowberly stepped away from me at once. I stared at the intruder, my face hot and tense with shame. Oliver looked from me to Mowberly frozen-faced. Before any of us could move or utter a sound, however, there was a step in the hallway and Dory, calling my name in a state of high excitement, bounded into the room. "Anne," she was chortling, "you'll never *believe* it! I *did* it, and even though it's a bit past midnight, I—Oh!" She looked from one to the other of the three statue-like figures in the room and realized she'd broken in on a scene. "Oh dear!" she mumbled awkwardly to no one in particular, "I *am* sorry. I didn't mean to..."

"That's quite all right, Dory," Oliver said, his mouth tight. "Anne was about to introduce me to her...companion."

I felt as if I were in a nightmare. "Oliver, this is Sidney Owen, Lord Mowberly. Lord Mowberly, my . . . guardian, Lord Fleming."

"How do you do, Mowberly?" Oliver said, icily polite. "I hope you will excuse both Miss Saunders and Miss Gilbart. Some of the guests are leaving, and they are wanted in the drawing room."

Mowberly bowed to Oliver and then raised my hand to his lips. Not in the least discomposed, he smiled into my eyes. "Until tomorrow, Miss Saunders," he said smoothly and stood aside to let me pass.

Oliver led us to the drawing room and disappeared. I did not see him again that evening. I tried to tell myself that it had all been for the best. Oliver had only been shocked by jealousy, I reasoned, and he would realize he loved me after all. But something else nagged at the back of my mind . . . a conviction that what I'd seen in his eyes was not jealousy but something else entirely. Was it disgust? Did he believe that I was turning out to be just like my mother? Had I made another major blunder?

After the guests had all departed, after I'd embraced Dory ecstatically in response to her news that Lord Dawes had indeed come up to scratch; after I'd thanked the Gilbarts and gone home with Grandmamma, after I'd told Miss Gribbin as many details of the affair as I could admit, and after I'd climbed wearily into bed (the first rays of the sun already creeping in behind the draperies), I lay awake pondering the problem. I hadn't believed for a long time that I would follow my mother's path. Nor had I really responded favorably to Mowberly's *amour*ous embrace. I knew that I had long since found a love that was more than *amour* and that I wanted no other. But what did *Oliver* think about what he'd seen?

I found out the very next morning. I was awakened shortly after eleven by Miss Gribbin, who said that Oliver was awaiting me downstairs. I dressed hurriedly and ran down, my pulses racing in alarm. I found him in Grandmamma's rarely used library, looking out the window at the cloudless sky. He had not bothered to remove his caped driving coat, but I was so distracted that I didn't stop to wonder why he wore it at all. "Good morning, Oliver," I said. My voice sounded strangely hoarse and tired.

He turned and gave me a wan smile. "I've awakened you too early, I'm afraid. You look uncommonly weary. But I'm off for Pentargon this morning, and I'd like to get started as early as I can."

"You're going *home?*" My spirits plummeted to a new depth. "So soon?"

"Yes. I've been away for more than a month. Too much has been neglected. It's time I went back."

"I wish I were going, too," I muttered glumly.

"Don't be a goose. After that spectacular presentation last evening, you'll be the toast of the town. I predict that you'll have the most successful season of any young lady in London."

I threw myself down on the sofa. "I suppose it would be of no use to repeat what I've said so many times before—that I don't *wish* for a London season, successful or unsuccessful."

"No, it would be of no use at all."

I clenched my jaw. I would not let him see me cry. "Then you've . . . only come to say g-goodbye to me?"

"Yes. And one thing more."

"Oh? What's that?"

He took a seat on a nearby ottoman and stretched out his booted legs, keeping a cautious eye on my face. "It's about Mowberly."

I tensed. "What about Mowberly."

"You are not to see him again."

I'd expected a scold, a reprimand, even an outburst of sarcastic abuse on my conduct, but I'd not expected that. "What did you say?"

"You heard me. You're not to see him again. Ever."

Oliver had never before spoken to me in so dictatorial a style. I didn't know what to make of it. "But why? Just because I let him *kiss* me—?"

"Don't be a ninny. My instruction has nothing to do with that."

"Then what *has* it to do with?"

Oliver's eyes fell from my face. "The fellow is the scion of a family of which I cannot approve."

"You can't approve his *family?*" The reason was so flimsy that I didn't believe I'd heard him properly. "What's wrong with his family?"

"They are a crowd of wastrels, gamblers and philanderers. There's not one of them who has an admirable quality." He looked up at me, frowning. "That must be reason enough for you."

"But it's not enough! This is the most peculiar demand you've ever made of me. I thought you *wanted* me to acquire suitors and—"

"I do. But not Mowberly. You have the whole of London society to choose from. Choose elsewhere."

I was utterly confounded. "You're not making *sense*. Mowberly may be a bit of a rake, but he's accepted in the best circles."

"I don't wish to discuss the matter further," he said, rising. "I am still your guardian, and this is a command to which I expect complete obedience. Is that understood?"

"It is *not* understood!" I jumped to my feet. "I'm sorry, Oliver. I would like to obey you in all things that I find reasonable, but in this I will *not—!*"

He grasped my shoulders fiercely. "I tell you, girl," he muttered through clenched teeth, "you have no choice. I will not permit any dealing with Mowberly. If you don't find my reasons adequate, then you must take my order on trust. I have not misled you in the past, have I?"

I looked up into his angry, troubled face. "No, of course you haven't," I said, softened. I wanted to say that I would do as he asked. What did I care for Mowberly anyway? But his order seemed to me an act of tyranny that was not only unnecessary but unkind. Not only was he going away and not taking me with him, but he was trying to restrict my movements in his absence. Bringing Mowberly to heel was the only entertainment I had to look forward to in the stultifying round of pleasure-seeking that the London season represented. "But how can I agree with you when I don't see—?"

"Damnation, Anne, will you cease this ridiculous discussion? We are speaking of the son of the man who brought about your mother's ruin! Isn't that enough reason to cast him off?"

My blood turned cold. "Is *that* what this is all about?" Furiously, I shook off his hold on me and turned my back on him. "You needn't worry, my dear," I told him icily. "The son will not ruin me as the father ruined Mama. You have my assurance on that score."

There was a long silence. Then he came up behind me. "I have no such worry, Anne. That possiblity never crossed my mind. I thought I'd convinced you long ago that I know you are not your mother's image but your own person. Why do you persist in flagellating yourself and me with this baseless accusation?"

I wheeled around. "What else am I to think when you make such a ridiculous demand of me?"

His face, which had been sadly tender, now hardened. "You are to think that I would not make the demand if it were not necessary. Confound it, Anne, why are you fighting me on this? Don't tell me that your heart is involved, because I won't believe it!"

"Why won't you believe it? He's handsome and dashing and less of a bore than any of the—"

"He's a self-indulgent, lecherous, conceited popinjay, and if you don't see it you're less of a woman than I thought. I'm sorry, my dear, if your heart has become involved, but even if it has, you'll get over it. Better a small pain now than a great one later."

I turned away and began to stride round the room. I didn't know what to make of this strange scene. I wanted to believe that Oliver was somehow crazed with jealousy, but there was no sign of the jealous lover about him. There was *something else* motivating his peculiar demand, and I had not a clue to what it was. "I think you've lost your mind," I muttered.

"Perhaps," he said curtly, "but I've said enough on this matter." He started to the door, in a hurry, as usual, to avoid any more of the sort of verbal confrontation that he so disliked. "You'd better heed me, girl. I will brook no disobedience in this matter."

He opened the door and threw me a look of such ferocity that I reacted with an unreasoning fury of my own. "I *won't* heed you!" I cried, angry, confused and devastated at the thought of his leaving. "How *dare* you come here, give me this un-warranted command and take yourself off? You've been my guardian, yes, but you rejected that role a while ago, didn't you? You sent me off to Grandmamma. Do you think you can drop the parental role when it suits you and calmly pick it up again and play the tyrannical parent when *that* suits you? Either you *are* my guardian or you aren't! And to tell the truth, I don't *want* you as a g-guardian any more!"

Hot tears began to course down my cheeks. He gaped at me, aghast, and then turned and closed the door. In two quick strides, he'd crossed the room. Taking me in his arms, he brushed the tears from my cheeks. "Don't, Anne," he said softly, looking down into my face with a worried frown. "I promise you that in time you'll realize this was all for the best. I'm not acting the tyrannical parent. Don't you believe that what I want more than anything is your happiness?"

I couldn't help but believe him. The tender words were a balm to my spirit. I slipped my arms under his, encircling his waist tightly, and dropped my head on his chest. "Oh, Oliver," I said tearfully, "why do th-things have to be this way?"

He seemed to stiffen. "Do you care for him so much?" he asked, the words coming from him with difficulty.

"Don't be a fool," I murmured against his coat.

He took me gently by the shoulders and held me off. "Then why won't you promise—?"

"Oliver, this is all so . . . so *ridiculous!* It's *you* I love, not Mowberly. If you really don't want me to take him, then marry me *yourself.*"

He seemed to be stricken speechless for a moment. Then he sighed helplessly. "Don't, Anne," he muttered. "Don't put me through this again."

"I can't help it. You *must* love me. I know you do. I don't understand why you won't—"

"I can't. Don't you see? I *can't!*"

"*Why* can't you?" I cried out like a heartbroken child.

He pulled my arms from him and turned away. "Because I'm betrothed to Eliza Gilbart. We're going to be married in the fall."

The floor seemed to fall away from beneath my feet. "I don't . . . believe you . . ."

He turned back to look at me. "Lord Gilbart has already sent the announcement to *The Times.*"

I don't know how long I stood there searching his face. I don't know what thoughts ran through my head. I was completely bereft of feeling. Eventually however, I felt my knees give way, and I sank down on the ottoman which was fortunately right at my side.

"Do you think, my dear," his voice came from somewhere above me, "that you could find it in your heart to wish me happy?"

"You won't be happy," I said dully.

There was a long pause. "Well, I certainly have not the time to get into *that* discussion," he said with abrupt decisiveness.

I heard his boots make their firm clatter as he crossed to the door. There he stopped once more. "Listen to me, Anne. Whatever passed between us just now is irrelevant to the primary purpose for which I came here this morning. There is to be *no further contact with Mowberly*. If I hear of you even so much as spending an evening in his company, I shall take the most decisive and drastic action. Believe me, my girl, for I have never been more serious in my life."

I heard the door close, but I didn't look up. I felt like a lump of sod, without feeling, without substance, without energy. *Perhaps,* I thought hopefully, *if I sit here for a while, I shall simply crumble away to nothingness. A pile of dust. And the maid will brush me away with her feather-duster until I am nothing more than tiny motes dancing in the air. I should have no past and no future to worry about, but just dance in the air and be happy.*

But after a time—I have no idea how long—feeling began to return. A strange, dull, aching anger. "I'll do as I *please!*" I shouted to the closed door. "I'll see Mowberly and anyone else who attracts me!"

There was no answering voice from the hallway, although I half expected to hear one.

"Who are you to give me such advice?" I demanded loudly. "You, who don't know what you're doing any more than I do! Go ahead and *wed* Eliza! You'll find out what a fool you are! She's another Harriet Worthing, don't you see that? Not enough spontaneity for you. You're making the greatest mistake, Oliver. Don't you *hear* me? The greatest mistake of your *life!*"

But he was long gone.

Chapter Eighteen

I REMAINED FOR a long while in Grandmamma's dusty library, trying to sort out the pieces of my life which seemed to lie before me like the wreckage of a landscape painted on glass. Whenever I'd thought about my future, I had always been set on one particular landscape—the castle and grounds of Pentargon. I had not been able to determine by what means I would manage to return there nor how long it would take me, but in the deepest recesses of my soul I had never doubted that Oliver would one day wed me and take me back to our Cornwall home. With one cruel sentence, however, he'd destroyed that expectation, and my vision of the future lay before me in jagged shards.

I emerged from the library that afternoon somewhat changed. I had touched the lowest point of my life, but I had survived. That is not to say that I didn't suffer the most excruciating agony. Rejection by a loved one is one of the most painful of human experiences, and in my case Oliver had been the object of my deepest emotions. I can't deny the enormity of my despair. But I didn't crumble under its weight. I didn't withdraw from life. I didn't even inflict my pain on anyone else. Instead, I began to sift through the pieces of my life to see what could be salvaged to help me face the days ahead.

There was not a great deal to salvage, but I was not without resources. I had a grandmother who professed to care for me and whose days I might enrich. I had a friend in Dory, in whose good fortune I might take pleasure. I had a mind capable of growth which I might improve by a program of organized study. And I even had an interesting game in the offering—that of capturing Lord Mowberly and then jilting him before the eyes of all of London's *haut ton*, a goal I fully intended to accomplish, Oliver's command notwithstanding. Life, though painfully restricted in its possibilities of happiness, was still to be lived.

I went about my business as usual. Grandmamma, exhausted from the exertions of the come-out, had suffered a fainting spell and had been ordered by her doctor to rest in bed for at least a week. I spent long hours at her bedside, but she insisted that I keep my social engagements. That very evening I attended the opera with Mowberly. The next day I spent a few hours with Dory, assisting her to select some items for her *trousseau*. And that evening, I attended a small dinner party at which Eliza sat just opposite me at the table. Rarely have I felt more miserable than when I had to watch her, elegant and smiling, at such close range. The awareness that I was facing the woman who would soon be taking what should have been my place as mistress of Pentargon and Oliver's wife made me almost ill. But I managed to speak to her with affability and even to wish her happy.

A few days later, Grandmamma startled me by appearing in the morning room at breakfast, fully dressed and bristling with purposefulness. "Good heavens," I exclaimed, looking up from my brooding examination of the tea leaves in the bottom of my cup, "didn't the doctor order you to remain abed for a week? You've two days left. What brings you down so soon?"

"You do," she said, taking a seat opposite without any more assistance than a slight pressure on her cane. "I'm better. And I don't intend to remain *incommunicado* for another moment. But I'm sick with worry over *you.*"

"Over me, Grandmamma? Whatever for?"

"Don't think to pull the wool over *these* old eyes, my girl. Something dreadful has happened to you, and I want to know what it is."

"Nothing dreadful has happened at all," I lied promptly.

Her shrewd eyes, moist with concern, met mine. "Is it something so awful that you can't confide in me? I haven't seen a look on your face like that since that evening when you discovered your poor mother's body on her bed. I can't force you to tell me, of course, but it chills me to the bone to see you like this. And to know nothing of the cause makes it worse."

I pressed my lips together firmly to keep them from trembling. "I assure you, Grandmamma," I managed when I'd recovered my stability, "that you're only imagining—"

She stretched her bony hand across the table and clutched mine. "Isn't there any way I can help you, my love?" she pleaded.

The touch of her hand on mind undid me. "Oh, Grandmamma, if only . . . But there's nothing . . . you will only think m-me a silly child."

"I never thought you silly even when you *were* a child. What *is* it, my dear?"

I shook my head. "It's only that . . . a bubble has burst. A dream. Such a s-silly dream, Grandmamma. About my future. About m-marrying someone I loved very much . . ." I covered my face with my hands. "I'm ashamed to speak of it. I was very foolish."

"Yes, of course you had a dream," she said with a touch of impatience. "To wed Oliver. What's so foolish about that?"

My hands dropped from my face. "Wh-what?"

"Did you think I didn't know? It was what I'd planned for you from the first. Why do you think I let him take you from me when your mother died? Didn't you think I would rather have had you with me?"

"Planned? Planned *what?*" I gaped at her in complete confusion. "What are you talking about?"

"Planned for Oliver to marry you. He needed someone quite special—I knew that long ago. And I knew that you—with the proper shaping, under influences which were not so debased and trivial as they'd been in your mother's house—could become that person. Here, with me, you would not have had the physical and intellectual stimulation that Oliver could provide. So I sent you to him."

"Do you mean to say that you wanted him to shape me? To make me the sort of woman he himself would wish for . . . to *marry?*"

"Exactly," she said smugly, reaching for the toast-rack. "Pass me the preserves, my love. All these revelations are making me hungry."

"But, Grandmamma," I persisted, unable to make sense of her disjointed explanation, "how could you think—? Didn't it strike you as unlikely that such a plan could work?"

"Not at all." She looked up at me, her brow furrowing. "It *has* worked, hasn't it? You've just admitted to being in love with him."

I winced. "Yes, I've admitted that. But that was only half your plan, isn't that so?"

She put down the toast she'd been carefully spreading with raspberry preserve. "What do you mean?"

"I mean simply that there was never any possibility that such a fantastic scheme could work."

"Buy why not? You're in love with him, and he's loved you from the first."

"Yes, I think he has. But whereas your plan has been completely successful in my case—for I seem to have followed the course you set with remarkable accuracy—the whole thing's gone awry with Oliver. Don't you *see,* my dear? He loves me in only a parental way. You've turned him into a *father,* not a husband."

"Oh, pish-tush!" She bit energetically into her toast and munched it with satisfaction. "If that's all that's been troubling you, then there's no reason for that tormented look to remain in your eyes. True, you've been a mere child to him until very recently. That why I took you back when I did. In time he'll see that you're a woman, and it will dawn on him that you're the perfect woman for him."

I didn't know whether to laugh or cry. "Oh, Grandmamma, we *are* a pair! I had counted on the very same scheme. We are both a couple of idiots!"

"Really, my love, I don't see why—"

"Don't you? Well, it serves you right for trying to play God. One can't do it, you know. Oliver once told me about the Greek *hubris.* Even those old Greeks knew that if one is arrogant enough to attempt to emulate the powers of the Gods, one will earn appropriate retribution."

"Retribution?" She put down what remained of her toast and looked across at me with newly aroused alarm. "What retribution? What on earth has happened?"

"Oliver has made his *own* choice for a wife, you see. And it is not I."

I was not prepared for the extent of her dismay. *"Anne!"* she cried in real pain, her face whitening. "Who—?"

"He's to wed Eliza Gilbart. An announcement will be appearing in *The Times* within the week."

"Eliza Gilbart! It's not *possible!"*

"It's not only possible, it's *true*. Oliver told me of it himself."

"But... she's not *at all* the sort of woman—"

I gave a small, wry laugh. "Grandmamma, if you say she's another Harriet Worthing, I shall scream."

But Grandmamma seemed not to hear me. She was staring out ahead of her, her mind apparently racing about like a mouse in a cage, looking for an exit. The look in her eyes, was, I thought, a mirror image of what my own must have been when I'd first heard the news—appalled. "The announcement has been *sent?*" she asked weakly. "Are you sure?"

"Yes, dearest, I'm sure."

"Then... there's no hope." Her voice had lost all vestige of its earlier energy. It was ineffably weary. "No hope at all. With a public announcement he is irrevocably committed."

"I know it." But hearing those words said aloud was like a stab at my heart.

She seemed as devastated as I was. "What have I done?" she mumbled, completely crushed. "I planned so carefully for your lifelong happiness... and I've given you only misery."

"Oh, Grandmamma, *don't!"* I reached out my hand to her as she had done to me.

But she took no notice. "I've failed you," she said, fumbling blindly to her cane. "Failed you... utterly..."

I got up and, putting the cane into her hand, helped her to her feet. She was trembling, but she looked up at me and said brusquely, "Let me be!" She shook off my hand and, unsteady, frail and leaning heavily on her cane, hobbled from the room.

Knowing well how she felt, I didn't run after her. She'd suffered a cruel blow, but she was strong. I knew she would recover. She would survive, as I had.

Grandmamma stayed in her room for another week, seeing no one but Mrs. Panniers. But on the day that the announcement

of Eliza Gilbart's betrothal to Oliver Fleming, sixth Earl of
Pentargon, appeared in *The Times,* she emerged from the bedroom brisk and firm of voice and limb. "Mowberly," she said
to me when we sat down in the sitting room at tea time, "cuts
a fine figure. And I'm told his income is close to eight thousand
a year."

"Really?" I asked, amused at the obviousness of her new
course of action in my behalf.

"Of course, everyone agrees he's past praying for. Never
even has come *close* to being leg-shackled. Even Clarice Glendenning tried to land him without success, and *she* was a veritable man-trap."

"Was she?"

"Yes, indeed. You might not credit it now that she's put
on so much weight, but five years ago—or was it more?—she
was considered the greatest beauty the town had seen in years."

I looked over at my grandmother curiously. She was sitting
opposite me, calmly stirring her tea and showing no signs of
the agitation which she'd exhibited when I'd seen her a week
before. "Grandmamma, are you trying to warn me *against*
Mowberly?"

"Not at all. Clarice Glendenning did not have anything like
your sparkle. It is quite possible that you may prevail where
she couldn't. If Mowberly is the sort you fancy, I've no doubt
you can succeed."

I cocked a suspicious eyebrow at her. "Does that mean you
approve of him?"

A shadow seemed to cross her face. "I wish to see you
settled and contented, my love. Whoever can bring you that
contentment will have my approval."

A disparaging response leapt to my tongue. Did Grandmamma really believe that I could find contentment as easily
as that? With a man so different from Oliver? How could she
be so ignorant of my nature?

But I bit back my words. With a jolt of sympathy I realized
that she *had* to believe I could find contentment. How could
she live with her guilt otherwise?

I put down my tea, crossed to her chair and perched on its
arm. I was tempted to confide in her the wicked purpose of
my involvement with Mowberly but I held back. The knowledge of my iniquitous motives might be upsetting to her, and

she might attempt to dissuade me. Besides, there was really no reason for her to know. I leaned down and kissed her brow. "Thank you, Grandmamma," was all I said.

From that day on, Mowberly was always warmly greeted when he called, and our association developed. I found myself in his company almost every day. He took me riding in his phaeton several afternoons a week, sought me out at every social event to which we were both invited, escorted Grandmamma and me to the theater, and accompanied me on shopping expeditions and any other outings where I felt his company was acceptable. Grandmamma tried to be cheerful about our growing intimacy, but Dory, who had heard more of his evil reputation than Grandmamma had, grew more alarmed with each passing day. "He wants you as his next paramour, my love, I'm almost certain of it," she warned one day when we sat together in her bedroom. "It is his pattern. Even my Theo is concerned. He tells me he's heard talk of it at the club. They are wagering on Mowberly's chances of wearing you down."

"You must thank Lord Dawes for me," I said drily. "However, your Theo should save his concern for other matters, like his upcoming nuptials. No . . . on the other hand, tell him to *take* the wager. He may quite safely put his money on me. Mowberly shall not wear me down."

"Really, Anne, you are the most shocking creature! As if Theo would put money on such a dastardly wager . . . or would bandy your name about at all! And of course *he* has no doubt of the impossibility of Mowberly's succeeding, but—"

"But what? If you both know that I shall not succumb to Mowberly's blandishments, I don't see why you worry so."

"Because, my love, when Mowberly discovers he can't have you on his terms, he may drop his pursuit of you and turn elsewhere. And you will have to suffer the pain and humiliation of losing him."

"Dory, dearest, stop worrying over me. I know what I'm doing, and I promise you that whatever happens, I shall not suffer the slightest pangs. Now, please, let's drop the subject of Mowberly and take up the much more interesting one of the design you've selected for your wedding gown. Is this ths issue of *The Belle Assemblée* in which it is sketched?

I felt completely secure in assuring Dory that I was not in

any danger at Mowberly's hands. While it was true his hints of desiring to become my "protector" had become more obvious of late, I knew just how I intended to play the game.

The game proceeded just as I planned. At first I pretended not to understand his little innuendos. But he, skilled in these matters, was shrewdly aware that I understood him perfectly; he merely eyed me with amusement and bided his time. After a while, however, his hints became too blatant to be ignored. It was then I played my trump card. After one particularly sultry attempt of his to underline his verbal warmth with a physical encounter of the type he'd once before attempted in the sitting room at Gilbart House, I slapped him soundly, burst into false but convincing sobs and ordered him to leave and never return.

He stayed away for almost a fortnight. When he returned (as I was almost certain he would), I refused to see him. He tried to speak to me at social events, but except for throwing him little looks of heartbroken despair, I avoided all direct confrontation.

The situation was so entertaining that I almost convinced myself that I was enjoying it. If I had really cared for him, I could not have played the game half so well. I couldn't have sidestepped his attempts to talk to me, to visit me, to convince me to climb into his phaeton "for no more than an hour, I give you my word!" The natural yearning of a girl in love to be with her beloved would have made me yield at least once. But I had no such yearning, and therefore I had a profound advantage in the game. *He* was the fish, and I was the angler who could play him on as long a line as the contest required.

I decided to let circumstances dictate the strategic time to reel him in. And one day, the morning after I had been particularly cruel by dashing out of Almack's as soon as he'd arrived seeking me there, he appeared at my grandmother's door in a highly emotional state. He brushed by Hewes (to whom I'd given strict instructions not to admit him) with a rudeness that could only be excused by his obvious agitation, demanding over his shoulder to know where the devil Miss Saunders was hiding. Hewes, following him down the hall and objecting vociferously to this high-handed disregard of protocol, refused to say, but Mowberly opened one door after another until he found me in the morning room. Without preamble, he pointed to the butler behind him. "Send this nincompoop about his business," he ordered curtly. "I will brook no more of your evasiveness, my girl!"

I took one look at him and knew the time was ripe. "It's all right, Hewes," I said quietly. "You may permit Lord Mowberly to join me for breakfast. But please be at hand if I should call."

Hewes gave Mowberly a reproachful look and nodded to me reluctantly. "Very well, Miss Anne. But I shall be right down the hall." And he discreetly withdrew, closing the door behind him.

Mowberly remained on his feet, glaring down at me with nostrils flaring. "How *dared* you make such a fool of me last night?" he demanded, raging. "You caused every dowager in the room to whisper about us behind their fans! Didn't you know how much people would gossip when you flew out of Almack's like the tearful heroine of a Cheltenham tragedy?"

I folded my hands in my lap and lowered my eyes sadly. "I *felt* like the heroine of a Cheltenham tragedy," I said with mendacious misery. "Or at least like poor Pamela in Mr. Richardson's novel."

He stared at me for a moment and then sank into a chair. Leaning his head in his hand, he groaned. "Blast it, Anne Saunders, you've driven me to distraction. I haven't been able to push you from my mind! I've found no surcease in any of my usual pursuits, I take no pleasure in cards, I've missed two meetings of the Four-in-Hand, and all the fellows at White's are laughing at me behind my back!"

"I'm . . . very sorry, my lord."

He lifted his head just high enough to throw me a withering look. "Ha! Do you take me for a fool? You're not in the least sorry—you're pleased as Punch!"

"Pleased? I? At what, my lord?"

"At having triumphed, as you once suggested you might. Youth and vitality over age and experience, I believe you said—or words to that effect."

"Triumphed?"

"Yes, triumphed. You've won, my girl, you've won. I've come to offer for you."

I permitted the words to hover in the air a moment or two, and then I rose from my chair in what I hoped was an attitude of pained and offended dignity. "Have you indeed?" I asked coldly.

He lifted his head slowly. "Oh, good *Lord,* what now?"

"If you think, Mowberly, that I can feel in the least trium-phant over this churlish proposal, you may think again. Those words I just heard did not sound like a sincere offer at all. But if you meant them to be, you now have heard my refusal and may safely depart these premises still unshackled."

For him, this was the last straw. With a cry of rage he leaped to his feet. "Are you saying, you vixen, that you don't wish to *marry* me?" he shouted, grasping my shoulders and giving me a furious shake.

"Unhand me! You could not have believed that I would accept so grudging and unhandsome a proposal. One would think you were about to take a dose of tar-water rather than a wife!"

"Tar-water!" He gave a snort of laughter. "Anne Saunders, you are the most obstinate, irritating, maddening female I've ever encountered. But you shall have your way. Here. I'm down on my knees. I've surrendered. Completely capitulated. Tell me you'll have me, ma'am, before I'm driven to distrac-tion. There, now, is that a more suitable proposal?"

"A bit more suitable," I said looking down at him with a small smile. "But of course you must give me time to think it over."

"Time? You've had months already. Don't tell me you haven't made up your mind long since to have me."

"Get up, Sidney and go away. I must be given time to think. I shall give you an answer in . . . in two days time."

After he'd left, I found myself giggling rather heartlessly at his frustration. It was so pleasant to see him squirming in the sort of discomfort he'd so often inflicted on poor innocent females. But two days later I accepted him, and Grandmamma, with what she hoped would convince me was a proud smile, sent the announcement to *The Times.* All that was left of my game was for me to plan how, when and in what sort of public way I would jilt him.

In the meantime we appeared together everywhere and ac-cepted—with the self-satisfied smiles of betrothed couples the world over—the congratulations of our acquaintances.

Less than a week after the announcement was published, I

was coming down the stairs in bonnet and pelisse, ready for Mowberly to take me up in his carriage, when I heard a loud knocking at the door. "I'll get it, Hewes," I called. "Tell Lady Marietta we shall be back in plenty of time to take tea with her."

I opened the door and found myself facing, not the expectant eyes of my betrothed, but the icy stare of my erstwhile guardian. *"Oliver!"* I gasped.

I had never seen his face so coldly implacable. One eyebrow rose in freezing disdain as his eyes swept over me. "Yes, Oliver. Can it be that you didn't expect me?" A tightly rolled copy of *The Times* was waved in my face. "Did you think when I saw this, that I would do nothing?"

"I don't suppose there is anything you *can* do, now," I said bravely, although the white fury of his face frightened me to the bone.

"Isn't there?" He tossed the newspaper upon a nearby chair. "I'm glad to see you dressed for travel. Get into the carriage."

"Oliver, have you lost your senses? I will certainly *not* get into the carriage, I am expecting . . . I have a previous engagement."

"Which you will not keep. Do as I say, or I shall have to—"

"Miss Anne, you've forgotten your scarf," called Miss Gribbin from the stairs. "Oh, my heavens! It's his *lordship!*"

"Good day, Miss Gribbin," Oliver said, taking my arm in an iron grip. "I'll take that scarf for Anne. Will you tell her grandmother, please, that I'm taking her back to Pentargon for a while and will send her a letter shortly with a fuller explanation?"

"Taking me *back?* Are you *mad?* Miss Gribbin, call Hewes at once. I'm being *abducted!*"

"Will you get into the carriage at once, or must I force you?" he muttered between clenched teeth.

"Miss *Gribbin*—!" I pleaded.

She laughed. "Oh, Miss Anne, *abducted*, indeed! As if Lord Fleming would—! Don't look so angry at her, my lord. You know how she likes her little jokes. I'll give Lady Marietta your message, but she will be very disappointed not to have seen you."

The pressure on my arm hardened painfully as he pulled me out the door. I felt as if I were living an insane nightmare as

Miss Gribbin waved smilingly from the doorway while Oliver dragged me down the steps. My flabbergasted outcries were completely ignored by Miss Gribbin above us and by Trewin on the driver's seat of the coach. Oliver propelled me, with cruel disregard for the safety of my limbs, up the coach steps and into the rear seat. Then, jumping up after me, he slammed the door. "Alright, Trewin," he shouted, "let's go. I want to be in Basingstoke by dark."

Chapter Nineteen

I EXHIBITED A wide range of emotions during the three-day journey to Pentargon—I pleaded, reasoned, wept, joke, ridiculed and scorned. Oliver made no response to any of it. He said not a word to me during the entire trip. That, more than anything else, infuriated me. I couldn't understand him at all. Why, if *he'd* rejected me, did he care what I did with my life or with whom I spent it? And by what right did he presume to dictate to me whom I should wed?

I had always dreamed of returning to Pentargon with Oliver...but not like this. This journey was nightmarish. Whatever we'd been to each other in earlier days seemed utterly destroyed. There remained not a shred of the closeness, the affection, the understanding that there once had been between us. Neither my words, nor my jibes nor my tears made any impression on him now.

I didn't tell him that I'd never had any intention of wedding Mowberly, for that would have been an act of surrender to his ridiculous tyranny. But I told him over and over that he was behaving as if I'd become Mowberly's mistress. "Dash it all, Oliver," I declared, "I'm not his doxie! I'm his *betrothed.*"

But Oliver only looked at me as if I were a creature beneath his contempt and said nothing. I pointed out to him that as long as I was properly betrothed—and to a well-born, well-to-pass, sought-after Corinthian of whom even my grandmother approved—his objections made no sense. "What has this to do with you, anyway?" I demanded repeatedly. "You're going to be wed yourself very soon. And you no longer wish for me in your life. Why then do you object to may making a life of my own?"

But he didn't deign to answer me. He behaved like the bored jailor of a miscreant prisoner. He spent the long hours of the journey either staring out of the coach window or looking at me with an expression of utter disdain.

By the time we arrived at Pentargon I *felt* like a prisoner. The castle itself, which I'd loved so much and for so long, looked different to me. Even the weather seemed to have conspired with Oliver to create an atmosphere of dark portentousness. Heavy clouds hung over the turrets, and the stone walls looked darker and thicker than I'd remembered. The facade seemd ominous and forbidding . . . and when Trewin ran up the steps and opened the door for us, he couldn't look me in the face.

Neither Mrs. Trewin nor Mabyn was anywhere to be seen as Oliver dragged me behind him up the stairs and down the corridor to my room. I was speechless with fury. He lifted me bodily from the floor, dropped me unceremoniously upon my bed and shut the door on me in the manner he'd used in bygone days—performing an act of physcial separation to avoid verbal confrontation.

I heard his key turn in the lock and his footsteps disappear down the hall. For the first time in all our years together he'd seen fit to lock me in!

I was indeed a prisoner. I could scarcely believe it. The very walls of my bedroom looked strange to me. I felt suddenly terrified by my utter confusion.

I got up and paced about the room like any caged creature, occasionally glaring at the locked door and demanding loudly to be released. But only the house answered, the wind whistling under the eaves and round the corners and filling the air with a pervasive and sibilant silence.

After a while, however, the silence grew familiar, and the room became once more my own. The wind died, and I, too, became calm. The was *Pentargon*, my beloved home, and the monster who'd locked me in was only *Oliver*. I had nothing to fear. I lay down on my bed and tried to make some sense of these strange events.

I knew that Oliver would not—*could* not—keep me locked up forever. Sooner or later he would open the door and make some explanation, and I would be free to go. My feeling of being a prisoner was more fantasy than reality.

But it was then that I perceived that the prison-fantasy was, in a manner of seeing that was beyond reality, quite true. I would always be Oliver's prisoner in my mind. Whatever he did to me, however he tryannized over me or ignored me, wherever he chose to live and with whom, wherever I chose to live and with whom, I would be his prisoner and bound up within these walls. And it was I, not Oliver, who'd brought me to this place. I had enchained myself. From the time I was sixteen and had realized I loved him, I'd build this prison in my mind. The *literal* incarceration which Oliver had foisted upon me was minor and only temporary. But my own imprisonment was permanent. I could think of no way to escape. Time and distance might help me to grow accustomed to my captivity, but I would never be free.

I had fallen into an uneasy sleep when there was a tap at the door, and Mrs. Trewin, key in hand, let herself in. She embraced me tearfully. Utterly confused by Oliver's behavior and the foreboding atmosphere of the house, she spoke in an awed whisper. "'Is lordship wants 'ee downstairs fer dinner. 'E's waitin' now. But there's time t' dress, if 'ee'd like t' change."

I washed my face and brushed out my hair while Mrs. Trewin rummaged through my old clothes to find something suitable for me to wear. Feeling a little refreshed after donning a clean muslin gown, I entered the dining room with some of my spirit restored. Mabyn stood at the sideboard, waiting to serve the meal. She was so awestruck by the obvious estrangement between Oliver and me that she was afraid to speak to me, but I greeted her with a cheerful word and a smile. Oliver, who'd been seated at the head of the table staring broodingly into a glass of Madeira, got to his feet. "Sit down and have your dinner first," he said brusquely, "and then we'll talk."

I nodded and took my place. Mabyn served my soup with a shaking hand, but I gave her a reassuring wink. I found, however, that I was quite unable to eat. My stomach was tightly knotted in dread of what Oliver had to say to me.

Oliver, too, seemed only to be playing with his food. When he saw that I was no more able to down a bite than he, he dismissed Mabyn, pushed his plate away and leaned back in his chair. "I know you think I've completely lost my mind," he began quietly. "I'd hoped, you see, to avoid any explanations by simply ordering you to keep Mowberly out of your life. The stratagem has not worked. I should have known from the outset that you'd be too obstinate to obey me blindly. I should have known, too, that I cannot keep you locked up in your room forever, which in my anger at your flagrant disobedience I fully intended to do. However, some calm reflection this afternoon made me see that there is nothing for it now but to reveal the reason for all this."

"Then there *is* a reason. Thank goodness for that. I was beginning to wonder if I'd lost *my* mind."

"Yes, there's a reason, but you won't thank goodness for it, I'm afraid, when you learn what it is. I hadn't wished to . . . I'd hoped it would never be necessary to show this to you." With a deep breath, he put a hand into his coat pocket and withdrew a folded packet of paper. "This is a letter your mother wrote to me shortly after your father—Reginald—died. Read it."

The expression of his face, his furrowed brow, the reluctance of his manner and the hesitations of his voice all combined to fill me with icy misgivings. "Is it . . . something very dreadful?" I asked, holding the letter gingerly between thumb and forefinger.

"The *paper* will not bite you." He pushed back his chair. "As for the contents, I wouldn't have struggled so long and so hard to keep them from you if I thought they would please you. I suspect you'll find the information very painful. I tried my best to save you from this, but . . ." He glanced at me with a look that bespoke both reproach and sympathy, and he rose from his chair. "I'll leave you to read it in private. Come to me in my study when you're ready."

After he'd gone, I held the letter in my hand for many moments. All semblance of courage deserted me. I didn't want to read this fearful message from the past. Too much emotion had been drained from me already during the past few days, and I suddenly realized how very weary I'd become. I was worn to the bone.

But if courage had deserted me, curiosity had not, and it was that which made me unfold the paper—yellow and worn at the creases—and spread it before me on the table. I moved the candelabrum closer to me and braced myself to face what it was I was about to discover.

There were two sheets of tightly-scrawled lines in my mother's cramped hand. I recognized at once her elaborately elongated consonants and the curlicued capitals which she'd always scattered over the pages of her writing with great liberality. I could almost hear her voice, with its rich tremor and girlish overemphasis, as I read.

My dear cousin Oliver, she'd written, *First let me Thank you for your words of Comfort to me at Reginald's graveside. Your sympathies were most Sincere and Kindly Expressed and gave me solace at a Difficult moment.*

But the Reason for this letter is only distantly related to my Husband's demise. I have been Weeping and Pondering the matter for many hours before writing this Missive, but I've decided that I must. There is no one else but You in whom I can Confide. My mother-in-law, your Aunt Marietta, has already Cast Me Off in disgust, and she knows only half the Truth. If she knew the Whole, she might expose my Beloved baby, and even Reginald, who knew All, did Not wish for That!

The Earl your father, who is, of course, the Head of the family, should (you will say) be the One to be told my Secret. But, Oliver, he is so very ill that it is clear that you will be the Head of the family very soon. Despite your Youth, you will have to assume the Burdens of all the family. Do you Mind very much having this one thrust upon you in Advance? I know you are not yet Twenty (Ah, so Young! I am only six years your Senior, but oh the Difference!), but I have long Believed that even at your age You are the Wisest and Kindest of us all. You are the only one of All the Saunders clan who has treated me with Affection and Respect despite the Malicious Gossip which you must have heard about me. For that alone you have won a Lasting Place in my Esteem.

So, Oliver, for all these Reasons, it must be You. You are the one I've chosen to be Custodian of my Secret. I pray with all my Heart that you never have to reveal to Anyone what is written here, but if something should happen to me, someone Else must know the Truth.

The story is not long. I married Reginald Saunders before

*I was Old enough to know what Marriage really is. Reginald
was always a Gentleman of great Sweetness and Generous
Affections, but you see, Oliver, he was not capable of what I
shall call Masculine love. We had, since almost the first month
of our Marriage, lived in separate apartments. I was content
for a While to live that way, but when Mowberly came along,
I lost my Heart. Amour is a very Powerful emotion, as you
will learn one day. Mowberly, being already a Widower at that
time, importuned me to Run Off with him. Although I was
Convinced that my Only Happiness rested with Mowberly, I
could not bring myself to Injure Reginald with such a Scandal,
and I remained with him.*

*Later, when I discovered that I was With Child, I confessed
to Reginald the Whole. He was unbelievably Forgiving. He
begged me to remain with him, pledging to Acknowledge the
child as his Own.*

*Please pardon the blots on this sheet, but I cannot restrain
my tears when I remember how much Reginald loved my Baby
that he knew was not his own . . . how he would play with her
for Hours and hold her in his arms when she Cried. No child
could have wished for a more Devoted father.*

*There is not much more to tell. I never revealed to Mowberly
that Anne is his daughter, for he has not shown the Slightest
interest in her. Isn't it ironic? But the greatest irony is that
now that Reginald has Passed On and I am free to remarry,
Mowberly has Lost Interest in me. The affair is Over. I am not
Bitter; it is the way of the World and the proper Retribution
for my Sins.*

*I know, Oliver, that You will wish, as Reginald did, for
Anne to grow up a Saunders, with the protection of the Saunders
name. A little, Innocent child should not have to pay for the
sins of its Begettors. With the legitimacy of the Saunders name,
my little Girl shall be able to hold up her Head before all the
World, despite her mother's foolish Mistakes. Only you and I,
dear Oliver, need ever know.*

*Nothing in my life has any Value any more except this dear
creature whom God has given me. I know not what the Future
holds in store for my child and myself, but I shall sleep better
tonight knowing that You can protect my Anne when I am gone.
For this and for all the other Kind Services, I remain Forever
and Always your Grateful and Devoted Cousin.*

I continued to sit staring at the page until the words danced before my eyes. A few of the candles were already guttering down to the sockets, nauseating me with their smoky odor. I had a sense of being somewhere else, in a past beyond my memory. For a while I seemed to be living another life—my mother's. I could feel her confusion in the early days of her marriage, her temptation under the blandishments of her first real lover, her shame at having to reveal to her husband that she carried a child that could not have been his. I had never before realized the reason for her *amours*. I had never sympathized with her weaknesses and her easy drift from one lover to another. But sitting there in the smoky, dimming candlelight, I lived for a few moments in her essence, and her tragedy, for a while, became mine. I mourned for her anew.

But after many minutes my head began to swim with other sensations, and slowly, very slowly, into my tired brain crept the awareness that there was more in my mother's tale than what I had thus far comprehended. There was a message for *me*. With a start, I grasped what it was—*I was not really a Saunders!* I was the illegitimate daughter of my mother's lover, Lord Mowberly, and therefore my betrothed's *half-sister!*

I think I laughed. *No wonder poor Oliver has been distracted,* I thought, giddy with a sense of the ridiculousness of everything. Poor Oliver. As the custodian of my mother's secret, he couldn't permit me to marry Mowberly. He'd had to stop me. How could he have known I'd never had any intention of going through with it?

I put my head down on my arms, intending to laugh and laugh at the whole thing. All this fuss, the abduction, the quarreling, the tears, the anguish, the revelations—the *enormous* revelations!—and all for nothing. Just because I'd decided to give Lord Mowberly a set-down. All because of a silly *game!* Wasn't it *funny?*

But I found myself crying. *Poor Oliver,* I thought as my shoulders shook with sobs, *went through all this because he hated to have to hurt me.* But I wasn't hurt. Losing Mowberly meant nothing to me. I had not really wanted him as a husband, and I certainly didn't want him as a brother. Then why was I crying like this?

I sat up and stared confusedly into the flickering candlelight. Something was hurting me, but I was too tired to understand what it was. I wiped my eyes, feeling peculiarly disjointed. I had no sense of myself. It occurred to me with a kind of horror that if I looked into a mirror, *the face looking back at me would not be my own*.

I blinked away the frightful vision and concentrated my mind on folding the letter carefully along the very creases my mother had made in the paper so many years ago. Then, like a sleepwalker, I got to my feet and let them take me where they would. They carried me to the door of Oliver's study. I pushed it open and leaned dazedly on the frame.

It was dark within, and I feared for a moment that the room was empty. But I heard a movement across the room and immediately saw his outline against the window. "Anne—?" he asked tensely.

He'd been waiting for me, standing at the window staring out on the ominous night sky. A glimmer of moonlight, shining from behind a great, black cloud, was the only source of light in the room. It outlined his form and revealed the swirls and curls of the cloudy configurations in the sky behind him. I remember wondering if the view signified that a storm had ended or that one was about to begin.

"Are you all right?" He went to his desk and fumbled with his Argand lamp.

I was so weary I could barely speak. "Oliver, I'm so . . . confused."

He started across the room toward me. "Did you understand the letter?"

"Yes, but . . . I don't know who I am."

He paused. "What?"

"Who *am* I, Oliver?"

"That's a ridiculous question. You're Anne Saunders, as you always were."

"No. I never was—"

A step in the corridor behind me made me jump. "Your lordship?" It was Trewin's voice.

"Yes? Dash it, let me light the lamp. What is it, Trewin?"

"A caller, my lord."

The light came up to reveal Oliver's impatient face and Trewin, blinking awkwardly, standing beside me in the doorway. Oliver put a hand to his head. "Now? At this hour? Who is it?"

"It's a Lord Mowberly. Says 'e want t' see Miss Anne."

I groaned. In some part of my overly fatigued mind, I almost believed it was my mother's Mowberly, come to claim me as his daughter. But I knew it was only a fancy, conjured up from too much stimulation and a draining exhaustion. I knew who it really was. "Tell him to go away," I said.

"'E won't go, Miss Anne. Says 'e 'as reason t' believe yer bein' held 'ere against yer will."

Oliver muttered a curse under his breath. "You may as well send him in," he said.

"No!" It was all too much for me. I couldn't face another confrontation—not yet. My knees began to buckle. I saw, with a strange, detached disinterest, that Oliver's brows had risen and that he was taking a quick, alarmed step in my direction. An enveloping, cloud-like lassitude spread slowly from my legs to my head. "Oliver," I said, my voice seeming to come from some other body, "I think . . . for the very first time in all my life . . . that I'm going to . . . faint."

Chapter Twenty

I WOKE TO bright sunshine, the clatter of dishes from the breakfast room below and the smell of coffee. Everything seemed
normal, orderly and cheerful. My bedroom looked like the
pleasant room with which I had long been familiar—the shabby,
slightly dusty bedhangings, my scarred but commodious dressing table, the sheer draperies which fluttered gently in the late-
spring breeze and let in the familiar, tantalizing whiff of the
sea. "Feeling better?" came Oliver's voice from above me.

I lifted myself on one elbow and blinked up. He was smiling
down at me in the fond manner of old times. He was wearing
his worn riding breeches, a pair of dusty boots and a shirt open
at the neck and unadorned by the formality of a neckcloth. He
was my Oliver of old. It warmed me just to look at him. "Yes,"
I answered, "very much better, I think." I was relieved to find
that my mind was so much more composed than it had been
the night before. "What happened?"

"You did as you threatened. You fainted. Frightened us all
to death."

"Us?"

"Mrs. Trewin, Mowberly, me, everyone."

"Mowberly?" I winced. "Is he still here?"

"Waiting for you in the breakfast room."

I sat up in alarm. "Good God, Oliver, you didn't tell him—?"

"That you're his half-sister? No. Nor will you. That is something no one else will ever know."

"Not . . . not even Grandmamma?"

"Not even she."

I shook my head, still troubled. "I don't know, Oliver. I have to think about all this."

"Yes, I suppose you do, but not now. You've been asleep for more than twelve hours. Now you must get up, get dressed and go down and tell Mowberly you've changed your mind."

I grinned wickedly. "I *haven't* changed my mind, you know."

His eyes narrowed. "What?"

"I *haven't.* I never *did* intend to wed him."

"Didn't you?" His brow knit in puzzled suspicion. "Then why did you betroth yourself to him?"

I dropped my eyes and fiddled guiltily with the bedclothes. "It was only to . . . to teach him a lesson."

"A *lesson?* What on earth do you mean?"

"He was as bad as Sir Averil, you know. Every bit as bad. Arrogant and spoilt and fully expecting me to become his paramour just because my mother had been his father's. I was determined to bring him to heel."

"I see. So you managed to get him to offer marriage instead, is that it? You triumphed. What did you expect to gain from such a *coup*, eh?"

"I expected to give him a taste of public humiliation when I later jilted him, don't you see?"

"So that was your plan."

"Yes. From the first."

Instead of being amused, Oliver looked as though he would very much have liked to throttle me. "Are you saying this has all been a *game?*"

"Yes."

"I see. And everything I've done—playing the stern parent, dragging you back to Pentargon, even showing you the letter— was all unnecessary?"

"Yes, Oliver, it was."

He remained silent for a long moment. "I'm sorry for it all, Anne. I would have preferred that you never learned what was in that letter. But you've been hoist with your own petard."

With a shrug he strode to the door. "I've had more than enough of playing the heavy-handed parent, my girl," he said before departing, "but I hope you'll take one last bit of advice from me. A betrothal is a pledge, and like most pledges of any consequence, a great deal easier to enter into than to get out of. It is *not* a game! In future, you'd better give the matter serious thought before you enter into it."

A short while later I paused on the threshold of the breakfast room, filled with trepidation. What was I to say to Mowberly now? I found him standing at the unlit fireplace, his booted foot on the fender, his elbow on the mantel, the very picture of the Corinthian Gentleman. His neckcloth was impeccable, his shirt-points unwilted, his hair brushed and pomaded to perfection and his boots aglow. One would have thought he'd brought his valet with him.

As if he felt my eyes on him, he looked up. His lips stretched into a wide, self-approving smile. "Ah! *There* you are. I've come to rescue you, you see."

"Good morning, Sidney. It was very . . . kind of you to concern yourself."

He came forward and lifted my hand to his lips. "Kind? I wouldn't say 'kind.' Brave, perhaps. Noble. But then, I *am* your betrothed, after all. Naturally I would concern myself. But your guardian tells me there was no need. Why did you run off without leaving me word?"

"I'm . . . very sorry, Sidney. I never dreamed you'd follow me."

"Didn't you? When Miss Gribbin told me how you'd been carried off, I suspected there might be something havey-cavey in it, even though she thought it all a great joke. So I followed you."

"Do you mean you thought I might be in danger?"

"Yes. It was the timing of the departure. You were supposed to drive out with *me*, you know."

"Yes, so I was. I'd . . . forgotten."

His eyebrows rose. "Forgotten?"

"I *am* sorry, Sidney. Do sit down, and I'll endeavor to explain."

He took a seat and watched me askance. Something in my manner was already warning him that there were shoals ahead.

"I came home, you see, because I had to . . . to think," I

said, improvising wildly. "I was not sure of my feelings."

He leaned back in the chair, crossed one booted foot over the other and surveyed me through narrow eyes. "Feelings? About me?"

His suspicious manner, though quite justified, irritated me. He was so confident of his attractiveness that he couldn't believe I might really be in any doubt. "Yes, Sidney, about you." I sat down at the table opposite him.

"But, my love, you are already *promised*."

"Yes, I know that. I should have done my thinking before, of course, but you . . . you swept me off my feet."

"What? What *is* this, ma'am?" He leaned forward and stared at me from across the table. "What sort of game are you playing *now?* You, my girl, were no more swept off your feet than . . . than an elm tree! You played me like a fish on a line, and you know it. Are you trying to tell me now that you've *changed your mind?*" His voice revealed more outrage than pain.

I lowered my eyes. "Yes, Sidney. I'm sorry."

"You've said you're sorry three times. Please don't say it again." He got up and walked round the table to confront me. "Has this something to do with your confounded guardian? Doesn't he approve of me?"

"It has nothing whatever to do with him."

"Perhaps not, but he *doesn't* approve of me. I could tell that from the first. Can't say I blame him. If I were a young girl's guardian, I would not approve of me myself. But you, you little wretch, knew my reputation from the first."

"This has nothing to do with my guardian and nothing to do with your reputation. I . . . I just don't think we'd suit, that's all."

His face darkened with fury. He'd taken the trouble to follow me all this way in the expectation of receiving a hero's welcome and an outpouring of my undying gratitude. Instead he was rewarded with this incoherent rejection. "Don't think we'd *suit?* Is *that* all you have to say?"

"I suppose I could say more, but that's the gist of it," I admitted frankly.

"After everything that's passed? Does it mean nothing to you that I've been laughed to scorn by my friends for having been cozened into offering matrimony to a slip of a girl barely out of the schoolroom? That I've left London at the height of the season to follow you all the way to the ends of the world?

That I've turned my life upside down for you?"

"What can it mean if I don't love you?" I asked quietly.

"It's a bit late in the day to make *that* discovery, is it not?" His eyes burned icily into mine.

"Better now than afterwards, I think."

He took an angry turn around the room. "And now, I suppose, you'll let it be known all over town that you've jilted me."

I suddenly felt sorry for him. "No, Sidney, I don't have to do that. I can say that you discovered you do not wish for marriage after all, and I released you. Your cronies will be convinced that you've recovered your senses and are quite your rakish self again."

He stopped his pacing and looked at me measuringly. There was no love, no anguish in the glance. It was as if he were weighing the possibility of acting on my suggestion. "What you suggest, ma'am, is probably closer to the truth than you know. I was beginning to wonder, days ago, how I'd managed to fall into your trap. I was beginning to feel that I'd made a huge mistake." He stalked to the door. "Thank you, my dear, for making it clear to me that I had."

With that, he slammed out of the room, throwing me not so much as a backward glance. I could hear his boots clattering rapidly down the hall. His pride more than his emotions had been dealt a blow. I had had my revenge, but I felt no pleasure in it. I couldn't help noting that this experience with Mowberly had turned out far more painfully for me than for my victim.

I sat there at the table trying to adjust myself to a new, radically changed sense of myself. I had just dismissed a suitor who was, in reality, my brother. I wished I could as easily dismiss that fact from my mind. I could not accept with equanimity the thought that the same blood flowed in my veins that flowed in his. How much was that self-important, superficial, arrogant creature like *me?* After having spent years trying to prove myself that I was not as weak as my mother, would I now have to struggle against whatever *Mowberly* weaknesses were in me?

I was deep in these meditations when Oliver looked into the door of the breakfast room. He threw me a quick grin. "You must have done well. His phaeton has just bowled off down the drive at a smart clip."

"Yes," I muttered glumly, my chin resting on my hand,

"even *he's* probably relieved to be rid of me."

"Instead of sitting there feeling sorry for yourself, run upstairs and put on your old riding breeches. Let's have an hour of good galloping before I put you into the carriage and send you back to your grandmother."

I went off to do as he bid, feeling both eager and despairing. It had been years since I'd last ridden with him; there was nothing in the world I would rather have done. But it would end before I knew it, and I would soon find myself alone in the coach wending my way back to the imprisoning life of loneliness and fruitlessness which London meant to me.

We raced over the fields and jumped hedges until our mounts and we were breathless. Then, both reluctant to make an end, we ambled slowly back. Although the sun was still high, I felt within my breast the shadowy sadness of late afternoon. Oliver reached over and took my bridle, pulling Belinda to a stop. "Don't look so downhearted. Nothing important has changed."

"Hasn't it?" I patted Belinda's mane dolefully. "I don't even know who I *am* anymore."

"Yes, I heard you say something of the sort last night. It's a very fanciful but nonsensical statement, isn't it? What does it mean?"

"It means that I thought I was someone I knew. Anne Saunders. Now I find I'm someone else."

"You're still Anne Saunders. Reginald was your father, my girl, legally, morally and every other way but one. There's no reason in the world for you to think of yourself as anyone but his daughter. If you've a grain of sense left in that overactive brain of yours, you'll put everything else out of your mind."

"I can't, Oliver. It's been difficult enough to think of myself all these years as the child of a mother who . . . who was not what she ought to have been. Now to have a father, too, who was—"

"Was what? Nothing so very wrong with the late Lord Mowberly that isn't wrong with most of the men in his class."

"You said yourself that the Mowberlys were a family of wastrels, gamblers and philanderers."

"Yes, and so I could have said of half the society of London. Don't make problems where none exist. All of us, whoever our parents may be, have to forge our own characters in the end, or what's the meaning of human will?"

I let the horse amble ahead unrestrained as I mulled over

his words. He was right. He had to be, or there would be no
hope for progress in the world. Human beings were not locked
into a prison of inherited weaknesses—they had strength, and
will, and the capacity for growth and change. As for me, I was
who I was, with hopes and visions of my own, quirks of my
own, and a will of my own. And surely I was strong enough
to shape my character to fit standards of my own. I could not
shape my circumstances, but I could shape *myself*.

I lifted my head, picked up the reins and nudged Belinda
into a gallop. I pulled off my cap so that I could once more
feel the Cornwall wind in my hair as I raced across the fields
to the stable.

Oliver caught up with me in the yard and came round to
help me dismount. "That's the spirit," he said softly as he set
me on my feet. "You'll do. A *rara avis*, you know, needs have
no concern about forebears." He gave me a last, fond grin.
"The rare bird, after all, is the one who broke the mold."

Chapter Twenty-one

I WAS HIS *rara avis,* but evidently not rare enough. On the long, long journey back to London I reviewed the scene repeatedly in my mind. I remembered the pressure of his hands on my waist as he lifted me from the horse. I remembered the soft, soothing words in my ear. I remembered wishing urgently for the moment not to end. I'd looked up at him, aching for him to pull me close and wondering why, if I was his rare bird, he so implacably resisted me. I'd closed my eyes and swayed toward him.

But he'd put me by. As soon as his hands released my waist, I'd opened my eyes, but he'd already turned and headed for the house, his stride swift and purposeful. He'd succumbed to me once before; he intended never to do it again.

I saw him briefly just before I left. He bid me goodbye from the doorway as the coach departed, but that was all. What I now had to face was the fact that the next time I saw him he would be as good as wed.

The London summer was hot, but at Gilbart House, wedding plans were keeping everyone busy as bees. Eliza's wedding to Oliver was to be held in September, and Dory's was to follow within a month. Lady Gilbart was beside herself. "Two wed-

dings almost at once!" she would chortle to herself and everyone
else. "It is almost too thrilling to *bear!*"

We spent the warm afternoons in the Gilbart sitting room,
stitching away at the lovely items needed for two *trousseaux:*
lace-trimmed silk petticoats, nightgowns of the finest lawn,
camisoles with embroidered trim and ribbon woven through
the straps, handkerchiefs with entwined initials, sashes of satin
and chemises of crape, corsets, drawers, singlets, smocks,
scarves and linens of all sorts. Never were two young women
about to be launched into matrimony with such magnificent
accoutrements for use under the surface.

Grandmamma, disappointed by my rejection of Mowberly,
had become waspish. The heat drained her vitality, and her
only pleasure was the twice-weekly gathering of her friends in
our drawing room for cards. "Why must you go out every day
to sit and sew with the Gilbart females?" she carped. "If you
won't play cards with us or ride in the park with young Ludbrooke, you might at least walk on the Strand with Miss Gribbin
and give the nod to a few eligibles."

I responded that (1) I'd been raised to believe that card
games were a foolish waste of time, that (2) Ludbrooke was a
bore, that (3) it was too hot to walk on the Strand, and that
(4) I liked sitting and sewing with the Gilbart females. This
last, however, was not strictly true. Although spending my
afternoons with Dory and Eliza was preferable to Grandmamma's other suggestions, it was not pleasant to have to
spend my time stitching a row of spidery lace upon the bodice
of a nightgown which Eliza would wear in bed with Oliver. In
fact, if I'd let myself dwell on such things as I sewed, I would
grow positively despondent.

Fortunately we kept our minds on other matters as we sewed.
One of us would read aloud as the other two stitched. Or Dory
would sing. Sometimes we just sat idle, sipping cool lemonade
and inventing stories about our futures. I could always set them
laughing by predicting for myself a marvelous career as a teacher
at the Finchlow Academy. I entertained them frequently by
creating special classes for which I would be a perfect instruc-
tress: Tripping Over One's Feet With Grace, for example, or
How To Pop A Button At The Back Of One's Gown At Significant Moments. A special course I devised, for advanced
students only, was How To Destroy A Dinner Party, giving
especially high marks to those pupils who could devise a scheme

to manage the destruction before midnight.

Those afternoon talks led to a revelation that made me look at Eliza with new eyes. One day, while Dory and I were on our knees pinning the hem of a *peignoir* for Eliza, which she was wearing over her dress so that we could measure properly, I looked up at her curiously. "Don't you *miss* him, Eliza?" I asked, permitting myself for the first time to inquire about something that had long been troubling me. "You haven't seen him since the come-out ball in May."

"Oliver, you mean? Yes, I suppose I *would* miss him if I weren't so busy. But getting ready for one's wedding is so complicated and time-consuming that I barely have time to think about him."

I sat back on my heels, stunned. "But, my dear, it's been more than three *months!* If it were I, I'd be dying of impatience."

Dory nodded in agreement. "I would, too," she said, taking the pins from her mouth. "I miss Theo if I can't see him for even a *day*."

Eliza gave her trilling laugh. "That's because you're both so young and romantic. Oliver and I are much more sedate."

"Sedate?" I had known Oliver in all sorts of roles—guardian, friend, botanist, estate manager, teacher—but I would never have called him *sedate* in any of them. *"Should* lovers be sedate with each other?"

Eliza looked down at me with indulgent patience. "I don't know if I like the word *lovers,* Anne. We are betrothed. We shall be husband and wife. *Lovers* sounds so . . . so improper."

"Improper?" I didn't understand. "Do you mean like a . . . a liaison?"

"Yes."

I was taken aback. Was it not proper for husbands and wives to be lovers? Was my understanding of married love distorted by my mother's *amours?* Was married love a sedate sort of thing and only *amour* intimate and passionate?

But Dory, too, was studying her sister with a puzzled frown. "Are you saying, Eliza, that I shouldn't think of Theo and me as lovers? I've never heard anything so silly."

Eliza gave the *peignoir* a little kick and turned around. "You may think what you like, Dory," she said with gentle reproach, "but you certainly mustn't say it aloud. To call yourselves *lovers* sounds a bit vulgar."

"But let's not confuse the matter with the word," I persisted. "It's the *idea* which confuses me. Whatever they call themselves, aren't husbands and wives truly lovers?"

"What do you mean, truly lovers?"

"Well . . . not sedate. Passionate, warm and . . . and . . ."

"Amorous," Dory added. "And, you know . . . *lusty.*"

Eliza's color rose. "I suppose there are *some* husbands and wives who are lovers in that sense," she said carefully, "but I would not consider them among the finest-bred—"

"Oh, pooh!" Dory exclaimed, getting to her feet. "I intend for Theo and me to be as lusty as peasants."

"Nonsense, Dory!" Eliza said, laughing at her sister's bluntness. "What do you know of peasants?"

"I don't. But I know what *you* mean by sedate and finely bred. You mean dressing screens and separate bedrooms and that sort of thing. Well, I won't have it. Theo and I shall be *lovers,* just as Anne says. We shall share the same bed and the same bedroom, we shall speak intimately to each other, and we shall kiss and hug as much as we like. We won't be sedate for *years!* And if you're too shocked to invite us to your parties, I won't care a fig!"

"*Dory!*" Eliza exclaimed, horrified.

I stared at Dory in amazement. *Her* mother had never had *amours,* and yet she was describing, with a natural, open honesty, what I'd imagined married love would be like. Was it possible that *her* attitude—and therefore mine—was healthier than Eliza's?

I helped Eliza off with her *peignoir,* my mind racing about in confusion. Did this lovely young woman really intend to live with my Oliver in the sedate way she'd described? "Are *you* going to have separate bedrooms, Eliza?" I asked bluntly.

She took the garment over her arm, sat down and began at once to work on the hem. "Yes, I am," she said, not looking up. "It's what all proper ladies do, no matter what Dory thinks. And I hope that neither of you will repeat what Dory said to a soul. Mama would be quite disturbed by it."

Dory made a face at her sister and winked at me. I smiled back at her in heartfelt gratitude, for Dory had, all unwittingly, taught me something very special: that my mother's kind of love—warm, passionate, generous and unrestrained, was *not necessarily sinful.* As Dory described it, it sounded positively *healthy!* If one wished for a happy married life, wasn't Dory's point of view sounder than her sister's?

Dory's Theo was going to be a happy man. His wife would give him so much loving warmth that he would never have to look elsewhere for a paramour. And, if Dory was more fortunate than my mother, her Theo would return that warmth in good measure. And loving warmth, I realized with a glow of delight, was *amour! Amour* between a husband and wife was a good thing—not something of which to be ashamed. Dory was not ashamed of her instincts. It was Eliza—proper, well-bred, perfect Eliza—who was putting feelings of shame into the prospect of married love—the same sort of shame that I had put into my mother's *amour*.

I thought the matter over all that night and decided that Eliza, proper and admirable though she was, was at bottom cold. She was probably worse than Harriet Worthing, who had merely "lacked spontaneity." And if she was worse than Miss Worthing, she was surely not right for Oliver. He deserved something more in his marriage than what Eliza was prepared to give, more than the sort of marriage my mother had endured, with its separate apartments and the need for outside *amour*. Not that for my Oliver!

If there was anything at all that I could do to prevent those nuptials from taking place, I would do it!

A few days later, in mid-August, Eliza came into the sitting room carrying a letter, and she announced to Dory and me that her betrothed had informed her of his arrival date. "He says he'll be here by the twenty-seventh, in plenty of time for the Pressbury dinner in our honor."

"And about time, too," Dory muttered drily.

"What else does he say, Eliza?" I asked, feeling a bit desperate at the swift approach of the wedding date.

Eliza knew how attached to Oliver I was, and she generously offered to read the letter in its entirety. "He says, *Dear Eliza, I was glad to learn that Lady Gilbart has acquiesced to my request to keep the guest list under one hundred. I'm very grateful to you both, for a larger assemblage would make me too uncomfortable to enjoy the affair. I am doing my best to finish the work on the estate in time to depart for London by the end of next week. Look for me some time after the twenty-sixth. In the meantime, please feel free to do as you suggested in your last—do select the ring yourself. It will save us time later, and I trust your selection completely. I am marrying the woman with the most exquisite taste in all of London, and she doesn't need my assistance to select a diamond. Have the bill sent to my man Watkins in Chancery Lane. My regards to Lady Gilbart and the rest, Yours, etc., Fleming."*

"Not very romantic," Dory said, nibbling a strawberry from a well-filled fruit bowl at her elbow. "'Yours, etc., Fleming,' indeed. He could have said 'with love,' couldn't he?"

"Oliver is not given to ardent effusions," Eliza responded placidly.

Perhaps he isn't, I said to myself, *but if that letter is the letter of a man in love, I've learned nothing of* amour *in all my life.*

Reposing at that moment in the bodice of my gown was the letter he had many months ago written to me. *I have never thought of you,* he'd written, *as anything but the bright, pure, sparkling, unique creature that you are.* That was a great deal more "effusive" than *I am marrying the woman with the most exquisite taste in all of London.* If Eliza could see *my* letter, she might think twice about her own.

I stiffened as an idea—blindingly brilliant in its simplicity and its potential for stirring up trouble—struck like a crackling lightning bolt within my brain. Why *shouldn't* Eliza see my letter? It might teach her something about love.

Surreptitiously, I slipped my hand into my bodice and withdrew it. Keeping it wadded in my cupped hand, I got to my feet and wandered casually to the door. "I don't know, Eliza," I said thoughtfully, "I've known Oliver to be ardently effusive at times." I opened the door, but before leaving I let the letter fall from my hand to the floor. *"Very* ardently effusive."

From the corner of my eye, I saw her lift her head.

"I say, are you leaving already?" Dory asked in surprise.

"Grandmamma wants me. See you tomorrow." And I strolled off down the hall.

I heard Eliza call after me, "Anne, wait! You've dropped something." But I pretended not to hear. I ran out the front door and hurried down the steps. I had to give Eliza ample time to read the letter I'd left behind. To read it and weep.

Eliza didn't join Dory and me in the sitting room the next afternoon. It was Dory who returned the letter to me. "You dropped this yesterday," she announced with dramatic intensity. "Eliza recognized the hand, and she . . . we . . . read it."

"Oh?"

"Eliza is very upset over it."

"Is she? Why?"

"Because it's so much more 'ardently effusive' than hers. Goodness, Anne, if one compared your letter and hers, one would think *she* was the ward and *you* were the affianced."

I tucked my letter back into my bodice. "Oh, I don't think so," I said innocently. "Besides, I thought Eliza *liked* a sedate, restrained style in a betrothed. Isn't that what she said? Otherwise it's so vulgar."

Dory met my eye, and we both giggled. "Eliza and her separate bedrooms," Dory whispered scornfully. "I think the Finchlow sisters made too deep an impression on her. Being a lady isn't everything. Frankly, Anne, I'm glad I'm a little vulgar."

We sat down and donned our thimbles. "Do you think, Dory," I asked, my eyes fixed on my needlework, "that there may be *trouble* over this?"

"Trouble?" Dory was tightening an embroidery frame with concentration. "With Oliver, you mean?"

"Yes. If my letter has upset Eliza, will she . . . quarrel with him over it, do you think?"

"I don't know. I hope so."

"Dory! How *can* you—?"

"I mean it," she said, jabbing a needle into the stretched fabric to emphasize her point. "If they quarrel, perhaps Oliver will be driven to write a letter like yours to *her*. Nothing like a good quarrel to stir a couple up. A pair can be *too* sedate, if you ask me."

"But if they quarrel, they may break it off, and then there wouldn't be a wedding after all," I suggested, failing to add, of course, that that was what I hoped would happen.

"Oh, I very much doubt if matters will go as far as *that*," Dory said with assurance, pulling the long, colored thread through the cloth with a most disturbing complacency. "I've never yet heard of a betrothal that was broken because the gentleman didn't show sufficient ardor in his *letters*."

Dory was right, of course. No one with a grain of sense would break off so desirable a connection as a marriage to the Earl of Pentargon for so flimsy a reason. As I fastened a row of tiny silk rosebuds to the neckedge of a lawn camisole, I tried to accustom myself to the fact of it: *Oliver was about to marry Eliza Gilbart*. I would have to stand by and watch it happen. I would have to smile and smile through it all, to offer my good wishes, and, once the ceremony was over and Oliver had taken his bride back to what should have been *my* home, to find a way to live the rest of my life with the finality of it. In other words, to hear the bars clang shut, and the key turn in the lock . . . and to face the knowledge that the rest of my days would be spent in this prison of my mind.

Chapter Twenty-two

YOU, DEAR READER, who have been so patiently following the trials and vicissitudes of my life's story, have probably guessed that Dory was wrong. Her sister was startled by the signs of deep feelings Oliver had expressed in my letter, and she brooded on the matter for the rest of the week. Her vision of a marriage between two restrained, unimpassioned, mature people was dealt a severe jolt. She realized that Oliver was capable of a depth of emotion of which she was not, and the knowledge frightened her. When Oliver arrived on her doorstep, a tired smile on his face and a bouquet of *Chrysanthemae coronariae* in his hand, she had a careful speech prepared. She declaimed it in a well-rehearsed, controlled—but to him completely incoherent—manner and dismissed him with surprising but unshakable finality.

I, of course, knew nothing of this until afterward, when Dory confided to me the whole tale. Thus on that August afternoon I was taken aback when, just before teatime, Oliver himself stormed into Grandmamma's sitting room. "See here, Anne Saunders, what were you up to when you told Eliza Gilbart that I'm ardent?" he demanded angrily.

Grandmamma had been trying to teach me to play whist.

("If you're determined to dwindle into a sour old maid," she'd said, "you may as well get some pleasure from it.") She'd spread the cards over a small table, separated them into suits, and was trying to explain how one wins a trick when Oliver burst in on us. "Ah, Oliver!" she said, brightening. "Sit down and assist me with this chit. She has no card sense at all."

"She has no sense in any matter," he declared brusquely. "Well, my girl, what did you mean by it?"

I got up from my chair, my knees trembling. "What did I . . . mean by it?" I echoed faintly.

"Yes! How could you tell her I was *ardent?*"

"I didn't mean it as an *insult,* Oliver."

"Dash it, girl, how could you, my *ward,* express a judgment in such a matter at *all?* It made me seem a veritable *lecher!*"

"What are you ranting about, Oliver?" Grandmamma interjected. "You haven't even greeted me. Bend down, fellow, and give me a kiss."

"Be still, Marietta. This is serious. Your bubble-headed granddaughter has caused a rift between Eliza and me, and I want to get to the bottom of it. Well, Anne, what exactly did you say to her?"

"Nothing very much, truly. What does she say I said?"

"You could at least have said good day," Grandmamma muttered, gathering up her cards. "Does your generation have no manners at all?"

Oliver ignored her. "She said . . . Oh, hang it all, I could make no sense of what she said! Something to the effect that the ardor I show to you is more—what was her word?—*effusive* than that which I show to her. Never heard such nonsense in all my life. When, my girl, have I ever been effusive to you?"

"I don't know, Oliver. It was only your letter, you see."

"Letter? What letter?"

"Yes," Grandmamma parroted. "What letter?"

"The letter you wrote to me the day I left Pentargon to go back to school. Don't you remember?"

He put a hand through his hair in distraction. "I have some vague sort of recollection. We'd had a quarrel, I remember, and you needed a bit of reassurance." He took a turn about the room, Grandmamma's eyes following him with fascination. "But, confound it, Anne, it couldn't have been *ardent!* You were a *child!*"

"Yes, but, to be fair, Oliver, Eliza didn't know that. The letter isn't dated."

He paused in his striding and cocked his head at me. "Didn't you tell her when I'd written it?"

I bit my lip guiltily. "Well, no . . ."

"Why not? Why ever *not?*"

"Yes, my love," Grandmamma put in interestedly. "Why ever not?"

"Because she . . . didn't ask me."

Oliver growled furiously. "Damnation, Anne, is this another of your mischief-making *games?*"

"It isn't my fault," I lied. "I dropped the letter in the Gilbart sitting room, you see, purely by accident, and I didn't know until the next day that . . . that it had been found and read."

"Purely by *accident?* That letter must have been written a year ago! Are you trying to make me believe that you just *happened* to have the letter with you a year later?"

Both Oliver and Grandmamma were looking at me with suspicion. I couldn't blame them. My words sounded, even to my own ears, completely unconvincing. I wanted to be truthful, but how could I admit to Oliver what I'd tried to do? Making a quick decision to brazen the scene out, I said proudly, "I *always* carry the letter with me."

Oliver, startled, stared at me. "Always?"

My eyes locked on his. "Always."

He wrenched his eyes away and shook his head. "Even so," he said, more quietly, "I don't understand all this fuss. There could have been nothing improper in a letter I wrote to my sixteen-year-old ward."

"Seventeen, by then," I corrected.

"It seems to me, Oliver," Grandmamma suggested, "that the sensible thing to do is to *read* the document in question and *see.*"

"I can't do that. I don't know where it is. Eliza probably threw the thing away."

"No, she didn't," I admitted. "I have it back." I turned away and pulled the letter from its place. "Here."

"Well, *really,* my dear," Grandmamma chided, "no wonder Eliza is upset. I hardly think it proper for you to carry your cousin's letters in your *bosom!*"

I felt myself color to the ears. "It's *my* letter, and I may carry it where I like!" I retorted.

But Oliver was paying no attention. His eyes were racing over his own words. Then he looked up, his eyes meeting mine over Grandmamma's head. There was something in that look that made my heart stop beating.

In a kind of shock, he sank down upon Grandmamma's Grecian-style loveseat. "Good God!" he muttered in an undervoice. "Did I love you like that even *then*?"

I gasped, breathless with joy. *"Oliver!"*

Grandmamma, agape, looked from his face to mine. "I think," she said after a moment of silence, "that I'll go and see about... about tea."

Oliver lifted his head, profoundly troubled. "I suppose... this *is* a bit ardent," he said guiltily.

"Yes, I suppose it is," I said, still scarcely breathing.

"If one thinks about it, one can see why a young woman might feel disturbed if her betrothed wrote a letter of this sort to another..."

"Yes."

He put a weary hand to his forehead. "I suppose we might try to explain to her..."

"Yes, we might," I said, "if..."

"If?"

"If you really want to, of course."

Grandmamma reached for her cane. "If you'll excuse me..." she murmured.

Oliver's eyes never left my face. "Shouldn't we go to her and try to explain?"

I took the bull by the horns. "If I were you, Oliver—"

"Yes?"

"If I were you, I would become betrothed to the one to whom I'd written the ardent letter in the first place!" I said in a rush of words.

"Oh, you would, would you?" He looked at me disdainfully, but it seemed to me that a hungry look flared up in his eyes. "Even if the recipient of this... this *epistle* is only half my age?"

"Yes."

"And hasn't had a chance to meet even a small sample of the dozens of eligibles from among whom she might choose a much more desirable suitor?"

I went round the table and knelt beside him. "Oh, Oliver, she's *had* a chance. For two years. And all that's come of it is an offer from a rake and a near-offer from a bore."

Grandmamma chuckled. "She means Mowberly and Ludbrooke. Not worth a groat the pair."

"Are you still here, Aunt Marietta?" he asked, not looking away from my face. "I thought you were going to order the tea."

"Yes, yes, I'm going, you rudesby."

"Good. For I must ask this idiotic young female how she thinks I'd feel a few years from now when she wakes up one morning and realizes that she's buried herself in Cornwall with a stuffy old husband, a raft of offspring, and all without ever having had a proper chance for romance."

I brushed his cheek with my hand. "Is that why you've held yourself off from me, Oliver?" I ask softly. "To give me a proper chance for romance?"

He took my hand in his and searched my face, afraid to believe what he saw there. "Yes, of course it is."

"No other reason? Eliza—?"

He lowered his eyes. "I only offered for Eliza because you'd convinced me you wouldn't cut yourself off from me otherwise."

"Oh, my love, what a fool you are. I shall never love anyone but you."

He uttered my name with a groan and pulled me to him. I buried my face in his shoulder with an almost unbelieving delight. "Oliver," I whispered, "I love you so."

Grandmamma chortled aloud. Oliver, without taking his lips from my hair, said firmly, "Aunt Marietta, I think you are becoming decidedly in the way."

"I'm going, nodcock, I'm going. Although why you should find me in the way, I don't know. After all, I foresaw all this years ago."

"Yes, Grandmamma," I said, "but if Oliver means to kiss me, I think it would be better if he did it unobserved."

"I didn't say I mean to kiss you, you wanton."

I lifted my head and peeped up at him. "No? Well, then, I mean to kiss you, which is the same thing in the end."

Grandmamma hobbled to the door. "I suppose Lady Gilbart will never speak to me again," she mumbled. "Oh, well, can't be helped. A raft of great-grandchildren will make up for it."

As soon as the door had closed behind her, Oliver bent his head. "My rare bird!" he sighed as his arms tightened about me and I melted into a warmer embrace than I'd dreamed possible.

When at last he let me go, I couldn't help laughing up at him. "That, sir, was not very fatherly."

"It's been a very long time since I felt fatherly toward you, you wretch," he grinned, pulling me to him again.

A while later, however, his eye fell on the letter which had fallen to the floor. A clouded expression crossed his face. "Tell me the truth, my love," he asked, tilting up my chin. "Why did you show Eliza the letter?"

"I *didn't* show—" I began, intending to keep my guilty secret to myself.

"I know you too well, girl. You did it on purpose. Didn't you realize how much trouble you would cause?"

"Of course I did," I admitted at last. "Making trouble was exactly my intent."

"You are utterly shameless!" He let me go and stood up. "And so am I. If I were any sort of gentleman I would go back there and try to patch things up again."

"Oliver!" I jumped to my feet and threw my arms about him. "I won't let you!" I put a firm hand to his mouth to stop his objections. "She had her chance. She doesn't deserve you, and she can't have you!"

He gave a reluctant laugh. "Doesn't *deserve* me? What a goose you are. She's the most gentle, considerate, soft-spoken, ladylike—"

"—sedate—"

"Yes, sedate, lovely, *perfect* creature."

"Oh, I agree completely."

He looked at me with suspicious amusement. "You do?"

"Yes, completely. But, perfect or not, she can't have you."

He pulled me into his arms again. "Very well, ma'am, I shall leave things as they are. But the only reason I'm surrendering to your blandishments is that I realize that Eliza is too good for me."

"Yes, but is she a *rara avis?*" I demanded.

"No, I don't suppose she is."

"And could *she* keep you in a state of constant anxiety because of her wild and impulsive games?"

"No, I don't think she could."

"And would *she* agree to share the same bed with you . . . or even the same bedroom?"

He gave me a sharp, arrested, quizzical glance. "Wouldn't she?"

"No, my dear sir, I don't think she would."

"Good God, girl, is *that* why you put a spoke in her wheel?"

"Never mind," I said with a laugh as I snuggled back into his embrace. "Just take my word that, although Eliza may be perfection to the rest of the world, I, my love, am perfect for you."

And so, in due course, I returned to Pentargon, not as a prisoner but as its blissfully happy mistress. Oliver and I spend our days contentedly breeding two lively offspring and a huge number of fruit trees and flowering shrubs. We have long, lively visits from Dory and Theo and their five progeny and from my grandmother, who, though well into her eighties, is still lively and sharp of tongue. Eliza Gilbart does not come, although she is contentedly wed to a gentleman of temperate manner and excellent means. She is childless, but in recent years has opened an Academy for the Education and Refining of Young Ladies and is doing very well.

It amuses me now to realize that Eliza's concept of *vulgar lust*, Dory's *passionate intimacy*, my mother's *amour* and my *married warmth* are really all very much the same thing. What a great deal of wasteful speculation I spent in my youth trying to understand their subtle distinctions. I don't feel quite so sorry for my mother any more; she had love, of a sort, and all love is wonderful. I've lost the feelings of shame about my heritage.

But I do admit, as I watch Oliver crossing the orchard with little Reggie on his shoulder and plump little Marietta running alongside, that love is especially wonderful when one is able to share it with one particular, lifelong partner.